Ghost Maven

The Haunting of Alice May

Tony Lee Moral

Ghost Maven: The Haunting of Alice May

Copyright © 2022 by Tony Lee Moral

Sabana Publishing

tonyleemoralbooks.com

ISBN: 978-1-838211561

Book cover design: Tony Lee Moral

For Josephine

Acknowledgements

Ghost Maven: The Haunting of Alice May was written during two inspirational years living in Monterey, Pacific Grove and the Big Sur. Hiking in the cypress forests, kayaking in the bay, and countless visits to the Monterey Bay Aquarium, Point Lobos and Point Pinos Lighthouse helped shape the backdrop of the story. This book is dedicated to my mother.

Chapter One: The Fog

I'd always been in search of my own private island, somewhere I could feel safe, a solace from life's miseries. In the rough seas off Monterey, I thought I finally found just that.

At first we didn't see the strange fog rolling in from the horizon because we were too busy concentrating on our strokes. It crept in as we paddled, draping itself over the water like a kind of gray ectoplasm, obscuring the horizon and the sea in front of it.

"Stay in a V formation!" shouted Priory, the hunky gym instructor in his twenties, a sun-kissed Californian jock. I couldn't help but keep my eyes focused directly on his masculine figure as he navigated the water like a swift sea otter, his strong muscles steering his kayak nimbly through the thick ocean swell.

Thrusting my paddle into the choppy water, I tried to keep my wooden kayak gliding in a straight line. Even though we were only half a mile out to sea, it seemed more like five hundred. I also obsessed over showing a brave face so no one would notice the terror in my eyes. Aquaphobic for as long as I can remember, I struggled with a real fear of drowning. Not afraid of dying, per se—but the nightmarish idea of ice-cold water pouring into my throat choking my tongue and filling my lungs, rendering me unable to breathe or speak, terrified me more.

We were all from Monterey High School, like a dozen ducks bobbing in the vast expanse of ocean. The surging swell shone a shimmering blue, draped with kelp like gaudy necklaces on a voluptuous body. I am no great fan of sports or athletics, but on that day, I had something to prove and fears to overcome.

"Hey Christian, what's the difference between an Irish wedding and an Irish funeral?" That was Lance, another thick-muscled jock deftly steering his kayak through the thick swell.

"Dunno. What?" replied Christian, a pleasant, fresh-faced boy. He had curly brown hair and a sunny disposition, exuding a good-natured charm. Although he was in his late teens, he still had baby fat around his face which made him look younger. I met Christian the first week after we moved to Monterey, outside church waiting for my dad and little sister. Since that very first day, he has always attempted to make me feel welcome.

There was a brief pause before Lance answered, "One less drunk."

"That's terrible," Christian said with a groan. "You know my ancestors are Irish, so I should be offended."

"You guys suck," shouted Ruth, an athlete in her own right, paddling a purple canoe.

The playful banter continued. I wanted to join in but I didn't feel I knew them well enough. After all, I was the still the new girl, having only been in school for a week. My homeroom class had already organized a kayaking trip for the end of the week, so I volunteered to go thinking it would be a great way to break in and make new friends.

Just before the fog had rolled in, I felt excited for a new beginning, like those random spring flowers that emerge along the coastal path. Despite my fears, it felt good to be out on the bay on such a sunny day. For a moment I almost forgot about the few painful months my family and I recently endured. The water lapping around me seemed to absolve it all.

In the distance, through the encroaching miasma, I spied Point Pinos lighthouse with its tall, white tower gleaming in the sunlight. We were still a couple hours away from sunset when the light would switch on but the lighthouse was still a reassuring beacon as we paddled through the waves. Between that and Priory, I convinced myself that I was safe.

A spiky-raven-haired girl as she paddled to the right of me shouted, "How you doin', Alice?"

"Good," I fibbed, grimacing a fake smile. Truthfully, I wasn't at all comfortable in the water, and I never had been.

Her name was Emily. She wore her black hair standing up like violet crocuses, her freckled skin was pale, even whiter than mine. Something of an eccentric among the girls at Monterey High, her style of dress was eclectic and for this outing she'd opted for a pink shirt, mauve scarf, black trousers, and handmade silver earrings. Emily befriended me right away when I started school.

"Look," she suddenly shouted, pointing. "A sea otter!"

I spied the animal in the distance, his paws wrapped around a clam shell with long whiskers quivering in the sea breeze. The sunlight caught the sheen from the oil on his greasy back. He watched our group inquisitively before disappearing under the water in a flash, a ripple across the glassy surface the only evidence suggesting he had been there at all.

A murmur of delight spread across the twelve kayakers but the elation soon turned to horror as everyone began to notice the white mass of clouds and fog sweeping in. The mass enveloped us and rushed toward the shore with its poisonous breath. I choked on the acrid air that engulfed us.

Priory's steel-gray eyes squinted at the horizon. "We'd better head to shore, NOW!" He angled the nose of his kayak toward the distant lighthouse and urged the rest of us to follow.

I quickened the pace of my paddle, my heart beat wildly—threatening to thunder out of my chest. The opaque blanket seemed like a terrible omen as it covered us, surrounding us with suffocating fingers. I had never seen fog so thick, nor had I ever experienced such a strange, nauseating stench that invaded my nostrils. It corroded my eyes and lips, pressing stingy salt water against my skin.

"I can't see in front of me," Emily yelled.

"Keep calm," Priory said. "Everyone turn your kayaks ninety degrees and paddle towards shore. Slowly now. Keep calm and follow my voice."

Visibility worsened and I lost sight of the other kayakers.

"Emily, are you there?" Priory cried out.

"Yes," said a meek voice.

"Christian?"

"Yes."

"Ruth?"

"Yes."

"Lance?"

"Yeah."

Priory continued going through the names until he came to mine. "Alice?"

Too terrified to move let alone speak, I offered no reply.

"Alice!"

Somehow, I steered my kayak away from the group, and they quickly disappeared into the dense cloud mass. I could vaguely hear them calling my name but their voices became fainter. "Hey!" I managed to shout. "Hey!"

I detected fear dripping from my voice and tried to calm my shaking hands. In spite of my efforts, I trembled fiercely and felt alone, like abandoned driftwood left to tarry at sea. "Hello?" I shouted again. "Priory! Christian! Emily!"

No reply.

Oh God, Oh my God, I prayed to myself. *What am I doing here? How stupid can I be? What am I trying to prove? Who am I trying to impress?* I took a deep breath and tried to motivate myself. *Confront your fears, Alice. Everything will be okay.*

A nearby splash startled me.

What was that? Another sea otter? I knew there were sharks in the bay, but looking around, I could see nothing through the thick, gray fog. The damp air seeped into my nostrils and throat with its suffocating clench. Feeling drowsy, I gasped for air, hoping not to succumb to a panic attack.

Then for a moment the fog lifted and I saw it—in the distance toward the middle of the bay, glowing in the sunlight like an aura—an island. I could see the sand illuminating with a golden-yellow hue on a pristine beach nudged up against clear, turquoise water. Rising above the shoreline stood two mountain peaks covered in green, stretching high into the heavens. It was one of the most beautiful sights I had ever seen, like a fancy vacation postcard deserving of a frame.

A strange calm descended over me.

I was perplexed as I didn't know of any island in Monterey Bay. Still, whatever it was, I could most definitely see land, so I paddled in that direction. Trying to keep my kayak in a straight line, I dug deep into my strength reserves and kept calm as I steered toward the land mass. All I could hear was the slop-slop-slop of my paddle hitting the water, as I focused on the silhouette of the island. It was so beautiful, I felt an inner peace and tranquility despite the grim circumstances.

Then—as quickly as it appeared—the island vanished. I looked again but saw nothing except the desolate sea and sky. The mist suddenly became so dense, I couldn't even see my hands on the paddle. Even my upper body seemed shrouded.

"Oh God," I muttered, convinced I would meet my Maker. The only consolation; death would guarantee a reunion with my mother.

My thinking became disoriented and muddled, and I felt uncoordinated and weak. Feeling seasick and having lost the will to paddle at all,

I dropped the oar in the water, and it ebbed with the tide, slowly drifting away. In seconds, it, too, completely vanished, just like the island.

I was left to face my fate.

A huge wave tumbled me overboard. When I hit the ice-cold water, it knocked the wind out of me cutting through my chest like a thousand knives. The murky depths enveloped me, the water chilling me to the bone. I gasped, and my mouth instantly filled with salty seawater, gagging me. I tried to take a breath but couldn't. My limbs went limp, and I was sure my greatest nightmare was about to happen. I knew I was drowning.

SPLASH! I could see the shape of something moving near me.

Another sea otter? A shark? Really, it didn't matter, for I was much too drowsy to care. I tried peering through the murkiness to see who or what splashed about, but the freezing water stung my eyes making it difficult to keep them open. To my amazement, I thought I saw a familiar face in the water beckoning me.

Then I could see a shape swimming toward me and trying to focus, I watched the figure swim with strong, steady strokes. Dark clothes floated in the current with hair that resembled golden seaweed suspended in the water. As the swimmer got closer I could see it was a boy. He had a pale face, like a luminous vision in the murky blue, and seemed at ease underwater. As he swam closer, I saw him looking at me with the lightest blue eyes I'd ever seen.

The sight of him strangely calmed me, like the quell of acceptance before death. An inner peace descended upon me as I lost control. I could no longer hold my breath and was sure I would drown as I lost consciousness. I told myself, *before you know it, the water will fill your lungs entirely, and it will all be over.*

Just as I sank and the depths threatened to swallow me forever, the boy reached out and grabbed my arm. With a touch so gentle it felt magical, he slowly pulled me toward the surface. As we ascended, he reached forward and kissed me.

His lips were lush and cool against my own and I forgot all about drowning. All I could think about was the magic of that kiss touching me in a way I never felt before. In semi-consciousness, I struggled over whether it was even possible to feel that kind of touch let alone feel it again.

Chapter Two: Henry

"Alice...Alice...Alice..."

The voice sounded hollow and empty, as if echoing inside my skull. It sounded strange and alien, yet sort of familiar. A distant memory of my mom calling me when I was a child. We were playing hide-and-seek, and I had hidden in the downstairs cupboard. It took Mom ages to find me, but I knew she deliberately took her time, prolonging my fun and my favorite game.

I'm dead, nothing matters anymore—maybe I'm in the fourth dimension, I thought to myself. *Pretty sure I'm not going to Heaven anytime soon.* These thoughts comforted me. If I was dead, I could see Mom again. I could remind her I love her, and if I had the chance to live again, I would promise to be nicer to Sophie and help out more with the housework.

I opened my eyes and coughed up an ocean of water. It felt like someone forced my mouth open and poured a bag of salt down my throat. My tongue was thick as sandpaper, as if it had rubbed against the sea in battle and lost. Both of my eyeballs stung from the salty water and when my blurry vision could finally focus, I saw four anxious faces peering down at me, as if I were some shriveled specimen, waiting to be dissected for a biology exam.

"She's coming around," Christian said, his face draining of the anxiety that had been building up in his furrowed forehead.

"Thank God," Emily cried, looking haunted. I could see from her eyes she had been crying. The tears left stained streaks on her cheek from the black mascara and her eyes looked like two black lumps of coal.

"Try not to move your head, Alice," coached Priory, placing his wet hands against my temples. "Somebody grab a towel from my kayak."

"Wh-what happened?" I managed to stutter.

"You capsized in the water," Christian said, his voice sounding grave. "We found you on the shoreline ten minutes ago."

"Capsized?" I tried to sit up. "Ouch!" My head hurt as if hit with a baseball.

"Take it easy, you're safe now," Christian said, smoothing my wet hair across my forehead. I noticed his nose was slightly bent to the right of his face, I never paid any attention to his face before. Looking down at me, his face seemed accentuated and at that moment, his crooked nose was all I could think about.

Emily began to cry as if she knew what I was going through.

Silence followed for a few minutes as I tried to collect my thoughts—then I remembered the boy who rescued me. "The boy. . .Where is he?"

"What boy?" Christian asked, looking at everyone else to see if they heard me too.

"I—he pulled me out of the water and saved me from drowning," I said, struggling to get up. Someone brought a towel and placed it under my head so my chin was touching my neck.

"We didn't see any boy," said Christian. "Take it easy now, Alice. You have a slight concussion."

I frowned, tasting the saltwater in my mouth again. Another memory wafted into my groggy mind, the distinct silhouette of a mysterious island in the bay with twin peaks stretching into the heavens. I recalled an irresistible allure, like a tide pulling me to the golden shore. "There was this. . .an island," I said. "I saw an island, right in the middle of the bay."

Priory frowned. "What island?"

"When the fog surrounded me, I saw it in the distance. Something sort of drew me there, so I paddled toward it, but. . ."

Sensing a murmur among the crowd of onlookers, I realized the other kids from my class were staring down at me like I was some helpless, floundering seal.

"Alice, honey, there's no island in Monterey Bay," Christian whispered. "Maybe you just imagined it, like a mirage or something."

"I did not! It was there! An island! I saw it with my own eyes," I insisted, struggling to get up. "Ouch!"

"Take it easy. The paramedics are on their way."

I closed my eyes, but all I could see was the memory of the island and the handsome face of the rescuer who saved me from drowning.

*

When the paramedics finally arrived, they checked me over brusquely and rushed me to Monterey Hospital for a checkup.

Thirty minutes after I arrived, my dad rushed in with my kid sister, Sophie, in tow.

"Alice, honey! My God! What happened? Are you OK? Does it hurt? Is it your head? You could have drowned, baby!" The torrent of questions poured out of him, his tone waivered alternately between concern and reproach.

I smiled and tried to calm him. "I'm fine, Dad. Honest." It was so good to see him. Out in the bay, there was a moment when I thought I might never see him alive again.

My dad, Oliver Parker, was in his forties, handsome with graying hair at his temples and a sun-kissed tan. He was even more handsome when younger, and ever since he was a kid, the ocean fascinated him. I found that odd, since water scared the hell out of me. Unfortunately, Mom's long illness took a toll on him and his kind, youthful features were replaced with worry lines, his dark hair flecked with gray. The burdens of bringing up two daughters on his own while juggling a full-time job and mourning the loss of his childhood sweetheart.

Even in my disoriented state, all I could think of was the mysterious boy who pulled me out of that water. The memory of his touch, his luminous face and golden hair, and best of all—the underwater kiss, still so vivid and magical. I closed my eyes trying to picture him again, but the painful stiffness in my neck proved too much distraction.

My little sister, Sophie, took after my mom with the same fair hair and blue eyes. Now, her face was solemn, and big tears ran down her pink cheeks. That surprised me; Sophie never cried. She was the toughest twelve-year-old I knew, even though she suffered from asthma. At Mom's funeral, while Dad and I wept, Sophie stoically held it together with a quiet strength. When Mom's coffin passed by within inches of me, Sophie squeezed my fingers tight. I can still remember that touch passing her strength on to me. Now, as she sat next to my hospital bed, I felt that same power. It was somewhat silly considering I am the older sister, the one supposed to be more responsible.

"Are you really OK?" Sophie asked, tears streaming. "I mean–really okay?"

I nodded.

She nodded and sniffled, then became angry. "Who falls into Monterey Bay anyway? That was a dumb thing to do." Then her voice softened. "Did you swallow a lotta water?"

"I think I spat half of it out, but I never wanna eat sushi again." I tried to make light of it, but I wasn't fooling anyone. They knew how close I came to drowning.

A short time later my memory returned and with it, all the emotions. I hated being in the hospital because it reminded me of our endless visits to see Mom. It is so difficult to go through the pain again. The memory of her looking so pale and fragile in that thin nightgown, propped up in bed. She always did her best to mask her own fear, and comfort Sophie and me with her smiles and kisses, but I knew how scared and sad she was. It was also tough watching Dad. I could tell from his eyes it was tearing him apart.

The doctor came in to take my pulse. He murmured soothing words and smiled at me in a genial fashion. As he spoke, I remembered that guy again, my unknown savior.

"Where is he?" I asked, looking around at the anxious faces of my family.

Dad asked, "Who, honey?"

"There was this boy in the bay. He rescued me."

Dad frowned and looked at the doctor and said, "I know nothing about a boy. The school brought you in."

"But there was a boy. He saved me from drowning."

"Hey, just try to rest. You took quite a bump on the noggin," the doctor said, gently pushing me back down on the pillow.

Dad exchanged quick, worried glances with him and I recognized that look on his face, the same expression he'd worn when I fell off a horse back home and when he suggested that we move to California, and during Sophie's sudden asthma attack when six-years-old. The look of a dad who is terrified, knowing he has no control.

"She took it really hard when her mom died," my dad said in a hushed tone to the doctor beside my bed. "She was seeing a psychiatrist in Chicago until we moved here."

"Well, I can recommend a dozen good psychiatrists here in the bay."

Great, I thought as my dad nodded and thanked the doctor. Just what I need, another freaking shrink. And that was my last thought before drifting off to sleep.

*

By the time I woke up, it was dark and cold outside, I could see the condensation freezing on the glass. Dad and Sophie were gone because the doctor asked them to leave so I could get some rest.

Looking around the empty, quiet room, I noticed the window offered a view of the sea. I crept out of bed to have a look. Feeling a bit chilly in the backless hospital gown, I watched as the sea changed from blue to a deep crimson to black. The pale moon crept up above the horizon and in the distance was the rhythmic pulse of the lighthouse.

*

Just after lunch the following day, Dad checked me out of the hospital. I was silent as he drove me home, along Route 68, until we hit David Avenue leading straight to the Monterey Aquarium. Turning left took us to the coastal road.

I turned my head to look out at the bay, watching the sunlight dance with malevolence on the water. The events of the past day seemed like a hazy memory, and the bright light of Pacific Grove bathed everything in a deceptively warm hue. All seemed okay in the sterile light of day. I could see some kayakers out in the water, and a group of divers wading into the shallows.

A small headland called Lovers Point jutted out into the bay, a signal we had arrived at Pacific Grove. Dad steered onto Forest Avenue, drove a couple blocks and stopped in front of house number 136, the large, white and blue Victorian clapboard we were renting.

"Okay?" he said, turning off the engine.

I nodded, and we went inside.

Over the weekend, I thought of little else except what happened in the bay. The memory of the boy who saved me haunted my thoughts. *Who was he? Where did he come from? What was he doing out at sea in all that horrible fog? What about the mysterious island? Did I imagine it, or was it really there?* I couldn't rest until I knew the answers. Slowly, I closed the shutters to my bedroom window and tried to get some sleep, hoping to block all of it—boy included—out of my mind.

On Monday, Dad went to work and dropped Sophie off at school leaving me alone in the empty house with only my homework to keep me company. I brought my book collection with me from Chicago and in the middle of stacking them on my bedroom shelf, I heard a knock at the front door.

When I swung the big oak door open, I wasn't prepared for the sight before me. An old woman stood on the front porch just inches from the door. She must have been at least eighty-years-old with leathery skin and a skull-like head shrunken on a slender neck. Her dark eyes glistened in sunken sockets as she stared at me so intently, I froze for a second.

"Hello," the elderly visitor said. "I'm Mrs. Prescott from across the street. I just came to welcome you to Pacific Grove." Her singsong voice full of nostalgia.

Wow. A welcome wagon? People still do that here? In Chicago, folks barely knew anyone's names.

"Thanks. That's real nice of you. I'm Alice," I said extending a hand. "Alice May Parker."

The old woman shook my hand, wrapping her gnarled, knotted fingers around it. Her skin was like ice, and I was glad to withdraw from her clammy touch. "Alice? A lovely name for a very lovely young woman."

"Thank you," I said again. My mother had named me after her grandmother, named after that much more famous Alice, the one who'd traipsed around Wonderland. I found that a bit ironic since I often wanted to disappear down a rabbit hole.

"Is your mom home?"

"No. She's gone. She's dead," I replied flatly. I could say it easier now, without flinching or embarrassment or the need to elicit sympathy. People told me it would get easier and easier, and I guess they were right.

"Oh, I'm so sorry. You poor dear." The old woman offered an outstretched hand to comfort me, but instead grasped the empty air. I didn't want to touch her again.

Mrs. Prescott's steel-gray eyes flickered from me, over my shoulder, and back again. Her gaze narrowed, penetrating my very soul.

"I didn't come only to welcome you," she said. Her tone changed, becoming ominous as she spoke in a low, strangled voice, "I must tell you something very important." She looked directly into my eyes, her skin tightening to expose her skull. When she opened her mouth, I saw the rottenness of her teeth. "Stay away from the water."

Chapter Three: The Dance

Monterey High School sat in the center of town, about a ten-minute drive from my house. Going back to school after what happened was tough. I felt the other kids staring at me, and one of the senior jocks whistled, I wasn't just the new girl, I was now the strange new girl who had fallen into the bay and almost drowned. I couldn't have brought more attention to myself if I had walked around with neon *KICK ME* sign on my back.

Before homeroom, I stopped by my locker, and a figure came rushing up to me and before I knew it, Emily had me in a tight hug. Then holding my shoulders at arm's length, she studied me for a moment, making me feel uneasy. She looked me straight in the eye and said in a hushed voice that for my ears only, "It's good to get away sometimes—to make a fresh start. It's good to leave the pain behind."

I glanced at her sideways, leave the pain behind? What in the world does she mean by that? Emily knowing more about me than I revealed bothered me. As though she could somehow experience what I felt at that moment. As a very private person, I found it unnerving.

I shoved my books into the locker, slammed the door shut, and turned the key firmly. "Leave what behind?" I asked, feigning ignorance. "I'm good."

Emily nodded knowingly, her gaze unwavering, "Okay Alice," she said, unbelieving. Then she changed the subject.

"Hey, guess what. Lance is having a party!"

"He is? When?"

"Next Friday, and we're both invited."

I shook my head. "I dunno. I'm not really in the partying mood. My head still hurts."

"Oh, c'mon! It'll be loads of fun. Besides, what better way to make new friends?"

"Okay. Well, we'll see," I said, sensing Emily's disappointment. But—I really didn't want to go, and wasn't about to make any commitments.

*

The rest of the week went by painfully slow, and it was a relief when Friday came. I saw high school parties as something of a chore. Dressing up, guys trying to impress girls, girls looking unimpressed. It was all such an amusing, phony ritual. I wondered why evolved human beings put themselves through it. I would much rather have sat with friends over coffee, talking about the latest book or movie. That might have made me sound a bit dull, but it was how I felt.

Nevertheless, I made an effort to go because I knew Emily wanted me to. I put on a nice white dress and my mom's silver necklace, which was one of the few things of hers that I wore. Staring back at my reflection was always something of an internal battle. I wasn't fat, but like most girls, I wished I could be taller and slimmer, so I could carry off a dress like my friend Elisabeth from Chicago. She was effortlessly chic, and I missed her wit and style.

I stood awkwardly at the door while Dad read *The Monterey News* in the front room.

"Wow! You look fancy!" he said when he finally took notice. "What kind of party are you going to again?"

"A guy from my class is having a birthday. Emily invited me, and I don't wanna disappoint her."

Dad nodded—much to my surprise. I assumed he would disapprove; but since it was the first party I'd shown any interest in since Mom's illness, he seemed relieved instead. "Have fun. Do you want me to pick you up?"

I shook my head. "No. Emily and I will catch a cab. I won't be late."

*

The party was on a boat anchored off Pier 39 in the marina. Emily was waiting patiently by the plaza, near a dolphin-shaped fountain. She was wearing dark purple dress and funky-looking costume jewelry. She had an odd fashion sense that included a mishmash of styles, refusing to follow any particular trend.

"Great dress!" my friend squealed when she saw me. As usual, she immediately pulled me into a hug.

"You think so?" I noticed her large silver talisman with a yin yang symbol on it. "I like that. What does it mean?"

"This? It's my lucky talisman," said Emily. "It makes me feel balanced, so I don't get seasick!"

I laughed. "I think we should be more worried about the seniors than waves or sharks," I joked, smoothing my dress. "I don't know who I'm trying to impress."

"Then why don't you just impress yourself?" said Emily, linking her arm in mine and steering us toward the pier.

When we climbed on board, I tried to steady myself on the deck, which wasn't easy on a boat packed full of teenagers. Hip-hop music drifted from the stereo across the bay. We were only about a hundred feet from shore, but it seemed like we were several miles out to sea. I watched with envy as the beautiful girls danced with 'jocks' whose muscles were hardened by hours of kayaking in the bay.

"Alice!"

I turned around and saw Christian coming toward me, accompanied by another boy. Christian had a huge smile on his face, as he looked me up and down. I wondered if he was ever in a bad mood.

"Wow. You look terrific."

"Thanks." I smiled, sheepishly. I certainly didn't feel terrific.

I turned to look at the other boy standing next to him with cropped, black hair and wire-framed glasses. The brown eyes behind those glasses stared at me without blinking. He looked sickly—pale. No warmth or friendliness radiated from him, and he made no effort to smile or even pretend to be curious like the others.

I held out my hand, waiting for the cold stranger to introduce himself, but he acted like a handshake was some alien gesture—embarrassed, I withdrew my hand.

"And this is Ethan," Christian said, sounding apologetic.

"Nice to meet you, Ethan," I said politely.

The boy nodded at me and uttered one word, "Likewise."

"Ethan's a member of that book club I was telling you about," Christian continued.

"Ah, okay." I nodded. "I may take you up on your offer to join. I love books."

"You do?" asked Ethan, still not blinking.

"Er...sure. I read a lot."

"What's your favorite?"

"I would have to say *Pride and Prejudice* by Jane Austen." It was true. I had read it at least ten times.

"Good choice," said Christian.

"And what's yours?" I asked Ethan.

"*Atlas Shrugged*," came the reply.

Christian asked me to dance, but I declined politely and opted for watching the other kids from the sidelines instead. I took a sip of punch, hoping it would relax me when I glimpsed one of the most beautiful girls I had ever seen. Tall with straight blonde hair, a flawless complexion, and perfect facial features. She held her head high upon a slender neck and wore a pink cardigan wrapped around slender shoulders. I couldn't help but stare as she walked gracefully past as though gliding on casters.

"Who's that?" I asked Emily, who was standing next to me.

"Heather Palmer," she whispered in my ear.

"She's beautiful," I said.

Emily shot Heather a rather mean look and shrugged. "She certainly seems to think so."

So, it seemed, did every boy on the boat because they were all looking at her like dogs gawking at a T-bone. Next to her stood a tall, handsome guy with a solid build. He started kissing the base of Heather's neck and she didn't resist. Instead, she laughed playfully as he slipped his hands around her waist.

I watched the couple together, my mouth agape. "Who's she with?"

"That's Channing, her boyfriend," Emily whispered again. "The high school jock, in case you couldn't tell."

Channing rested his hands on Heather's neck. I studied the hands for a moment; they were big and powerful from throwing so many footballs and scoring touchdowns.

"They're stunning together," I said with a sigh, wondering if I'd ever look that good with a guy. I also wondered if anyone would ever look at me the way Channing was looking at Heather. My boyfriend's back in Chicago had been bookish or music types, quirky individuals. They were not drop-dead handsome, and they definitely were not high school jocks. In fact, I had met my last boyfriend at the local chess club. It lasted a few months, but then he seemed to run out of moves, and we reached a proverbial stalemate.

The girl turned her head to face me as if sensing my gaze. Our eyes met for a few seconds and something registered between us, a kind of female solidarity. Heather smiled at me while enjoying Channing's kisses. I blushed, feeling myself going bright red for being caught staring.

All around me kids were dancing, flirting, and laughing with the ease of familiarity. Emily chatted with one kayaker, Christian and Ruth, the athletic girl kayaking with us the day I almost drowned, were engaged in deep conversation. I started to feel unsteady, wishing I wore Emily's lucky talisman. Everything seemed to just swirl around me, and I knew I had to get off the boat. I made a move toward the ramp.

"Where are you going?" Emily called. "Are you okay?"

"I just need to go for a walk. I'll be back."

*

I walked along the docks, breathing in the cool night air. The place was dimly lit by the glistening moonlight. As I made my way along the squeaky boardwalk, the gentle lapping of the water ebbed and flowed around the stilt legs.

Out of the corner of my eye, I saw something in the air. It flew toward me, its movements fluttery and jerky. The iridescent wings of what looked like a giant moth seemed to catch the moonlight. I watched in awe as it danced in the rays of light, circling around my head, then headed toward the end of the dock.

The pull was irresistible; it was urging me to follow. As I reached the edge of the dock, I saw protruding rocks, and behind them was a huge expanse of ocean. The moth finally settled on one of the rocks, its wings coming to rest. I longed to hold it in my hand, to feel its delicate vibrations on my skin, but it remained just out of reach.

Despite my fear of the water, I delicately stepped out onto the rocks, feeling the magnetic pull of the tides. The moth was mere inches from my hand, and for a moment I almost considered jumping.

"Stop," said a sharp voice behind me.

I whirled around—atop the boardwalk stood the young man who saved my life. I hadn't imagined him after all since I could see him, as handsome and stately as the pines growing in the forest that overlooked the bay. I noticed he was wearing the same dark brown trousers and shirt as when he'd rescued me.

"Step away from the water," the boy said, his voice stern and commanding, like he was accustomed to giving orders. So firm was the demand, I wondered if he was in the military. The Monterey Naval

Academy was nearby, and I often saw the cadets in town, hanging out in the bookstores or coffee shops. They always looked dapper in their beige uniforms and caps. One or two had even wolf-whistled at Emily and me, making us giggle.

I stared at the hottie on the dock, wondering who he was and what he was doing here. The sight of him again made me giddy, and it had nothing to do with the fact I had chased an overgrown moth out to some slippery seaside rocks. I gripped a tall, jagged peak, being careful not to scrape my palms.

He continued to glare at me. His whole body was rigid, like the mast of a yacht. Only his hair moved, ruffled by the sea breeze, sun-bleached tufts framing a tan face, as if he'd spent most of his life in the sun. Heather could have Channing; this boy was the most beautiful guy I had ever seen.

I was silent for a moment as I turned around to face the dock. The movement caused the moth to rise into the air and disappear into the blackness of the sky over the ocean. With a hint of disappointment, I watched it go.

"Wh-who are you?" I asked, finally finding my tongue.

"A sailor of these waters," he vaguely replied.

I thought about his answer for a moment; then it all made sense. He was a sailor, but he didn't look like the typical guy in the US Navy. Still, he couldn't be an ordinary seaman either. There was something more *otherworldly* about him—something very refined.

Most of the young sailors and guys who worked on the boats around Monterey were cute, but they all had a cookie-cutter look to them: the same cropped haircuts, Ralph Lauren polo shirts, and flexing muscles. This guy who had rescued me was more like an antique Rolls-Royce among a fleet of Fords.

"You're the guy who rescued me from the bay," I said, more of a statement than a question.

He nodded. "That is correct, and I prefer not to jump in the bay after you again. The water is cold tonight."

I thought I detected irony or perhaps some humor in his words, but I couldn't be sure. I waited for some expression to register on his face, yet he remained emotionless.

Then his tone of voice seemed to soften a little. "Please step away from the water. It is unsafe."

I noticed his speech pattern was slow and measured. He spoke like a hero in one of the novels I liked to read—a leading man Jane Austen or Charlotte Brontë would write about. None of the boys at school spoke with such precise diction. Most of them preferred to use indecipherable slang like "Yo" and "Waz up?"

I tentatively climbed over the rocks toward him. Eventually I got close enough to get a good look at him. He was even more handsome than I remembered with his blonde hair messy from the salt spray, and those piercing blue eyes as deep and unfathomable as the bay. His bronze skin appeared lightly freckled, but otherwise, he had a flawless complexion. His strong nose began in a crease within his brow.

He stretched out his right hand toward me, and I studied it for a brief second. It was large and masculine, browned by the sun, with clean fingernails. His hands looked weathered as though they sailed many a stormy water.

I reached out my own slender hand and tentatively took his. As his strong fingers gripped tightly around mine, I felt a charge of electrical energy pulsing through my body. He pulled me clear of the rocks. I was almost breathless when I found myself back on the dock, right beside him.

"Thank you," he said, his body inches from mine.

Wait. He's thanking me? I couldn't believe it. "What for?" I asked in surprise. After all, he was the one who had saved me from certain death.

"For stepping away from the water as I asked you to."

It was then I heard Mrs. Prescott's warning in my mind saying, "Stay away from the water." I took a glance back at the sea and foaming waves splashing around the dark rocks. What is it about this bay that makes it so dangerous, that makes everyone fear it?

Before I could ask, he spoke again. "I would like for you to do something else for me," he said in his commanding voice.

"What?" I asked at once, willing to do anything to win his approval.

His eyes narrowed, his expression hardened, and his voice dropped to a low, hushed tone.

"Keep away from here and from me," he replied emphatically.

I was so taken back by the anger and venom in his voice that I stepped back a couple inches. He sounded as if he hated me with every fiber of his being. When I looked into his eyes, I saw no compassion, only contempt. I wondered why he had said it and why he was looking at me with such a hateful expression; I had no choice but to feel sorry for myself.

Then, swiftly, he turned to walk back up the boardwalk. He stopped halfway and untied a small boat from its mooring, a boat I hadn't even noticed before. I glimpsed the name on the bow, *Evening Tide*.

"Wait!" I called after his disappearing shadow. "Just. . .please tell me your name."

He stopped abruptly but didn't turn around. I watched his shoulders droop a little as if weighing the decision to answer me. He hesitated a moment longer before slowly turning his head to face me.

I caught a flash of his eyes in the moonlight.

"Henry," he replied.

Henry? Henry. I repeated the name to myself. It was an old-fashioned name, of sorts, but the sound of it was as sweet as the smell of jasmine. I opened my mouth, willing him to stay longer. "Why did you save me, Henry?"

Henry hesitated again, then for the first time, he spoke with a soft tone, "Because I did not wish for you to drown."

Chapter Four: Evening Tide

Evening Tide—that was all I had to go on, the name of his boat etched on the boards of the bow. It was such a simple name yet mysterious and alluring. If I could find the boat, it would lead me to Henry.

I had the rest of the weekend free to do my detective work. After helping my dad with the groceries on Saturday morning, I walked down the coastal path into town. Once in town, I headed toward the harbor knowing it would be occupied by yachts and sailing vessels.

Approaching the harbor, I could see tall masts pointing toward the sky like silver needles sewing in a blue canvas. I searched among the wooden shacks for a white one with a blue door, the one I had seen while kayaking in the bay.

U.S. Coast Guard headquarters was a small hut on the end of the pier, right next to San Carlos beach park. The sea lions were making their usual cacophony, and I curled up my nose at their salty stench as I walked along the pier. A rusty old sign hung outside the coastguard hut, and I knocked on the peeling blue paint of the wooden door.

"Hello? Anyone in?"

No answer.

I turned the knob slowly and entered a sparsely furnished office with a couple chairs and a metal filing cabinet. A wooden desk stood in the corner, littered with papers, seismic charts, and reports. Above those, on the wall, was a large maritime map of Monterey Bay.

"What can I do for you?" asked a voice coming into the office behind me.

I nearly jumped out of my skin—feeling like a snooper—and turned around to see a stout man in a blue uniform and a white cap standing at the entranceway. "I uh…I'm looking for the Coast Guard," I said.

"Well, you've found 'im," the man said gruffly. "Pickard, Captain John Pickard, and I'm very busy—unless you've come about the missing surfer."

"Missing surfer?" This piqued my curiosity.

"Yeah. Some out-of-towner went surfing yesterday morning off Carmel and hasn't been seen since. His car is still in the beach parking lot. We have every available fishing vessel looking out for him."

"That's bad. What do you think happened?"

"Well, it's likely that a riptide has taken him out. We'll probably find his body in a couple days, ten or so miles down shore, if we're lucky. Most of the time, we don't find any sign of them."

I shuddered. While we were kayaking, Christian had told me that the bay had a strange habit of gobbling up swimmers, that there were tales of people mysteriously disappearing. Over the years, many had gone unaccounted for. "It's like the Bermuda Triangle of the Pacific Coast," Christian eerily surmised.

The captain squinted, fixing his steel-blue eyes on me. "What can I do for you, anyway?"

"I'm looking for a boat."

"Plenty of those in the water. Just take your pick."

"No, not just any boat. It's wooden, kind of old-looking."

"Does this boat have a name?"

"*Evening Tide*," I said.

"*Evening Tide*," Pickard repeated, then shook his head. "Nope. I don't know of any boat by that name registered in these waters—but it still rings a bell. What kinda boat did you say it is?"

I gave the best details I could recall from the night before.

"Hmm. Sounds like a skiff," Pickard said. "You know, one of those boats that operate off a fishing vessel." He paused, and then he laughed. "You ain't much of a sailor, are ya?"

I shook my head. "No. I hate the water." I wasn't afraid to admit it. Still, for someone who despised it, I seemed to spend an awful lot of time around it.

"Why do you need to find this boat so bad?"

"I'm looking for its owner, a guy."

"A-ha! Another missing person, eh?"

"Well, he's not exactly missing," I began, wondering how to explain my predicament.

"Hey, wait a minute. Haven't I seen you before?" the captain interrupted, realization spreading across his face.

"Yeah. I'm the girl who fell into the bay while kayaking last week." My dip in the ocean had given me instant notoriety, for better or worse.

"I thought so! I was the one who called the paramedics. You're one lucky young lady. The bay has a powerful undercurrent and coulda easily taken you under. I reckon that's what happened to the missing surfer."

Okay, okay, I thought to myself, growing more and more frustrated by the minute. The last thing I needed was another lecture. My dad had spent most of the week telling me about the dangers of Monterey Bay. I had even been hauled into the principal's office, where I heard more of the same. I was the new girl, but I had an infamous reputation already.

"It's important that I find this guy," I persisted. "Maybe he's a sailor or a fisherman."

"Do ya know his name?"

"Only his first one, Henry."

Pickard shook his head. "Sorry. I don't know any Henrys. What does he look like?"

"Blonde hair, blue eyes, bronze skin, fine cheekbones," I said, then stopped, realizing that my description made me sound like a lovesick teenager. "He's a little different from most of the boys around here. If you met him, you'd know what I mean," I continued. "It's almost like he belongs in another time and place."

"Another time?" asked Pickard, cracking a smile.

"You're not taking me seriously, Captain," I said.

"Alice…You don't mind if I call you that do you?"

I shook my head; he must have remembered my name from the incident.

Pickard gestured toward a hard wooden chair by his desk.

I sat down. I liked the man; there was something unique in his straightforward saltiness. He reminded me of a benevolent uncle.

"I've been living in this bay for over thirty years, and nothing surprises me anymore. People have all kinds of strange stories about Monterey. You must understand that the bay—well—folks see things."

"What do you mean, see things?" I repeated in a whisper.

"Lights at night, ghost ships, strange noises, that kind of thing," Pickard said; his voice becoming hushed and serious. He stood and walked over to a large brown book sitting on his shelf. "My captain's log is full of such reports," he said, flipping through the heavy book.

"I've heard that the bay is haunted," I replied. "But surely you don't believe in those old ghost stories, do you?"

Pickard looked at me steadily, peering into me with blue, wolf-like eyes, and then he laughed. "Yes, of course I do. How could I not? I've seen too many strange things in my time to be a doubter." His voice went quiet for a moment as he looked out to sea. "Many of them can't be explained."

"Can't be explained," I muttered to myself.

"I believe there is something out there," he concluded as he continued to gaze through the window out to sea.

I believed as well, and I wanted to share my thoughts with him, but something prevented me from telling him about the mysterious vanishing island, for the same reason I didn't tell Emily. It was as if I would break some sacred pact—that uttering one word about it would betray some sort of oath.

"Have you seen anything…odd?" he asked, noticing how quiet I had become.

I shook my head.

Pickard continued to gaze at me with his steady eyes, saying nothing.

I tried to change the subject. "And your log book has no record of a boat called *Evening Tide*?" I asked.

Pickard shook his head. "I know where you can check though. Go to Pacific Grove Library. They've got a maritime section with a comprehensive record of boats docked in these waters. It goes back over a hundred years."

The local library? Of course! It was only a few blocks from my house. Embarrassed that I hadn't thought of it myself, I stood up to go.

"Right. Well, I'm up to my eyes with work," Pickard said, "So if there's nothing else I can help you with. . ."

"No, you've been very helpful. Thank you."

"The bay is strange, eh? The way people just—disappear," Pickard said, just as I reached the door.

"Does it really happen that often?" I asked, turning back.

"More than most people realize, I guess. They seem to vanish into the bay. It's like the water claims them or something. People disappear, and the bodies are never found."

I felt a lump in my throat. "Bodies never found." What could it mean? Silently, I walked back along the coastal path, kicking at the round pebbles underfoot. I thought about what Captain Pickard had told me: mysterious lights in the bay, lost ships, and strange phantom noises. Once or twice since we'd arrived, I'd woken up at night, looked out the window, and thought I had detected something shimmering in the water. Maybe the bay does make people see things, I thought. Maybe there is something out there.

I had always been the type to go looking for answers whenever confronted with questions, and now I had an obvious place to start. The entrance to Pacific Grove Library sat directly opposite Jewell Park, on the corner of Grand and Central. I hadn't gotten my library card yet, so that was the first thing I did when the soft-spoken librarian greeted me at the reception desk. Luckily, I had my ID with me, so the registration process was quick and painless.

She kindly directed me to the maritime section, in the left-hand corner of the library. I thumbed through the index of ship names, looking for any record of *Evening Tide*, but I found nothing. I jumped onto a vacant computer console and started Googling *Evening Tide* + Monterey Bay, but even the Internet couldn't seem to help me.

Feeling a bit rejected, I wandered back to the librarian. "I can't find what I'm looking for," I said, disgruntled.

"The computer records and the index only go back so many years," said the librarian. "You may have to resort to the microfiche, which contains local newspapers and maritime charts from 1850 to 1950."

I nodded. "Okay. I'll give it a try."

The librarian walked into a back room, then came back and handed me a microfiche file marked: *Shipping News Index*. I scanned through the list of boats beginning with the letter E: Esmeralda, Evelyn, Evening Tide. There was a listing! The record mentioned the boat in *The Monterey News* on November 14, 1915.

I frowned, realizing that was almost a century ago. Why are the records so old? I wondered as I made my way back to the helpful librarian. "Do you have a copy of *The Monterey News* from November 14, 1915?"

"We only keep hard copies of that newspaper since 1980. The rest are stored on microfiche, but I'm afraid the library closes in ten minutes. We close early on Saturdays."

"I'll be very quick," I said, breathlessly; it was vital I find out about *Evening Tide* right away. I couldn't survive another night of suspense.

"Well, all right," said the librarian, sensing the desperation in my eyes. She went back into the room, then returned and handed me another microfiche. "This contains all of the papers of 1915. I have to lock up in ten minutes."

I nodded, thanked her, hurried back to the microfiche station, and inserted the file. I quickly scanned through the calendar months of the newspaper until I reached November. It seemed to take ages to scroll through to the fourteenth, but I finally found the date I was looking for. The front-page news was plastered with Coast Guard warnings due to a heavy storm at sea. Scanning the microfiche from left to right, I tried to read the small print of each article, looking for any mention of *Evening Tide*.

"Five minutes until closing," the librarian announced to the patrons. She cast a meaningful look in my direction, and I nodded.

C'mon! I urged. Where are you?

Then, on page twenty of the paper, something caught my eye—an announcement:

EVENING TIDE CHARITY DANCE
800 OLD CANNERY ROW
MONTEREY
8 P.M. SATURDAY

There it was, in black and white, the name of Henry's boat. I hurriedly scribbled a note of the time and address. Excited, I took the microfiche out of the slot, handed it back to the librarian, and thanked her again. Then I hurried out of the library and crossed the green expanse of Jewell Park, eager to get back home to sort it all out and try to piece the clues together.

*

In the solitude of my bedroom, I contemplated what I had found. What connection does that dance have with Henry and the boat? It was Saturday, a couple of hours before eight and twilight had already fallen. Outside my window, I could see the sea turning a deep shade of crimson.

Something compelled me to go out that night. I wanted to check the address on Cannery Row, as it was the only lead I had to find Henry. I had to make up an excuse so that Dad wouldn't get suspicious.

"Going out again, honey?" Dad asked, surprised. He was reading a story to Sophie on the sofa.

"Um, Emily and I are going to a movie, if that's okay?"

"Okay, just don't be out too late. Remember, we have church tomorrow. And don't you have schoolwork?"

"My homework's all done, Dad. I won't be late." They might have had church, but I hadn't set foot inside one since Mom died. I knew there was no reason to bring that up, though, so I just waved goodbye and headed out.

I took the coastal walk to the Old Cannery. It was one of my favorite strolls; meandering along a path lined with colorful flowers and bushes. When I arrived at the edge of Cannery Row, the first building I saw was the Monterey Aquarium. The row was dark, with the exception of a few lights on the far corner. The address in the article, 800 Cannery Row, was just past the aquarium. I continued on to the old canneries, their wooden doors exposed to the street.

Finally, I reached 800. I had to step into a shadowy alcove to find the old wooden door. There didn't seem to be a bell or a knocker, so I turned the brass knob. To my surprise, it opened with an audible click to a long, dark corridor.

Soft music played behind a closed door at the end of the hallway, flickering light seeped from a crack underneath. Quietly, I walked along the damp, musty passageway to the source. I paused at the end then pushed the door open. The music enveloped me, and for a moment I stood in awe of what lay before me.

They converted the large cannery, with its high wooden ceilings, into an impromptu dance hall filled with elegantly dressed dancers. The women wore ball gowns with elaborate braids in their hair, and the men dressed in button-down suits and bowties. They didn't seem to notice me as I moved through the crowd, but I certainly noticed them—and wondered who they could be.

As I made my way around the edge of the room, a woman in a lacy black dress grabbed me by the elbow. "Thank you for coming," she said. "We have been expecting you."

"You have?" I asked in surprise, as I had never seen the woman before. I frowned. How could they have been waiting for me? Who are they? And why are they even here?

"Of course. Do you have a dance card?"

I shook my head, *what is a dance card?*

"Here you are," she quipped, thrusting a card into my hand.

As I looked into her eyes, I saw they were dark and hollow. It was then I noticed everyone's eyes were cast in shadow. They seemed to look right through me. As they danced, they were careful not to bump into me or each other, floating around as if moving on casters.

Then, out of the corner of my eye, I saw a familiar face. Henry was standing against the wall with his arms folded, watching the dancers and looking bored. He moved his head slowly back and forth, surveying the room, until he caught my eye. Instantly, he unfolded his arms and walked toward me.

I froze. He wore no smile as he stalked toward me like a predator closing in on its prey. I had nowhere to run or hide, so I could only brace myself for the verbal onslaught.

To my surprise, though, when he got within a couple feet of me, his solemn face broke into a smile. "Welcome," he said. "I am pleased you could come."

I frowned. "You are?" Only yesterday evening, at the boat dock, he looked as if he hated me, like mortal enemies. *What could have possibly changed, quite literally, overnight?*

"Of course," he replied lightly. "We have been expecting you," he said, parroting what the woman had already said.

I frowned, confused, with a million thoughts racing through my head. How could I have been expected when I wasn't even invited?

"Would you care to dance?" he said, offering his large masculine hand.

I nodded, feeling my adrenalin rush when I touched his fingers.

He gently led me through the dancers, onto the middle of the dance floor. The tune that was playing was a minuet. He put one arm around my waist in a cordial fashion like a gentleman, and then raised my right palm with the other, his thumb rubbing against my fingers. His touch was electrifying, the same sensation I'd experienced when he had saved me from drowning.

Lifting my chin, I gazed into his intense blue eyes. Never let go, I thought to myself. In a trance, I glided with him around the dance floor. Somehow my feet obeyed and danced, though my knees were trembling.

"You're a good dancer," I complimented. He had such exquisite manners, so unlike the boys at Monterey High or my old school in Chicago.

"Thank you. I practiced at the old dance school in San Francisco."

That piqued my curiosity. "Oh? Do you spend a lot of time in the city?"

He nodded. "Yes. I was a fisherman, working at the docks off Pier 39."

"So how did you end up in Monterey?"

He hesitated before answering. "I took a job delivering a consignment. That was what brought me down here."

I digested it for a moment. Henry's eyes were so blue they reminded me of sapphires sparkling in the light, my favorite of all gems.

"You dance rather well yourself," he said, returning the compliment.

I smiled a little in acknowledgment. "I did ballet a lot when I was kid."

"But no longer?"

I shook my head. The truth is, I haven't really danced since Mom died. I hadn't felt like it. My legs were listless and didn't feel like dancing, no matter how many times Dad tried to coax rhythm into me. In the end, he always let my stubbornness win out. But being with Henry, I felt animated again. It felt good to be alive and in his arms.

"Who are all these people?" I asked. "Why are they here?"

"It's a sort of—society."

"A society? A society of what?"

"We meet up for charity," Henry replied. "We get together once in a while."

The music changed to something a little more upbeat, and a smile crossed his face.

"Have you ever danced *contra*?"

I shook my head.

"There is nothing to it," he said. "Let me be your guide."

Suddenly, I sensed that we were the only couple still dancing, and when I looked around, I saw everyone staring at us. We glided around in the center, and even after the lively music stopped, we carried on dancing.

I could feel myself falling for him. "I'd like to see you again. Will you meet with me tomorrow afternoon for coffee?"

He hesitated, bowed his head, and inhaled deeply. Then to my elation, he nodded. "Okay. Meet me by Lovers Point, at a quarter past three tomorrow."

I nodded, and a surge of adrenalin rose inside me.

I didn't remember leaving the party, walking home in the darkness, entering the house, or climbing into bed. All I could think of was my first date with Henry.

*

The next morning I woke up and wondered where I was. At first, I thought I was back in Chicago, and when I saw the pale blue shutters, I knew I was in Pacific Grove. Then I remembered the dance! The memory was so vivid, but for a moment, I wondered if it was real or if it was all a dream? I looked for signs of evidence of the night before, but since I have the habit of putting my clothes away before I go to bed, not even the dress I was wearing could persuade me I hadn't imagined everything.

"How was the movie?" asked Dad when I came down to the kitchen for breakfast, his bleary eyes slightly puffy with sleep. He and Sophie sat at the table enjoying a plate of scrambled eggs.

I had to think quickly. "Er, Emily and I decided to hang in after all," I said, reaching for the cereal box on the top shelf.

Dad looked at me for a moment and then nodded before returning to his Sunday newspaper. Again I thought of the music and the dance, the brush of Henry's fingers against my waist, and I wondered if it really happened or if I was going crazy?

If it did happen, I remember we arranged to meet at Lovers Point, the headline that jutted out from Pacific Grove between Monterey and Asilomar. It's a popular place for trysts, even though two lovers had drowned themselves in the bay.

I arrived eagerly at three o'clock after being preoccupied all day with the thought of meeting Henry. Sunday brunch had been only a mere distraction as I waited for the afternoon to come around. I sat on the rocks overlooking the park watching a couple of kids playing on the sandy beach below and seeing families picnicking in the small crescent of green. I thought I heard whispering in the trees bordering the park, but maybe it was the wind.

I glanced at my cell phone's clock, worried over whether Henry would stand me up, or worse, I had dreamt the whole thing. Maybe I'd put him on the spot. Maybe not showing up is his gentle way of letting me go, I thought with a sigh.

"Hello."

I looked up, startled, and saw that he had appeared from behind the rocks. "Oh! Hi," I said, almost in relief, that I really wasn't losing my mind. "I'm glad you came."

"I really should not have." His words made our meeting sound forbidden, which made it even more exciting for me, even though we were just going for coffee.

"There's a place near here called Magnolia Bakery. They have the most amazing carrot cake. Does that sound okay to you?" I asked. "It's my small way of thanking you, and how can anybody refuse coffee and carrot cake?"

He paused for a moment, thinking deeply. Then slowly he nodded. Elation swelled inside me when he agreed.

We walked a couple blocks, past the park, and made a left on Fountain, then onto Lighthouse Avenue. I had the sense that Henry knew where he was going, like he knew the layout of the town. I was still getting used to my bearings; he practically led me right to the café.

Together, we sat in a shady corner in the back yard of Magnolia Bakery. The boughs of a large sycamore tree seemed to weep over us, providing us with welcome shade, partly obscuring us from the bakery itself. It was already my favorite place in Pacific Grove, calm and tranquil, one of the few places where I couldn't see any sign of the ocean.

"I just love this place," I said. "You know, it's mentioned in one of John Steinbeck's novels. Cannery Row, I think."

Henry nodded. "Yes, I know."

"What would you like?" I asked. "We have to go up to place our orders here."

"A coffee," Henry said.

I nodded and went to the counter and ordered a coffee for Henry and a vanilla latte for myself. "And some of that carrot cake, please. It looks so good."

"Comin' right up, hon" said Candy, the friendly blonde waitress. By now, the staff was getting to know me, as I had been there twice already.

I brought it all back to the table and took a couple nervous sips from my latte, but Henry hadn't bothered with his. The untouched carrot cake stood between us like unspoken territory.

Henry sat across the table, his gaze lowered, ever so often glancing up at me under his thick eyebrows. He was achingly handsome—with the crease of his brow, tan skin, straight and perfect nose, and piercing eyes. An aura of mystery and magnetism surrounded him.

I punctuated the awkward silence with another sip.

Henry continued to study me with watchful eyes, still not touching his beverage. After a time, he spoke. "How long have you been in Pacific Grove?" he asked.

"Almost a month now," I replied, then paused to think about it. It's really been a month already? Wow! I couldn't believe how quickly time passed, so convinced our first few weeks in a new place would drag on. So far, my time in Monterey had been very eventful.

"What about your family?" he asked.

"My dad works at the aquarium, and I have a kid sister. Her name's Sophie. She's twelve and adorable."

"What about your mother?"

I paused and took another sip of latte. Sometimes when talking to new friends, I skipped the part about Mom dying because I didn't want their pity. No one at school knew, not even Emily. I just hadn't found the right time to tell her yet; I didn't want it to alter her behavior toward me. Since I didn't feel that way with Henry, I answered honestly, "She died six months ago. Cancer."

"My condolences," he said.

I thanked him. "What about you? Where are your parents?"

"They died a long time ago," he said, then paused.

I waited for him to continue, when he didn't I didn't press him knowing firsthand how private grief needed to be. "I'm sorry, too," I said, studying him for a moment, thinking about how his parents died, and realized he must have been very young when it happened. He didn't look any older than eighteen. The reality of losing one parent was tough enough, but the thought of losing two was too much to bear.

We sat in silence, sharing our grief. It seemed a bit strange, but ever since my Mom died, I'd felt a kinship with those who experienced losing a loved one. We formed kind of a club, exclusively open to the heartbroken.

"Are you from around here? I mean, is Pacific Grove your home?" I inquired, trying to play it cool but secretly wanting to know everything about him; where he comes from, what his favorite food is, his favorite music, and what movies he watched.

He shook his head. "I'm from San Francisco originally, North Beach."

"Really? It's a beautiful city." In reality, I had only been there once, when we moved from Chicago. "And you said work brought you here?"

"I was employed on one of the squid-catching boats and have stayed here ever since."

"Oh," I said, digesting it for a moment. "Didn't you go to high school?"

Henry shook his head. "My family was poor, and we needed the money. Besides, what good are books if all you do is haul in fish all day?"

"True," I said, though honestly, I couldn't live without my books. *Where would I be without Thomas Hardy, Jane Austen, and all the Brontë sisters?* I thought with a shudder.

"Your family…Were you close to them?" I asked.

"I was, until they died."

"What's your last name?"

"Raphael."

Henry Raphael. There was something very old-school, almost biblical about the name. It was unlike any other I had heard before except for the archangel Raphael in Milton's *Paradise Lost* who warned Adam and Eve about the dangers of temptation. I liked it and repeated the name in my head. *Henry . . .*

Taking another sip of my latte, I looked into his blue, unfathomable eyes. It was like diving into the ocean—deep, mysterious, and full of hidden danger. I was only too eager to plunge in.

"What are you thinking?" he asked.

"About an old woman named Mrs. Prescott, my neighbor. She said something strange to me the other day."

"What?" he asked, clearly curious now.

"She told me to stay away from the bay, that it isn't safe."

"She is right. You should listen to her."

I shook my head. "But if I had stayed away from there, I wouldn't have met you."

Henry was silent and fiddled with his untouched mocha. He seemed to be absorbed in thought and took a deep breath before speaking. "Did you see anything else when you were out in the bay?" he asked, looking at me intently.

I paused for a moment. Part of me wanted to tell him about the island, but something prevented me from saying anything. Not that I didn't trust him. It was, just as it had been with Captain Pickard, that I felt it would be like betraying a secret. "No, nothing—only you, when you rescued me," I fibbed.

He continued to gaze at me with his impenetrable stare, making me uncomfortable.

I shifted in my seat, sensing he didn't believe me.

"Alice. . ."

I liked how he spoke my name. It was the first time he had done so, and it sounded so sweet rolling off his lips. "Yes, Henry?" I said.

"You must believe me when I tell you the bay is not safe. Your neighbor is right. It is full of danger. You must stay away from it. I implore you."

"I'm not afraid," I said with conviction forgetting, for once, my terrible fear of water. I was even prepared to swim at the deep end if that was what it would take to be with him, even if my aquaphobia was lurking underneath like some terrible sea monster waiting to pounce.

"What are you afraid of, then?" he asked.

I swallowed. I was afraid of a lot of things: never seeing Mom again, us being alone, Dad being so sad, and Sophie growing up without her mom. All those things preyed on my mind every day, gnawing away like hungry demons.

"I'm afraid this carrot cake will go stale unless we eat it," I quipped, changing the subject. I took a bite. It was delicious. I savored the taste of the butter cream icing melting in my mouth, then offered my fork to his mouth. "Try it? It's good."

He opened up and took a bite. I watched as the cake passed his lips and he swallowed slowly. I thought of the kiss he'd given me and wondered if I would ever share another moment like that with him again.

"The cake here hasn't been so good since the last baker passed away," Henry said, chewing casually. "Dropped dead in the kitchen of a heart attack. It was a real pity. He was a good guy."

I frowned, pausing mid-chew—*he knew the previous baker? How long has he been here?*

Later, after coffee, we stood outside the bakery.

"Take care of yourself, Alice," he said to me evenly, with an unspoken finality dripping from his words.

I nodded and said goodbye. I didn't want to leave him. Reluctantly, I walked down the street back toward my house. Every so often, though, I turned to look back. When I did, I saw that he watched me go. I carried on walking for a few more steps, but when I looked around again, he had mysteriously vanished.

*

The rest of the week passed painfully slow, and I could do little but think of Henry. Why does he have such a magnetic hold on me? I wondered. There was something so mysterious about him—so unlike the boys in my class, that it made me wonder who he really was and where he had come from. I didn't mention him to Emily. I wanted to keep the memory of Henry to myself, and just like the secret island, I felt that speaking his name or mentioning him would betray my protective oath to keep him a secret.

On Saturday, Sophie and I went to the farmers' market to stock up on fruits and vegetables for the week. We enjoyed browsing the stalls and kiosks, chatting to the farmers, and savoring the samples. There was a fine selection of cheeses so I bought a half-pound of my favorite, Monterey Jack, for tonight's lasagna.

After Dad came home from work, he wanted to take Sophie and me on a drive up to Santa Cruz.

"I, uh, have a few things I want to do today in Monterey," I said. "Besides, I have some research to finish at the library, a project for school," I lied, knowing that homework would be all the excuse I would need to get me out of the trip.

"Okay, honey. You win," said Dad.

I waited until they left, but instead of going to the library right away, I headed for Cannery Row.

Chapter Five: Sailing

Passing the clam-chowder stalls, several cafés, and the Plaza Hotel, I walked to the far end, where there was a ramshackle collection of dive shops. One had a sign on the front of a large dolphin riding a wave. Intrigued by the sign, I paused to read the ads plastered on the window.

I went into the shop and walked up to the good-looking guy behind the counter. He had blond, curly hair, freckles, and blue eyes—the typical surfer-dude, dressed in a neoprene wetsuit, revealing the muscles bulging underneath.

"Hey," he greeted, showing a set of movie star, perfectly white teeth.

"Hi. I wanna learn how to sail."

"Well, you've come to the right place," he said and introduced himself, "I'm Connor, and I will be your instructor. I teach sailing diving here."

He looked to be twenty or twenty-one, the kind of guy who wakes up every morning with a sunny disposition.

"I do sailing lessons on Sundays, starting at eight in the morning," Connor stated. "It's fifty bucks an hour."

Fifty dollars was a lot for me, but I did have some money saved up, so I agreed.

"Why do you wanna learn how to sail?" Connor asked.

"Er...well, I figure since I live in Pacific Grove, I should take advantage of the bay." The truth—I wanted to try and find the island. I knew that overcoming my fear of the ocean by learning to sail might give me some peace of mind and the answers to all the questions floating through my head since I'd seen the vanishing land mass.

"Sounds good to me. When do you wanna start?"

"Next Sunday would be great."

"Eight o'clock sharp then." Connor beamed another sunny smile at me, looking like he'd just stepped off the set of toothpaste commercial. "We meet by the marina, at Lovers Point. You know where that is?"

"Yep," I said. "Here's the money for my first lesson. See ya then."

*

Bright and early the next day, I woke up excited about going sailing next week. Dad and Sophie were already having breakfast downstairs, and I could smell the pancakes throughout the whole house with their maple goodness. After greeting my family, I reached for some plates in the cupboard and pulled out a carton of soymilk from the refrigerator.

"Sophie and I are going to church," announced Dad, pouring honey on his pancake. "Mass is at eleven."

I sighed and offered out my plate, waiting for the pancake. "I don't think I'm gonna go," I said, not having forgiven God for taking Mom away from us and exactly why I hadn't bothered to set foot in one of His houses since the funeral. I felt God had betrayed me and my family, and until He made make amends, I saw no need to waste my Sunday mornings.

Dad nodded. "Okay, but it would be a good way to meet the neighbors, get to know people. You want to make friends, don't you, Alice?"

I honestly had no desire to meet anyone, and I already had friends. If it were up to me, I would gladly stay home and keep to myself, except for my quests to discover the island.

"I just started a great book, Dad, and I wanna catch up on my reading. Besides, I've already made some friends and even joined a book club at school."

"Fine. Whatever floats your boat," said Dad with a defeated sigh.

The two of them left for church a short while later. I've never been very religious, even though my mother was. She took us to church every week and made sure we said our prayers every night. Even though he wouldn't admit it, my dad wasn't especially religious either, but since Mom's death, he seemed to take some kind of comfort in the church. I couldn't knock him for that and respected his feelings—we all have to grieve in our own way, but I want him to respect my feelings, too.

I puttered around the empty house for a while, trying to decide what I should do first. Maybe a visit to the local library down the street where I can work my way through titles by Charlotte Brontë, starting with *Jane Eyre. Would the library have a copy?* I also thought about a copy of *Villette*.

Oddly enough though, something changed my plans that morning, and I felt an inexplicable yearning for church after all. I found myself putting on a sweater, my running shoes, and reaching for the house keys.

The Our Lady of the Cross church building in Pacific Grove was only a mile up the hill, and I enjoyed the morning walk in the warm sunshine. When I arrived, I stood outside the building for a few moments, contemplating the white façade. Our Lady of the Cross was a large white clapboard church with solid brown crossbeams. The first thing I noticed was how sturdy it looked. It looked strong enough to withstand a hurricane standing there steadfastly, surrounded by a green lawn, right in the middle of a neighborhood block.

As I approached, I heard singing coming from inside. It sounded like they were nearing the end of Mass. I reached the oak double-doors, but instead of going inside, I plopped down on the marble steps and waited for the service to end and everyone to pile out.

Silently, I watched the seagulls performing their acrobatics in the sky above. The sea sparkled in the distance and the morning sun shimmered above the water. Pacific Grove was built on a sloping hill so it was nearly impossible to be anywhere in the town without glimpsing the bay.

The singing continued as the parishioners crooned, *Amazing Grace* loudly, whether they could carry a tune or not. It had always been one of my favorite hymns, even though I wasn't so sure about the words . . *.and grace will lead me home*, I thought as the noise came to an end.

Not long after that, I heard the hollow sound of people shuffling down the aisles toward the exit. I stood to wait for Dad and Sophie.

"Alice!" shouted a voice.

I turned around and saw Christian standing in the arched doorway of the church. He looked handsome in his chocolate-brown Sunday-morning suit, crisp, white shirt, and dark tie. The ensemble differed greatly from the casual clothes he'd been wearing at the book club, but he still had that same sunny smile, wonky nose, and the sparkle in his green eyes.

"Hey," I said. "What a coincidence, huh?"

"Yeah. Good to bump into you. Did you attend Mass? I didn't see you inside."

"No. I just came to meet my dad and little sister."

"Well, you should stop in sometime. My dad's the minister here," Christian said with a nod.

Surprised, it took me a moment to digest the information. "So you're—"

"Yep," he said, cutting me off, "a certified preacher's kid. Don't hold it against me, though. That's my dad right over there," he said, pointing.

The minister was a thin-faced man with graying hair, dressed in the typical high white collar and black suit. He was talking to my dad and Sophie, welcoming them to the parish, and for a moment, reminded me of the Chicago car salesman who'd sold us our Volkswagen.

"The guy he's talking to is my dad," I said.

"Hmm. Looks like a decent guy. I bet he's proud of you," said Christian.

"Not always, but yeah, we get along pretty well. We're a close family."

We studied our fathers and I noticed how strikingly different they were. My father was burly, with strong hands—a real son of the earth. Christian's dad, on the other hand, was thin and delicate, and holding a thick leather-bound book in his hand—a son of God. I wondered if Christian had noticed and was thinking the same.

"I'm glad they joined our parish. Why didn't you come inside?" he asked gently.

I shrugged. "I haven't been going to church lately."

"Why not?" he probed. "Sorry. I don't mean to pry. It's really none of my business. Everyone's always telling me I'm too direct."

"No, that's okay. Direct is good," I said with complete honesty. I preferred open and honest people to those with hidden agendas. "I don't talk about this much, but—well, my mom died a few months ago, and ever since then, I haven't been able to make peace with God, I guess."

"I understand," Christian said.

I wasn't sure if he truly understood or not. How could he know the pain of losing a parent unless it happened to him? *Now Henry...he would understand*, I thought. Still, it was nice of Christian to try.

I darted my eyes around at the happy parishioners, chatting and laughing after the service. It was a bit ridiculous, I knew, but I resented how content they seemed.

A few moments later, I saw Heather Palmer walking down the steps wearing a pretty white dress with lace trim. Her hair done up with a headband, she looked radiant. For some reason, I was surprised to see her there. I wouldn't have taken her for much of a churchgoer. An older woman accompanied her. She had more blond hair than gray tied up in a bun at the nape of her neck. The two of them looked like the epitome of pretention.

Christian saw me watching Heather as she glided down the steps in almost angelic fashion. "You know her?" he asked.

"Yeah. She's in my biology class. I never would've expected to see her here, though."

"She comes every week with her mom, never misses a Sunday."

"She's beautiful," I said and sighed. "I wonder what it's like to be so gorgeous."

"Er, she's okay, but she really doesn't have that much going on upstairs." He tapped his forehead. "She's a little too—self-involved."

I watched as Heather paused at the bottom of the marble steps, expertly greeting the parishioners with a radiant smile. She cocked her head in my direction but I didn't want to be caught staring at her again, so I turned my back to her.

Standing in the crowd, I sensed someone watching me, just as I watched Heather. Right then, I glimpsed the old lady who lived down the street. She was at the back of the crowd of parishioners, glaring at me, again with that strange look in her eyes.

"Who's that old lady in the green dress?" I asked, feigning I didn't know her.

Christian followed my gaze through the crowd. "Oh, that's Mrs. Prescott, the local ghostbuster," he said, with no trace of sarcasm or irony in his voice whatsoever.

"Ghostbuster?" I repeated, puzzled.

"Yeah. She's convinced that Monterey and Pacific Grove are haunted, and she often takes tourists around the harbor to show them the most haunted places. Monterey is the oldest town in California with some of the oldest buildings—of course, all that history comes with a fair number of ghosts."

"Ghosts?" I said. "You don't believe in that stuff, do you?" I asked, incredulous.

"I do," said Christian, looking me straight in the eye.

"Have you seen any?" I asked.

"Growing up in Pacific Grove, you see a lotta strange things, especially near the bay. Once or twice, I've seen lights and heard strange noises, that kind of thing."

Suddenly, my world seemed to be so far from metropolitan Chicago with its tall buildings and bumper-to-bumper cars. "That old lady gives me the creeps," I said. "There are some strange people living in Pacific Grove, that's for sure."

"Oh, Mrs. Prescott's harmless. She's lived here all her life. She dutifully helps the church, always pitching in on flower arrangements, local collections, and things like that."

"She said something strange to me the first week we moved in."

"What?"

"She told me to stay away from the water."

"Ah, well, maybe that's because of her kid. He drowned in the bay a long time ago."

"Drowned?" I shuddered, feeling aghast and sympathetic for the old lady at the same time. "That's awful. I feel sorry for her."

"Yeah, well, she hasn't been quite the same since."

I now looked at Mrs. Prescott from a new perspective, with new compassion and sympathy. I had heard that losing a child was worse than losing a parent, but she still gave me the creeps.

"Why did you move to Pacific Grove if you don't like it?"

"I never said I don't like it," I countered. "My dad's a marine biologist, so when he got a job at the aquarium, we all moved here."

"A marine biologist? Really? That's so cool! Well, you're in the right place if you love the ocean."

I nodded and let his remark pass. I couldn't bear to admit to Christian that I was terrified of the ocean and didn't want to go near it, even if my dad had no problem diving in and checking out the sea creatures.

Christian's face immediately turned serious. "Just watch out for the sharks."

"Sharks?"

"Yeah. This town kinda feeds on new blood, like the high school jocks who stalk Heather like great-whites on a poor seal."

"Oh. Those sharks," I said, almost with relief. "Don't worry about me. When it comes to land-sharks, I can take care of myself."

"Good." Christian beamed at me, as if I had passed some matriculation test. "Hey, wanna go grab a coffee? There's a great bakery near here that makes the most amazing bagels, especially on Sundays. We can talk about the book assignment."

"Er, not right now. I've got some things to do." Christian was sweet, but I didn't want to send him any signals or make the wrong impression. To be honest, I just couldn't see myself dating the son of a minister; it was a little too close to God for my comfort.

Christian nodded. "Well, okay then. Enjoy your Sunday," he said cordially then left me alone and went to talk to his father.

*

I wanted to go sailing, knowing it would make me feel closer to Henry somehow. After a cinnamon bagel and a cup of coffee, I walked down to the small marina, near Lovers Point.

Although it was early the following Sunday, the marina buzzed with activity. A group of divers prepared for a boat trip out in the bay, putting on their aqualungs as I approached the marina, dotted with sailing vessels readying themselves for a day cruise.

Connor waited for me at the end of the jetty. He was onboard a small sailing boat about twenty feet long, a broad smile on his sun-kissed face.

When I saw the boat, I immediately started sweating and couldn't catch my breath. I heard my heart pounding in my ears.

I hadn't expected that we'd traverse the waters in a vessel so tiny. It was much smaller than the boats I was used to, by at least thirty feet. My experience on the kayak had made me very wary of small boats, and this one looked very insignificant floating in that giant sea.

"Ready to go?" asked Connor, flashing a smile.

"Uh, I didn't think I'd be sailing in such a small boat," I said, nervously looking up and down the short length of the hull. I'd already read the manual, but the act of sailing would be something different.

"Oh, you'll be fine. There's nothing to worry about. It's a calm day, and I'll be there to catch you if you fall overboard." He smiled again, showing those white teeth.

I couldn't possibly back out; not without Connor thinking I was a chicken or a weirdo. I wanted to go through with it, had to, for my own sake, but when I moved toward the sailboat, my legs turned to jelly.

"I can't go through with this. I can't. . . .I can't," I said, breathing heavily. "I'm sorry—you can keep the fifty dollars."

Connor paused. "I'll tell you what, how about you take one of the small paddle boats and just stay inside the marina? It's sheltered, and I'll give you a life vest. That way you can acclimatize to being out in the water and if you're good, next week we can go out sailing. Huh?"

I nodded. *Baby steps. Yes, that is a good idea.*

Connor took me to some paddleboats tied up to the jetty and selected a bright red one. I felt like a kid as he strapped on a life vest that
hugged my chest, but at least I knew I wouldn't drown.

"Okay?" he asked.

I nodded and breathing deeply, I waved goodbye to Connor as he
returned to the surf shop.

"Hey!" shouted an angry voice as I climbed into the paddleboat.

Out of the corner of my eye, I could see a figure running down the
jetty at great speed toward me. I couldn't believe my eyes—Henry? I
hadn't seen him look so angry as he paced up and down on the shore,
fists clenched.

"Do you have a death wish? I told you to stay away from the bay!
Why will you not heed my warning?"

Shocked by the venom in his voice, I couldn't find the words to
answer. Once again, he looked and sounded like he hated me. "I-I just
wanna learn how to be on the water; that's all," I stuttered. "I don't want
to be terrified anymore," I reasoned, sounding like a little girl being punished for stealing from the cookie jar.

"Did I not tell you it is dangerous?" he said, exasperated. "Do not
go out into that bay, Alice. Ever!"

I pushed the paddleboat out, but Henry grabbed the stern and
pulled back on it, with amazing strength.

"Okay, okay!" I said and relented. "I won't go out." Frustrated, I
walked back up the jetty with Henry behind me. "I hope you're satisfied," I said over my shoulder. "Fifty dollars down the toilet!"

"You have a stubborn streak, do you not?" Henry said, striding up
the pier after me.

"So my dad says," I replied, "but it's my life, and I'll do what I want
with it."

"Why do you do it?"

"I told you, I'm trying to get over my fear of the water. I figured I'd
take some lessons, ease into it myself. If no one else wants to help me,
I've gotta help myself. What's it to you anyway?"

Henry pulled my arm to stop me from walking. Then he paused and
squared his hands on his hips, looking out over the bay, thinking as
though weighing a decision. "You are that determined to go into the
water?"

I nodded. "Yes. If I will ever cure my aquaphobia, I have to get
back out there. Do you have any idea what it's like to live in fear every

time you're on a boat or near a swimming pool? It's horrible living here, surrounded by all this water."

Henry looked straight in my eyes, his blue irises glinting in the sun. "Fine," he said. "Then come with me."

I curiously followed him down the shoreline, still wearing my life vest. We left the Lovers Point marina behind and walked half a mile down the beach, past some old sycamore trees to another jetty with a couple of boats docked. Henry stopped at a small sailboat at the end. It was about twenty feet long, with a huge main sail the color of sky-blue. On the side of the boat the words *Evening Tide* were scrawled in dark blue; this is the same vessel I saw the night of the party.

"Welcome aboard," he said, ushering me onto the boat.

"Is this yours?" I asked, marveling at the old boat I'd been so eager to find.

"If you are so determined to go in the water, someone has to teach you; I would rather it be me."

I smiled, still terrified of going in the water, but being with Henry calmed me down somehow, so I climbed aboard.

"Sit up there, near the front," Henry instructed.

I did as I was told and took my position near the bow, on one of the wooden crossbeams. Henry untied the boat from its dock. Then he expertly steered the boat out of the harbor and into the bay.

From my position, cross-legged near the bow, I watched him hoist the sail. His face solemn with the breeze blowing through his hair. His blue eyes narrowed as he faced the wind, looking out to sea—his handsome, chiseled features exposed to the salty elements. I enjoyed the scent of the breeze as it caressed my own hair, and for a moment, I was at peace.

"How do you feel?" he asked.

"I'm okay. I mean, I'm not seasick, and I don't sense a panic attack coming on or anything," I answered truthfully. Being with Henry gave me a sense of safety, just like when he'd pulled me out of that watery tomb.

The wind huffed, and the sail billowed; we soon found ourselves gliding out of the bay. I saw a distant Connor outside his surf shop and waved. The town of Pacific Grove left far behind, its quaint houses and rooftops but a distant memory, as we headed out into the expanse.

I leaned back and settled into the nook of the boat. The sea breeze ruffled my hair and the white waves danced like graceful ballerinas around us—I was having the time of my life!

A confident sailor, Henry's whole body took on an imposing stance as he steered the boat. I felt at his mercy but that was all right with me.

"Where did you learn to sail?" I asked.

"Oh, I've been sailing for a long, long time," Henry said cryptically as he pulled the main sails with the rope, "ever since I was a kid."

"In San Francisco Bay?"

"Yes," he said, his strong chin jutting out to sea. "My Pa taught me how to sail before I could run. We took fishing trips around the bay when he was not working. We would sneak out of the house early, before Ma got up. Often, we stayed out all day, just the two of us, fishing in the bay."

"Sounds nice," I said, finding something adorable about the old-fashioned way he spoke of his parents, especially calling them "Pa" and "Ma." It reminded me of the times I'd spent with my own dad. We'd had some quality times together, but over the past few months, those had been overshadowed by my mother's death.

"How are you feeling now—seasick?" Henry's voice full of concern, "Not afraid are you?"

"No, I'm fine," I said and meant it. No signs of the terrible nausea or the overwhelming fear that usually assaulted me when on the water. "For some reason, I feel very calm when I'm with you."

Henry nodded and seemed pleased, but he kept his eyes out to sea, on the distant horizon.

I looked furtively around, wondering if I would catch another glimpse of the mysterious island.

"What are you searching for?"

"Er…just keeping my eyes out for dolphins," I said nonchalantly, "or whales. It's almost their migration season," I said, having learned from my father that we sailed directly into the path that grays would take when moving on to warmer waters.

I raised my right hand theatrically over my eyes, trying to shield the glare of the sun as I made a point of spying imaginary dolphins. I started to wonder about the island. Had I really seen it or was it just a hallucination?

Henry squinted at some far-off horizon, and a frown appeared. "A storm is coming in. I should take you back."

"A storm? Connor said it would be calm today." I looked out to sea, but saw only a blue sky and endless horizon.

"Connor was wrong. I see trouble brewing," my young captain said sternly.

"But I don't see anything," I replied, lifting my hand over my eyes and straining to catch a glimpse of any thunderclouds that might herald a storm.

"It is coming; believe me," said Henry. "When you have been on the water as long as I have, you can tell the signs." He pointed to the sky at a couple seabirds flying rapidly toward the shore. "Storm petrels. They always fly inland just before bad weather. We are heading back."

He turned the boat around, disappointment crept in. I actually wanted to stay out in the bay a little longer. Scanning the horizon, I looked for any approaching storm. I saw nothing, but I recalled how quickly the fog crept in while kayaking with the group. I knew the sea to be a moody monster since experiencing one mood-swing firsthand.

Henry steered the boat back toward the marina, expertly pulling the sail and taking advantage of the winds. Ultimately, the strong winds proved him right, and I was glad he'd known enough to steer us back to shore. By the time we reached land and docked at the marina, a strong gale moved through, one that rivaled the windiest day in Chicago.

"Thanks," I said, eyes shining with happiness. "I never thought I could feel at home on the water." I found it quite the paradox to say those two words in the same sentence, "home" and "water."

"My pleasure," he said.

His politeness tickled me and how unlike other boys I knew at Monterey High. There was something strange about Henry and his manners plus the precise diction—certainly not modern.

"Can we go out again?" I asked hopefully.

He hesitated then slowly nodded. "Sure. Why not? Same time next week?" he asked.

I nodded, elated.

"Yes, and thank you. You've helped me more than you can ever know."

Chapter Six: Ghost Stories

I smiled broadly, deep in thought as I walked up my road to the house. It had been a beautiful, memorable morning. I noticed the white chrysanthemums that grew on the lawns; they looked so lovely as their petals caught the glorious sun. Something about being with Henry made everything seem so much brighter.

Someone waited on our front porch, sitting in the old rocking chair. I almost didn't see her because she sat so still with her back rigid, and her gnarled fingers joined together as if in prayer; her unwavering gray eyes staring trancelike at me.

"Mrs. Prescott?" I asked hesitantly, wondering how long the old woman had been sitting there. "Uh…what are you doing here?"

She stared at me with furious eyes. "I told you to stay away from the bay, but you did not heed my warnings."

"Excuse me?"

"You didn't listen to me, and now you have brought great trouble for all of us."

"I'm sorry, but I don't know what you're talking about," I said. *This old lady is really beginning to scare me.*

"The bay has taken him, just like it took my Johnny."

"Taken who?" I asked, confused by her words. I assumed the *Johnny* she had referred to was her son, the one Christian had told me had drowned.

"That boy from the bay, the one you've chosen to keep company with…He is not one of us."

Not one of us? What's that supposed to mean? And how does she know anything about Henry?

"Mrs. Prescott, I'm sorry, but I don't have time for this," I said, walking past her.

The old woman sprang up from the rocking chair with surprising strength and agility for someone her age. Instantly, she stood just inches away from me, eyes unwavering and trancelike—so close I could feel her breath on my face.

"You can see it in his eyes. He has been taken by the bay."

"Whose eyes?" I asked, doing my best not to tremble.

"The boy who rescued you. You may think he is like the other boys, but he is not. He has been taken, just like my Johnny."

"What do you mean by taken?" I asked again, my voice wavering. She really did her best to scare me, and I began to wonder if she was certifiable. I heard sometimes the grief of losing a child can make someone go mad, and the self-proclaimed ghostbuster was definitely well on her way if not there already.

"There's an evil menace floating over the water, an ancient curse. It is not safe. You are not safe."

Ancient curse? Menacing evil? Christian also told me that Mrs. Prescott claimed to be the town ghostbuster, but I couldn't fathom someone believing in such nonsense.

"I don't know what you're talking about," I said, trying to brush past her.

Instantly, Mrs. Prescott grabbed me by the arm and started to shake me, her nails digging into my sleeve like tiny sharp knives. She wouldn't let go, her fingers clamped around my arms like deadly vises.

"What are you doing?" I exclaimed, wrestling with the old woman. Finally, I managed to shake her off without hurting her.

She looked at me, long and hard. "I have warned you twice." Then, without another word, she disappeared quickly down the garden path and hurried down the street.

I ran inside and slammed the door shut, trembling violently. She might have been just a crazy old woman who'd lost her son, but I had no idea why she had to involve me. She doesn't know anything about Henry.

The house was empty, and silent other than the tick-tock of the clock in the hall. Dad and Sophie went to morning Mass and had obviously gone somewhere else afterward. I was glad, though, because I wanted to be on my own, and I didn't want to have to face either of them in my frightened state. Tears began to well, and I wanted to bawl my eyes out.

I went into the kitchen and sat down. *Pull yourself together, Alice*, I urged myself. Once my knees stopped trembling and my eyes dried a bit, I noticed Dad's note pinned to the refrigerator. I plucked it off and read it out loud: "Gone to the aquarium for a long lunch. Calamari is on the menu. Call my cell if you want to join us. See you later. Love, Dad."

I crumpled up the note in my hand and immediately decided I preferred to stay home alone to think—especially about Henry.

The realization came to me that I didn't know much about Henry either. He told me he came from San Francisco and he'd grown up on North Beach. He'd gotten a job on one of the fishing boats that trawled Monterey at sixteen. A first-class sailor, completely familiar with the waters along the coastline. He could predict the turn of the winds and tides, but even more uncannily, he seemed to understand what I was feeling. I knew nothing else about him.

The longer I pondered Mrs. Prescott's strange words, the more troubled I became. In my attempt to answer the many questions swirling through my head, I needed to seek solitude and some fresh air, so I took a stroll to Magnolia Bakery on Lighthouse Avenue.

"Hi, Alice," said Candy, the pretty blond waitress. "This is becoming your regular haunt. The usual? Skinny vanilla latte with an extra shot?"

"Sure," I said.

"Comin' right up," she said with a smile.

I watched her pour the coffee into the polystyrene cup. Sitting on the marble shelf in front—carrot cake. It reminded me of the conversation I had with Henry.

"You know, your cakes are so good. How long has the baker been here?" I asked, leaning on the counter.

"Who, George? Honey, George has been here longer than you and I have been alive, for over twenty years."

"Are you sure?"

"Sure as the day is long."

"What about the last baker?"

"I don't know too much about him. I just heard that he dropped dead in the kitchen a long time ago, a heart attack on the job. That's dedication for ya."

I frowned. Henry told me the last baker's carrot cake was better, but—he wouldn't know that if the last baker passed away two decades earlier. It made no sense, he's too young. . .hmm. Maybe he got it mixed up with some other bakery.

"That's strange. Remember when I came in here the other day, when I ordered the coffee and latte?"

"Sure, hon'."

"Well, the guy with me said something about the former baker dying."

"You were with a guy? I thought you were on your own."

"No, I wasn't alone. We sat in a corner, under the sycamore tree. I ordered two drinks and carrot cake, remember?"

"Yeah, I remember you coming in, sweetie, I just didn't see your fella." She then smiled, offered me my fresh latte, and went on to wait on the next customer behind me in line.

I walked out to the yard and sat in the same spot, under the boughs of the tree, where I'd had coffee with Henry. Mrs. Prescott's words still rang in my mind as I sipped the latte.

As I sat there, the image of a particular person kept floating into my mind. From the first time I met him, he had been kind and understanding so I felt I could trust him. With excited urgency, I stood up to leave, half my latte sat untouched on the table.

*

Since it was a Sunday afternoon, I figured he might be home instead of out enjoying the sunshine. In the distance I saw Our Lady of the Cross church gleaming like a great white whale in the sunlight.

The minister's house was a Victorian white clapboard, sheltered by a canopy of pine trees. It stood just up the hill from Lighthouse Avenue, just a few blocks from my house on Forest. A nice, roomy house, similar to the other houses in the neighborhood.

I skirted around the side, to the main door, and knocked on the pane of stained glass, hoping that someone would be in.

A shadow appeared through the glass, and Christian opened the door wearing his brown Sunday-morning suit, the same one he'd worn to Mass when I'd seen him. His face broke into a smile when he saw me. "Alice! What a surprise!"

"I need to talk to you. I'm not interrupting, am I?"

"No. We just finished lunch. You look worried. What's wrong?"

"Mrs. Prescott thinks the bay is haunted," I blurted out, hoping I didn't sound stupid.

"Okay. Well, uh. . .I think you'd better come in," he said, gesturing me inside.

It was strange walking into a preacher's house after months of shunning God and the Church. Even though I was still a little angry with

Him for letting my mother die, I tentatively entered hoping I would find some forgiveness there—if not some answers.

As is the case for most homes in Pacific Grove, the furniture looked antiquated and Victorian. An imposing grandfather clock stood in the hallway, with black-and-white family portraits adorning the walls. I looked them over, noting the baby pictures of Christian. He was really cute as a kid, with large eyes and a mop of hair, but no hint of the wonky nose. Portraits of his mom and dad hung beside his.

I followed Christian into the living room, and he shut the door behind us. All of a sudden I felt rather foolish being there, but it was too late to make a convenient exit.

"Now, tell me what happened," he said, sitting down next to me on the lace-covered couch. "Would you like something to drink? I have some great herbal tea."

I shook my head and started to tell him about the strange encounter with Mrs. Prescott. I skipped the part about going sailing with Henry or ever meeting Henry. "She was waiting for me when I returned home this afternoon. It was like she was possessed or something. She had the craziest look in her eyes."

"Where were you before that?" he asked curiously.

I didn't like his interrogation tactics, so I hesitated before answering. "Out in the bay with…a friend. See, I had this notion that I might be able to cure my aquaphobia by taking some sailing lessons, facing my fears head-on, but Mrs. Prescott keeps telling me to stay away from the water. She had the strangest look on her face today."

"I see," Christian replied, studying me intently.

My eyes wavered, and I wondered if he believed me. "You don't seem entirely surprised by Mrs. Prescott's superstitions," I offered, trying to steer the conversation away from my sailing trip with Henry.

Christian paused then said, "I don't believe they are just superstitions."

"What? Don't tell me you are buying into them, too," I said, incredulous. Christian was a bright boy, well read and intelligent—and ran the local book club. Granted, his father was a minister, but that didn't prevent Christian from being an independent, free thinker. At least I'd had that impression from the beginning—now I began to wonder.

Christian sighed. "There are many things we can't explain, Alice. Yes, I do believe in the supernatural. As the son of a minister, I know there is an afterlife. I believe in heaven and hell."

"How can you believe in that?" I asked in amazement. "C'mon! You can't really believe in hell!"

Christian didn't seem to be offended. He smiled and decisively stood up from the couch, peering down at me. "We may need a second opinion. Will you come with me?"

"Where?" I asked curiously.

"I want you to meet someone. He may have the answers to some of your questions."

*

Christian drove his father's car—an old, rustic sedan. We took Route 68 to Carmel and then Highway 1. My driver suddenly appeared a few years older behind the wheel of his dad's car, with a relaxed smile on his face and the wind ruffling his brown, curly hair.

"Where are we going?" I asked, enjoying the ride. For a moment I had forgotten my troubles. I liked getting out of town and the liberation that came with travel.

"To see an old friend," Christian replied. "He lives in an ancient house just on the outskirts of Carmel. I haven't seen him in a while, but I think he may be able to help us."

We drove through the quaint town of Carmel, with its polished streets and houses, along the beach road. Finally, Christian pulled the car to a stop outside a ramshackle house, shaded by tall pines.

"Who lives here?" I asked curiously, looking at the peeling paint on a front door in desperate need of repair.

"You'll see," said Christian as he opened the door to get out.

I followed Christian up the garden path to the house. Outside the front door sat the skull of a large mammal. From the shape of its jaws it had to be a whale, I remember from pictures in the books my dad brought home.

Christian knocked on the wooden door. "I hope he's in," he said, looking around the exterior of the house. "Sometimes he goes fishing along the coast."

We heard the hollow sound of footsteps then an old man opened the door. He must have been in his seventies. Wisps of gray hair had grown around his ears with eyes as dark-blue as the sea. He wore a clean white shirt and britches, and there was a grandfatherly thing about him that made me like him immediately. "Christian!" the man bellowed with surprise and genuine warmth.

"Hi, Sam." Christian smiled and pulled the older man into a friendly hug.

"You get taller every time I see you. Nice of you to drop by. Who's this?" asked Sam, squinting at me with inquisitive eyes.

"This is Alice, a friend of mine. We have some questions, and we were hoping you might be able to help us with some of the answers."

"I'll do my best. Come in." He gestured, and I followed Christian into the house.

The décor had a distinctly nautical motif, filled with antique bric-a-brac and miscellaneous maritime knickknacks. The antique glass cabinet housed ships in bottles, and oil paintings of sea-faring vessels and ocean panoramas decorated the walls. I even spotted some seismic charts in the corner—cluttered without being untidy.

We settled into a pair of comfortable cushioned stools opposite Sam, who took his position in a big leather armchair. He took out a pipe, lit it with a match, and started to smoke.

"We need to know about a little local history," Christian explained.

"Well, in that case, my boy, you've come to the right place. What's on your mind?"

"We're looking for information about an ancient curse, the curse of Monterey Bay," said Christian.

Sam's eyes grew heavy with nostalgia. "Ah, yes, and what a strange and unfortunate curse that is."

"Can you tell us about it?"

"Sure. Well, long ago, this whole region was inhabited by the *Esselen* Indians—a hunter-gatherer tribe who lived peacefully in the hills and valleys surrounding the bay."

I listened carefully to Sam's words. I had recently learned of the tribe he mentioned, and back when I lived in the Midwest, we had visited an Indian reservation belonging to the Sioux Indians. I sympathized with their predicament and had even joined a campaign protest, organized by my school, to save Native American land.

"When the first white settlers came to Monterey in the eighteenth century, they quickly colonized the region. A fort was set up for a garrison of soldiers. Among them, a young lieutenant—Charles Drake. A dashing young fellow from Texas with a love of life. He was an expert marksman; I heard he could shoot a jackrabbit at a hundred paces.

"The soldiers tried to make peace with the Esselen and offered gifts to Chief Gray Wolf. A wise old soul but also stubborn and fiercely protective of his people. He had a feisty daughter named White Dove. She had long hair, as dark as a raven's feathers, and large brown eyes and skin as brown as the winter sun.

"When young Lieutenant Drake first laid eyes on White Dove, he instantly fell in love with her. She was equally dazzled by the white man's charm. A secret romance ignited between the two of them, and they met on the peninsula of what is now Lovers Point. She brought flowers to Charles, and the two would sit by the bay and watch the seabirds from the shore.

"One day, though, White Dove's father followed his daughter and caught her holding the lieutenant in a passionate embrace. A terrible fight ensued between the old chief and his daughter. She said some harsh things to her daddy—told him his stubbornness would cause the demise of his people, since he refused to bargain with the white man. Enraged, the chief forbade her to see Charles again.

"Every day, White Dove wept for her lover, and she longed to be with him. She became more heartbroken with each passing day. Charles missed her just as much, and one night he stole into the Esselen camp and took White Dove. He planned to run away with her, so he had hidden a sea kayak in the bay for them to make their escape. Unfortunately for the young lovers, a terrible storm raged, and White Dove drowned. Her body later washed up on shore, along with Charles Drake's, since he had drowned trying to save the woman who'd stolen his heart.

"The old chief, mourning the loss of his daughter, wept and raged. Gray Wolf cursed the moon and the heavens and prayed to Sedna, god of the sea and the underworld. He asked Sedna to put a curse on the bay."

I shuddered, caught up in the story. "What kind of curse?" I asked.

"Well, the chief became furious with Drake, so he asked his god to make sure that anyone who drowns in Monterey Bay is destined to stay in the fourth dimension. They cannot leave this area until they atone for any harm against others. Although they walk among us and they look like us, they are…different. They may have a heart, but it does not beat. They are ghosts to us."

"A heart that does not beat?" I repeated. "But how is that possible?"

"They belong to the souls of those who have drowned in Monterey Bay," Sam continued. "There are tales of a green light along the shore. Some say it is the lantern of White Dove looking for Charles. The sound of the wind along the coast is the Indian woman calling for her lost love."

"Such a sad story," I choked out past a lump in my throat. "Poor White Dove."

"And poor Charles," Christian said, also touched. "That's quite a story, Sam. Thanks for sharing it with us."

"What about the curse, though? Is there any way to break the spell?" I asked.

"Some say the only way is for them to act out services to humanity or sacrifice what they love most. Old Gray Wolf was so angry, he demanded his daughter give up her love for Charles Drake."

"How can these poor drowned souls move on?" I asked. "Being stuck in the fourth dimension can't be fun."

"Some are afraid to look closely at how they've hurt others through their own selfishness and they refuse so are destined to remain there forever, watching friends grow old and loved ones die while they stay the same."

The thought saddened me deeply. I couldn't imagine the pain of those stranded souls, being stuck on earth forever and condemned to watch their loved ones die. "It must be a very lonely existence," I said. "I feel sorry for them."

"Me, too," said Sam as he bowed his head. "May their poor souls eventually find peace."

The three of us maintained a moment of silence in reverence for those poor souls, interrupted only by the ticking of the hallway clock.

As we sat there, I wondered if I should mention the island. Sam seemed friendly and knowledgeable and not as skeptical as many of the folks in Monterey. I took a deep breath and plunged in. "There's something else," I said hesitantly. "When we were all out kayaking a few weeks ago, I-I thought I saw something." As soon as the words tumbled out, I glanced sideways at Christian, but he nodded in support.

"Well, what did you see?" asked Sam.

"I saw—I saw an island," I said, drawing out the sentence in a long breath.

"An island?" repeated Sam. "What kind of island?"

"It rose from the sea and had a golden beach with two mountainous peaks. I saw it through the fog, but when I paddled toward it, it disappeared."

Sam stared at me. "You say it had two peaks?"

"Yes," I nodded. "Why? Do you know about it?"

Sam shook his head. "No, I didn't say that. An island in the bay, huh? Now that is mysterious."

"It sure is," Christian replied.

They probably thought I'd just hallucinated it. "I was wondering if it might have anything to do with the curse you mentioned," I persisted.

Sam just looked at me with silence, I sensed he held something back. Finally, he spoke, "No, I've never heard of an island linked to the curse." Then he shifted in his seat and gave me the brush-off, "Well, I think that's all I have to tell you folks."

"Thanks for your help, Sam," Christian replied, getting up.

"Anytime…and don't stay away so long next time," Sam said, then took a puff on his pipe.

As we walked away from Sam's house, a distinctively chilly feeling came over me. I remembered his words: The dead walking among us. *How is any of that possible? And if it is, who's dead, and who's not?* This discovery chilled me like a sharp icicle through my heart.

We rode in silence during the journey back as Christian drove along the darkening, winding coastal road to Pacific Grove. My head turned toward the bay, I watched the seemingly benign waves dance on the water.

Once or twice, Christian glanced over at me. "You okay?" he asked. I nodded.

"You know something, don't you?" he said, gently nudging me.

I turned to face him. "What do you mean?"

"When you fell into the bay, did you see something other than the island?"

I contemplated answering then said, "No," I wasn't ready to tell Christian yet about Henry, not until I found out the facts for myself.

Christian let it pass and kept his eyes on the road.

"Do you believe what Sam told us?" I asked.

"There are a lot of strange tales," Christian said, "but yes, I believe there is some truth in it. I don't believe things are over when we die. I believe that life carries on in another form or state."

I paused to ponder his idea. I had never been sure what to think about an afterlife, but since my mother had died, I had some doubts. I wanted to believe she was an angel in heaven, that she had gone on to some peaceful place free from illness and worry. Maybe she is watching out for Dad, Sophie, and me. I wanted to believe this, but I wasn't sure.

In any case, the hope of it gave me a sense of peace and the feeling that one day I might join her.

"Here we are," said Christian, turning off the engine as he pulled up in front of my house. He glanced across at me, with concern. "Are you alright?"

I shook myself out of my reverie, smiled weakly and nodded. "Yes. Thanks for taking me to see Sam."

*

Dad and Sophie were making dinner in the kitchen when I walked in. I smelled popcorn so that was obviously on the menu. Sunday nights our family had a ritual of eating popcorn and settling down in front of the TV for a movie.

"We had an awesome day!" Sophie cooed. "Daddy took me to the aquarium. We saw this jellyfish with the biggest tentacles ever! Then I saw a pair of seahorses that Daddy keeps in a beautiful tank. Did you know they mate for life?"

"Where have you been, honey?" asked Dad, handing me a bowl of popcorn.

I paused. "I went for a drive along the coast with Christian O'Neill."

"The minister's son?" Dad said with some surprise, as I hadn't spent much time with any boys since Mom died. "That's great. From what I know of him, he's a nice kid."

I nodded. Christian was nice, but Henry was the one always on my mind.

"Are you going to join us? We're watching *Mermaids*."

I shook my head. "No. I have some homework I need to do. Algebra tomorrow," I said, then excused myself to go upstairs with my bowl of popcorn in hand.

More important than algebra, I thought about the ancient curse Sam had spoken about. A heart that does not beat—I couldn't get those few words out of my mind. If their hearts do not beat, how can they love? And are they even still—human?

Chapter Seven: The Shipwreck

The Monterey High homecoming parade was in two weeks, and the whole school was in a rapturous state of excitement. A homecoming queen and king were to be elected by ballot, and Principal Philopolis had scheduled an assembly at which the results would be announced.

Five finalists vied for the queen's crown: Heather Palmer, Laura Ellis, Becky Goldman, Eva Laing, and Juanita Sanchez. All had grown up in Monterey County and as beautiful as the light that shimmered on the bay. Dark-haired Juanita originally from Mexico; Becky and Eva grew up in Monterey; Laura came from nearby Moss Landing; and sunny Heather was Pacific Grove born and bred.

"It's all so predictable," Emily said with a frustrated sigh. "Why can't we have a transgender homecoming queen up for nomination? I never thought Orange County would be more progressive than Monterey."

"Wait. If we had a real queen—as in transgender or drag—what would that make the king?" I quipped.

Emily laughed, then announced with theatrical finality, "Doesn't matter anyway. Heather's gonna win."

"How can you be so sure?" I asked as we took our seats in the assembly hall, just before lunch, next to some rowdy seniors. Heather was certainly very beautiful and popular, but Juanita and Laura had their own fan clubs, especially among some of the older students.

Emily shrugged. "I just have a feeling. Call it my woman's intuition." She seemed so certain. I wondered how she knew, but Emily had an acute intuition, so I didn't doubt her prediction.

All that morning, the ballots had been collected and counted. Now, Mrs. Philopolis walked up to the stand. She searched for her glasses, opened the folded results, and got right to the point. "And this year's homecoming queen is…" As if the weight of the world rested on the principal's next words, she paused, then finally blurted out dramatically, "Heather Palmer!"

Heather smiled radiantly and stood up to a tremendous round of applause as she stepped up to the podium to be congratulated by the principal. She looked so gorgeous in her pink cashmere sweater and jeans, with her long, fair mane falling softly around her shoulders, and she moved so gracefully.

I wish I looked like that, I thought to myself, envious as the seniors started chanting Heather's name and wolf-whistling at her. I knew I would never be the queen of anything, let alone homecoming queen—not that I wanted that kind of attention, anyway. I always shied away from the limelight and preferred to stay in the back.

Heather gave a short speech—a sweet, sincere promise to do her best to represent Monterey High.

"No surprise there," said Emily, clapping her hands not so enthusiastically. "I guess we'll have to wait till next year for our transgender queen." She had never been a big fan of Heather, something I determined from her distasteful remarks at the boat party.

I watched Heather smiling on the podium, her blond hair shining radiantly under the fluorescent lights, and again that twinge of jealousy. It seemed as if the girl had everything: beauty, adoration, brains—all the things a sixteen-year-old girl craved and more.

*

Later, in the cafeteria, I sat with an untouched bowl of limp pasta in front of me. I watched Emily across the table as she went about her rituals of preparing her lunch. Like she often did, she had brought in some wild herbs from her garden to make a special tea. Mixing it with hot water from a flask, she made an intoxicating brew. It was just one of the many eccentricities about her which I found endearing, but caused the other students to stare. I had a sip of her brew once but thought it tasted bitter and thereafter politely declined.

Finally, she looked up, having noticed my inquisitive stare. "What?" she said, wiping the corners of her mouth. "Do I have something on my chin?"

"How did you know Heather would win?" I asked.

"It's really just simple arithmetic. One girl plus all the popularity in the school equals homecoming queen," she explained. She took a sip of her herbal tea. "Besides, the kids at this school aren't progressive enough to elect anyone else."

"I think there's more to it than that," I said. "You seem to have an uncanny way of knowing things, predicting what's gonna happen. It's like you have this innate ability or something."

Emily continued drinking her tea, her green eyes as glassy as a cat's. "What are you saying?"

"Nothing. I'm just asking if there's anything I should know," I said. "I mean, we're friends, aren't we? And friends tell each other stuff."

"Oh yeah? Are you keeping any secrets from me then, Ali?" Emily countered, her eyes flashing as she studied me intently.

The question silenced me for a moment. I hadn't told her about Henry or the trip to see Sam. I let the matter drop, but I still wondered. "No, I guess not."

I hadn't told Emily about Henry because I needed more information about him before I went public with it. Too many unanswered questions, and our meeting with Sam only opened a new can of worms. I decided to seek answers of my own after school, and I knew just where to start.

*

After the last bell, I headed back to Cannery Row. The sun slowly set over the bay, and the fishing boats started returning to the harbor, groaning with the weight of the day's catch.

"Hey, Alice!" shouted a voice, followed by the sound of screeching brakes.

I turned and saw Connor, from the surf shop. He straddled his bike, smiling as usual, and his tan face seemed even more freckled.

"How did you get on out in the boat the other day?" he asked pleasantly.

"Fine," I said. "I ended up sailing with someone experienced, and he helped me."

"You had a sailing buddy?" Connor asked in surprise. "I thought you wanted to go solo."

I looked at Connor and frowned. "Yeah. You didn't see him? I waved to you from the bow of the boat, and my friend stood at the helm. Don't you remember?"

"Gee, Alice, I can't say I do."

I stared at Connor for a moment, wondering if he was going a little crazy. "But I-I was with a guy," I said, punctuating my every word. "You saw us—right?"

Connor looked at me, puzzled, and shook his head. "Okay, if you say so. Anyway, good seeing you. Let me know if you want to go out sailing." Then he waved and pedaled off.

I continued down Cannery Row, snaking alongside the old canneries and past Doc Ricketts's house. I hadn't been back to 800 since the night of the dance, and I wanted to see what I'd find inside.

The corridor was dark and musty. I fumbled for the light switch but found none. I creeped to the end of the entranceway, but this time, no music greeted me from the other side of the door. The second door creaked as I pushed it open. No dancers, no costume ball—only silence, and the entire place appeared deserted.

I looked around the room for clues, searching among the pile of boxes. I stared at the floor, covered in dust. I found it all quite strange. I'd only been at the dance a couple weeks ago, quite the extravagant affair, yet now the place looked like it hadn't been touched for many years.

"Can I help you, Miss?" a voice echoed out of the darkness.

"Ah!" I screamed, almost jumping out of my skin. I turned around and looked into the eyes of an old man. "Wh-who are you?" I stuttered.

"Perhaps I should ask you the same question. I'm Elias Jones, the caretaker. And who might you be, and why are you in this cannery, Miss?"

"My name's Alice, and I'm looking for someone," I said, my heartbeat slowly returning to normal. I felt I had aged about ten years, and wondered if my hair had gone gray with fright. "I was here the other night, and there was a dance. I'm looking for someone I saw there."

The old man frowned. "A dance? There have been no dances here for a very long time. It's nothing but canned storage now."

"But there was a dance," I said, looking around the old warehouse for vindication. "Over there sat a piano." I pointed toward the far wall and started to move in that direction. "And here a harp. . .and right over there—about twenty or thirty dancers doing a slow waltz."

"A slow waltz, eh?" said the old man who started to chuckle. "Looks like I missed a good party. Well, as I said, there hasn't been a dance here for over a hundred years."

"A hundred years?" I repeated.

The man nodded. "At least. They used to hold charity dances here every Saturday night, but those stopped a long time ago. It's been nothin' but an old cannery since."

I rubbed my head with my right palm. I knew I hadn't dreamt up the dance. It was all real. *I really did see Henry, and I can still remember the smell of him—and the perfumed dancers.*

"Are you sure you didn't just—imagine things?" said the old caretaker. "There have been some strange sights in the cannery, light tricks, makin' people see things."

I started to move, albeit in somewhat of a daze. *None of this is really happening. It can't be,* I thought, shaking my head and asking for the first time—*Is it just me? Am I losing my mind?*

"You all right, Missy?"

"Yes. It's just been a rough couple of months." I thought again of my mom.

"If you want to find out more about those dances, I can tell you where to look."

"Where?" I shouted, almost startling the old fellow.

"In the Monterey Maritime Museum, down by the plaza."

*

The museum had once been known as the Monterey Maritime and History Museum and stood in Custom House Plaza, near the town center. I hadn't had the chance to visit since my arrival, but it had been on my radar. After all, I did love history and reading so I wanted to find out more about the coastline. Exhibitions featured the colonization of the Spanish and the development of the squid and fishing industries. It also housed a huge selection of material on the nautical history of the city. I wondered if there was any record of that elusive little vessel, *Evening Tide.*

The maritime section of the museum was in a curved and dimly lit hall. The exhibit began in the 1600s, with the Esselen Indians. I gazed at the lithographs and photographs of the Native Americans, with their long limbs and painted faces. I thought of White Dove, the poor lovestruck girl who had drowned in the bay, and I studied the designs of the teepee houses.

One painting displayed Indians standing on a cliff face in Monterey with the cypress trees bent over in the wind while a terrible storm raged at sea. In the middle of the waves, the figure of a drowning victim. I shuddered at the wide, helpless eyes, the eyes of a person who knew they were going to die, to be swallowed by the bay.

As I walked past the Native American section, the exhibition led to the arrival of the Spanish. There were drawings of Franciscan priests and US soldiers in their navy-blue uniforms. I wondered if I would find a portrait of Charles Drake, the man who had dared to fall in love with an Indian chief's daughter.

The first black-and-white photographs appeared when the exhibition moved on to the early nineteenth century. Pictures of old Monterey, horses and carts, some fishing boats, and the canneries. I marveled at the images and how small the town used to be, so unlike the bustling port I lived in now.

By the start of the twentieth century, big boats moored in the harbor and the first cars were on the streets. This led to a section in the exhibit reserved for famous shipwrecks such as fishing vessels, cargo ships, and even a small liner—all lost at sea.

My heart skipped a beat when I arrived at the next display, headlined *Evening Tide*. The fishing boat had apparently docked in San Francisco and sank in the bay in 1915. I quickly scanned through the pictures from *The Monterey Herald* and read a caption underneath one of them:

Evening Tide, a fishing vessel hailing from San Francisco, wrecked and sank during the violent storms off Monterey Bay last night. All aboard have been lost at sea.

As I read on, I discovered the crew came from San Francisco, and presumed drowned. Thirteen sailors lost at sea, but no bodies were ever found. The boat had been fishing in the bay to take advantage of the large glut of squid in the area but were caught in the storm.

A black-and-white photograph, taken in San Francisco Bay sat as a memento of the crew catching a record shark only a month before. I studied the young faces, smiling and proud as they clustered around the big animal. Scanning each one of them closely, I recognized a face at the back and I froze.

There, in an old black-and-white photograph, stood Henry. No mistaking it, with his wavy hair, perfect features, straight nose, and inquisitive smile. And he didn't look a day younger or older than the last time I'd seen him. *But how could it be possible? How could his picture be in the archives of the museum, in a newspaper that was a century old?*

I almost cried out and lifted a palm to my mouth to prevent myself from gagging. A heart that does not beat, I said to myself, remembering Sam's words.

I continued reading the rest of the article. It stated that a memorial plaque in memory of the sailors was to be erected in Pacific Grove Cemetery.

"Miss, we're closing in five minutes," called the museum curator.

"Thank you. I found what I needed to," I mumbled as I rushed past the startled curator and made my way toward the exit.

*

Pacific Grove Cemetery was situated behind Our Lady of the Cross. I arrived early in the evening, and the fading sunlight cast long shadows on the grass. It was a tidy, well-kept cemetery, with fresh-cut flowers at each gravestone. Trees obscured much of the view, but in the distance, a glimpse of the bay in the twilight.

Slowly, I walked through the graveyard, kicking up the red and brown fall leaves underfoot. I had only visited my mother's grave the day of her funeral and hadn't stepped foot in a cemetery since. Dad and Sophie had gone back to place flowers, but I told them I preferred to remember Mom as she was, like some smiling angel in heaven. Dad said he respected me for that, and he wouldn't make me do anything I didn't want to do.

I walked carefully among the granite headstones, examining the names on each—names of past husbands, wives, children, and lovers. The dates spanned 150 years. I must have spent the next twenty minutes searching for the headstone I sought.

When I saw it, a black plaque engraved with thirteen sailors' names, I read them out loud: "Saul Baslow, George Billings, O'Reilly Bradford, Henry Fuchs, Joshua Harvey, Robert Jones, Neil Kent, Lincoln Matthews, Jamie Monroe, *Henry Raphael*. . ." I paused for a moment—then took a deep breath before reading on, "Jackson Rawlings, Andrew Salt, and Blake Woodrow."

Henry Raphael. I saw his name etched in stone—forever captured in hard granite, as permanent as death itself. I stared at the headstone in disbelief, certain that I was caught in some waking nightmare, a dark world of my own imagination. My feet sank into the ground, and for a moment, my world felt like it would crumble and I would lose my balance—just topple over. *How could it be possible that there is a hundred-year-old headstone for a young man named Henry Raphael behind a church in Pacific Grove?*

The picture and the headstone were undeniable proof that Henry was indeed dead. . .Still, I'd spoken to him and seen him walking around Pacific Grove as real and alive as the other people in this town. Most of all—I felt his lips on mine and *that* was real. *How is this possible? If he has a heart that isn't beating how will he ever be able to—love me?*

Chapter Eight: Swept Away

All that week in school, the black-and-white photograph of Henry haunted me. *Is he a ghost or some kind of spirit? Just a figment of my imagination?* But I knew it all actually happened. He rescued me from drowning and without him, I would have been at the bottom of the sea.

I started to wonder about my own mental health. For all I knew, Mom's death had taken more of a toll than I had realized. *Am I losing it?* After all, it had been a tough six months, with a lot of necessary changes and adjustments, all entrenched in grief and loss. *Maybe the cracks are beginning to show. I wonder if I should see a shrink again.* For sure, the photo was real, as was the gravestone. But how could the lady in the coffee shop and Connor the Surfer claim they didn't see him when they saw me. I knew he existed—even in century-old form.

"What's eating you?" Emily asked as we sat in trigonometry. "You've been acting strange all week, like you're sleepwalking or something."

"Um, nothing."

Emily stared at me for a moment, not entirely convinced. "You know you can tell me anything, don't you, Alice?" she asked, her green eyes wide. "I mean, I know we haven't known each other long, but I am your friend."

I nodded. I trusted Emily, but I wasn't ready to confide in her yet, not until I had some answers for myself.

*

On Saturday, I went about my chores: groceries in the morning, picking up mail that had been rerouted from our address in Chicago, and general housework. Then I settled in and did some biology homework, but my attention continually veered in another direction. I dreaded seeing Henry the next day for my sailing lesson. I thought about skipping out on it altogether, but I didn't want him to wonder about me. *But how can I face him? What can I even say to him? Do I tell him what I know? That I read about his—death?*

His gaze seemed to penetrate my very soul, and even if I didn't want to tell him the truth, I was sure he could draw it out of me without so much as a word.

Sunday morning came quickly. I had spent most of the night awake, consumed by the thought of the picture and the tombstone, tangible evidence Henry was truly dead—it was literally written in stone. If not, there was no way he would still look the same after a hundred years of decay and deterioration.

Eight o'clock, and I still hid in my bed. Dad and Sophie sang loudly downstairs, but all I wanted to do was bury my head under the covers, afraid to face Henry. In an absurd way, I felt I had betrayed him.

There came a knock at my door.

"Hey, sleepyhead, are you gonna get up anytime soon?" my dad said. "Alice?" When I did not answer, he slowly turned the handle and poked his head inside my room. "Honey, are you all right?"

I managed to lift my head from under the covers and nodded meekly.

"You're not sick, are you?"

"No. I'm…just a little tired," I said groggily. "I didn't sleep very well."

"Well, Sophie and I are getting ready for church. Wanna come?"

I shook my head. "No. I've got a tennis lesson," I lied, throwing off the covers. "I'm getting up now."

"After church, how about lunch at Poppodors?"

Poppodors was a Mexican café down the street, and they served the most amazing chili and nachos. It had quickly become a family favorite.

"Okay," I said, not really caring one way or another, even though I loved their salsa and the warm tortilla chips they put on the tables as an appetizer.

Ten minutes later, I heard the front door slam. The engine revved, and the car disappeared down the drive. Finally alone in the house, I managed to pull on some clothes and look at myself in the mirror. Dark circles had formed under my eyes, and I looked like the living dead myself.

I walked along the winding coastal path to the marina, dragging my feet as though encumbered by heavy weights. The gray clouds, thick and ominous, hovered above the sea in a blanket of gloom. In the far distance, I could see a thunderstorm brewing.

Henry waited down at the jetty. He looked even more handsome with the sun shining on his tan arms, eyes sparkling like the Hope diamond; well he is one fine-looking guy for a hundred-year-old corpse, to be sure.

He turned and smiled when he saw me. When I didn't return his smile, he instantly knew something bothered me. "What is the matter, Alice?" he asked.

I tried to avert my gaze, afraid that if he looked into my eyes, he would read my thoughts which would lead into my soul. "Nothing," I lied. "I just didn't sleep very well last night."

He looked at me steadily. "Is it the water again? Are your phobias troubling you?"

I shook my head. "No, it's not that."

"Do you still want to go sailing?"

"I don't know. I am feeling kind of . . .," I trailed off without finishing—in an instant I was overcome with everything so I covered my face with my hands and started heading back.

"What is the problem? Tell me." He ran over and in front of me, grabbed my shoulders and kissed me.

Drowning in the touch of his kiss, everything melted away. I ran my hands over his neck and down to his chest. With my right hand, I searched then finally laid my palm to rest on his heart. "I can't feel it," I said, just loud enough for Henry to hear. "I can't feel it!" I repeated, my voice rising in urgency.

"Feel what, Alice?"

"Your heartbeat. I can't feel your heartbeat," I said, starting to panic. I pressed my palm more firmly, noticing how muscular he was, but then I jerked away from Henry and stared at him in horror. "Oh my God! It's true! You're…dead!"

"Alice, calm down," Henry said, raising his palms in the air.

"No! Don't try to deny it. I know all about you, about the ancient curse, about it all! I know about the shipwreck and the twelve other sailors who died." My words tumbled out like a furious torrent of water.

Henry looked as though I'd struck him for a moment then bowed his head in shame when he realized he couldn't deny it. He breathed deeply then looked straight into my eyes. "How did you find out?" he asked quietly.

"A picture of you at the museum—in an old newspaper article dated 1915. Explain that to me. I mean, it is you, isn't it?"

Slowly, he nodded. For a moment, he almost did look a century old as if all the troubled years escalated to that point. Now, his face resigned to confession. "Yes, it is true," he said finally.

"Oh my God!" I exclaimed, cupping my hands over my mouth. I thought I would keel over or faint right in front of him. It felt like I swallowed a barrel of salty seawater and had the wind knocked out of me. "But how? How is it possible?" I asked, gazing at his perfect, angular features and youthful skin. One-hundred-seventeen years and he looked only seventeen.

"I have been cursed, I am stuck in Monterey Bay, Alice. I have been here for the last century."

"So you're dead?"

"Not exactly."

"What do you mean, not exactly? I saw your picture in the newspaper. Are you a ghost?"

"No."

"Then what are you?"

"I'm neither alive nor dead. I am...undead."

Undead? I couldn't believe my ears. It was like a scene out of some horrific movie, but clearly not a Hollywood script because Henry still stood there in the flesh, right in front of me.

"Undead?" I said. "And what is that? Some state of existence that Webster hasn't bothered to define yet?" I asked.

"I reside in the fourth dimension—a different plane," Henry said, "neither alive nor dead. I am trapped in my own private hell."

Fourth Dimension. The word conjured up a place where people were forced to stay as punishment for wrongdoings, a place where the dead stay until they evened the score—service to humans. *But what did Henry do for such punishment?*

"What year were you born?"

"In 1897."

"1897?!" I asked. It was incredible to hear him say it, to admit that he was born in an entirely different era, at the end of the nineteenth century.

"I realize it does not make sense, but we are the undead," Henry said. "We walk among you, but humans know not of our existence."

We? So there are more like him? I suddenly had an image of an army of ghosts marching through Pacific Grove. It was too terrifying to imagine; the stuff of nightmares. I wanted to run away from him, but, for some reason, I stayed rooted to the spot like one of the cypress trees that bordered the shore.

"How many of you are there?" I asked.

"A few," he conceded.

I wondered who the few might be. *The librarian? The florist at the mall? Mr. Johnson, my schoolteacher?* The thought terrified me: ghosts and ghouls; pulseless, empty shells living among us; lurking about in our supermarkets, schools, and streets. It all sounded too fantastic to be possible.

Henry studied me for a minute, registering every look, every mental process, every breath that I took. Finally, he spoke. "Do you still want to go sailing? I mean, that is the reason we have come here, is it not? To help you overcome your fears?"

"I-I don't know," I stuttered, turning my head away. I wasn't sure about anything anymore. "Right now, I just wanna be alone."

I started to walk away, heading down the coastal path, but I sensed him watching me as I turned. I could feel his penetrating gaze on my back, like the striking heat of the sun, but I didn't dare turn to look at him, partly out of fear and partly because of my confusion, so unsure of my own feelings. I could no longer look at him in the same way. I thought I fell for a charming, old-fashioned guy, but now I had no idea. *How can he live without a beating heart in his chest? Is it even possible for him to love? And, even more, how can I ever love him back?*

*

Monday morning during biology, I doodled away in my notebook. Even though I wasn't much of an artist, I managed to pencil a relatively decent sketch of Henry. All I could conjure up was how his hair curled at the base of his neck. Not something I should have focused on in biology, but far more interesting than the mating rituals of the amphibian.

Emily nudged me.

Quickly, I covered up the drawing with one hand, shame registering on my face.

"What's with you, Ali?" she asked. "You're acting all strange again."

"I just haven't been feeling like myself."

"Hmm. Well, you've been acting weird for a week now," she said with a sigh.

I sensed that she was beginning to get impatient with me, finding me exasperating, and I couldn't blame her. I received similar comments from my father and sister, but I was stuck in a place difficult to move out from under, almost as stuck as Henry.

I shrugged. How do I tell my friend that I've been dating a century-old ghost? Then again, he isn't really a ghost, he is still flesh and blood, even though his heart doesn't beat.

I spent most of the day in anguish. I wondered what Henry did during the day, where he spent his time, and who kept him company.

The bell finally rang for school to end, and I carried my books and walked out into the schoolyard, ignoring the cries of some of the jocks calling me over.

"Hey, Alice!" Christian yelled.

I carried on walking, as I had no desire to speak to him—or to anyone, for that matter.

"Alice, wait up."

"Sorry, Christian. Not now," I said and rapidly walked toward the gate, leaving him staring after me.

*

Then, right there at the gate, I spotted him, looking more handsome than ever. His wiry frame stood tall, like a sentinel or the mast of a proud ship, not at all like the other guys, who tended to slouch, all scruffy-looking in their low-hanging trousers and t-shirts. Henry wore a battered leather jacket, jeans, and a checked shirt, and he looked like the coolest kid on the block. Whenever I saw him, my heart flipped wildly, and I felt a rush of oxygen to my head.

"What are you doing here?" I asked. I wanted to see him, but at the same time, I didn't—something like my own personal curse.

"I needed to see you," Henry said. "I have been unable to think about anything save you."

I nodded. "Me, too. How did you get here?" Knowing it was a long and steep walk up to my school.

"I drove," said Henry, pointing an old truck in the parking lot. For a moment I was impressed. Maybe he was human after all.

After a short pause, I asked, "So…where do we go from here?"

"Well, how about a walk?" he offered.

We left the school behind and took the coastal path over the peninsula. Down below sat Monterey Bay, with the late afternoon sunlight glittering on the water.

I glanced at him sideways, walking next to me, his arm lightly brushing against mine. Being so close to him seemed to push every button in my body, intentional or not. Even dead he could make me feel more alive than ever.

"So you're really dead, huh?" I said. "What is it like?"

"Like anything, it has its drawbacks."

"What kind of drawbacks?"

"Always being around this bay, for a start." He glanced around the huge expanse of water and cursed, then said, "God, it is so beautiful— but I am weary of this place."

"Yeah, I see how that might suck to be here for so long. I've only been here a while, and it's not so bad, but I couldn't imagine spending a full century here."

We smiled, bonded in our mutual dislike for Pacific Grove.

"Can everyone see you? I mean here in the bay?"

Henry shook his head. "No, not everyone. It depends if they are looking or not. It's amazing how many folks don't pay attention to what's right in front of them."

"So...what else?" I probed, running my hand through my hair as the wind started to pick up.

"It is difficult getting to know people, because long after they die, I will carry on here—not living but not dying either."

I was silent for a moment, pondering his dilemma. I tried to imagine the tragedy of outliving everyone he cared about. I knew being left behind felt like, but I'd only lost my mother so far. "It must be hard losing the ones you love," I sympathized, recalling my own pain. My mother was young, only in her early forties, and so full of life. I could only hope at least a slim chance exists of an afterlife, so I might be with her again.

"Everyone dies," he said, "except us. We are not so lucky."

Lucky to die? I wondered, the thought twisting in my head as I struggled to make sense of it all.

"After you drowned, did you try to contact your parents? I mean, did you ever try to let them know that you weren't—gone?"

Henry shook his head. "That is not an option. There are no second chances."

I stopped abruptly on the path and looked at him. I thought back to the waitress at Magnolia Bakery and Connor, the surfer dude, both of whom had denied seeing Henry in the flesh. "Are you trying to tell me you're just a figment of my imagination?"

Henry shook his head again. "No. I only meant that when you die in the bay, you are unable to return to your family or the ones you love. Those are the rules."

Rules? Drowning in the bay has a rulebook? This really is some kind of ancient curse, because the afterlife didn't seem to make sense. Then another thought came to me. "Is that why you rescued me? Because you didn't want to see me drown, for me to end up like, uh. . ."

"Like myself," Henry finished for me, nodding. "Yes. I refused to allow you to be cursed, to have to suffer this same cruel fate."

Silent for a moment, I tried to fathom how it I would feel to be in the same predicament. I wouldn't be able to see Dad and Sophie, and I wouldn't be able to see Mom again. It would be a terrible and lonely situation, for sure. For a moment, I truly pitied him.

He seemed to sense what I was thinking. "Have no pity for me. I do not wish it, and nor do I deserve it." His eyes remained steady as he gazed out over the bay.

"I don't pity you, but what do you mean you don't deserve it? What have you done?"

"Nothing." He shrugged the question away and kicked a pebble.

I studied him for a moment, not sure if he spoke the truth.

We had reached Cannery Row and wandered along the sidewalk, looking at the shops and the wares for sale. An array of goods and good eats: clam chowder, ice cream, and toffee apples—things we could see, smell, and taste.

"I bet you've seen a lot of changes over the years," I said, motioning to the storefronts.

Henry smiled and nodded. "You could say that. That was Doc Ricketts's place." He pointed to a blue and white shack that faced the ocean, but it is now a hardware store.

I knew of Doc Ricketts because I read *Cannery Row* by John Steinbeck. The good doctor was the hero of that timeless tale and a real person. "You knew him? What was he like?" I asked, intrigued.

"He was a good man and a fine naturalist. He appreciated the details of the world around him, a great sailor too. He and I often went sailing in the bay. I was sad when he died, and I miss him still."

"I would have liked to have met him," I said.

"Over there was the old salt bathhouse," he said, pointing to a building now home to a restaurant.

"A bathhouse!" I exclaimed. "That sounds so cool. I bet the water was cold though."

"It was. It caused quite the sensation when it opened. Nobody had seen the likes of it before. A gentleman named William Smith opened it in the early 1900s. Over at Lovers Point, there was also a Japanese tea-room and garden."

I giggled. I never would have imagined that sleepy old Pacific Grove teeming with such a colorful history. Henry witnessed so many of the changes, and I somewhat envied that. "I would have liked to have been here then," I said.

"They were fun times," he admitted, but then his face darkened. "But that was all before the shipwreck."

"That must have been a terrible time for you. Did you just wake up and find that you had drowned?"

"No. The current carried me a few miles. I washed up on Asilomar Beach with the morning tide."

"How did you feel when you woke up? I mean, you were dead."

"Very strange," he replied. "I had a weird perception of the world. I could no longer feel cold or pain. My body seemed alive, just empty inside. I had this terrible feeling of being utterly alone."

I tried to imagine what it was like to be a ghost.

We passed John Hopkins Marine Station and continued on. The purple flowers nodded their heads in greeting as we passed by. Up ahead, the rocks of Lovers Point shimmered in the distance, and it wasn't long before we arrived at the lane leading up to Forest Avenue, where I lived.

I stopped under the boughs of one of the large Monterey pines. "I've never dated a dead guy before," I said.

"I would hope not," he said, smiling back at me. "But I do hope you would consider it."

I nodded.

*

The next few days were some of the happiest in my life. Henry took me on a number of dates around Monterey. He was gentle and kind, old-fashioned and considerate, qualities absent in the boys that went to my school. Some of my classmates were kind, like Christian, but never before had any managed to challenge my mind or fill me with so much life. More than anything, I loved the way Henry looked into my eyes, like he shone a light into darkest corners of my inner soul.

We visited the aquarium and strolled around the glass exhibits, watching the sharks, rays, and jellyfish glide through their underwater worlds. Henry had a fine appreciation of nature; quite like my dad in that respect. He was familiar with the Latin names of every animal and plant in the aquarium and could pronounce them correctly, too.

When I questioned him about that, he smiled and said, "When you live for over a century, you find a lot of time for studying."

Some white jellyfish floated in a large tank, their bodies seemingly suspended in the water. With a squeeze of their bell-shaped bodies, they gently pulsated through the aquamarine environment, tentacles trailing in their wake.

"They're beautiful. What are they?"

"Moon jellies," said Henry. "They drift with the tide, and they often migrate for hundreds of miles, floating with the ocean current. Occasionally, there are blooms in the bay. It's a truly spectacular sight. I do hope you manage to see it sometime."

I marveled at the creatures' graceful movements through the water and their diaphanous beauty, like dainty sea-creeping ballerinas. "They're so delicate, like miniature clouds lined with silver."

"Swimming among them is something else," said Henry. "I have had the privilege of swimming in some blooms once or twice. The whole sea appears tinged with tiny clouds, like it is a sky all its own. It truly is beautiful."

We watched the moon jellies in their large tank, and in that very moment, I felt more glad to be alive than ever before.

*

On another occasion, Henry and I had a picnic at Lovers Point. I had brought my favorite blanket, a checked woolen tartan, and I spread it out over the grass bordering the sea. We watched the waves crashing against the shore. Henry had brought some cold chicken for us to share, and I had made a salad with my favorite sun-dried tomatoes and artichokes.

After we had eaten, Henry reached into his jacket pocket and pulled something out. "For you, Alice," he said, handing me a small book.

I took the book curiously and read the cover. It was by Edgar Allen Poe. "Poetry?" I asked in amazement. I carefully opened the tiny tome to the copyright page and read it was a first edition, published in 1896, a year before Henry was born.

"His writings are a bit—macabre, but I hope you like it," Henry said.

"Yes! I mean, no one has ever given me a poetry book before," I answered, fondling the cover. This is true; the only gift I'd ever received from any boy was a box of candy, in the eighth grade, and my love for the candy ended up lasting longer than the relationship. "It's very sweet. Thank you."

"Sweet? Since when has poetry been sweet?"

"It's just. . .I'm not used to guys giving me anything, that's all. So you're a Poe fan, huh?" I said, flipping through the pages.

"Yes," said Henry. "An incredible writer. I enjoy his short stories as well."

Inside was a page of lilac paper and I was instantly drawn to it, since purple is my favorite color. I read the inscription: "To Alice, with fond and sincere wishes, Henry." I smiled over at him. "It's beautiful, thank you." I turned the pages and settled on one of Poe's most famous poems, *Annabel Lee*.

"Will you read it for me?" Henry asked, jointly holding the book between us.

"Um. . .okay." I looked down at the book and read, "It was many and many a year ago, in a kingdom by the sea. There lived a fair maiden whom you may know by the name of Annabel Lee."

Henry's arm brushed against mine as I read the poem, and again the thrill ran through my spine like an electric current.

"And this fair maiden had no other thought than to be loved and be loved by me," I continued, my voice becoming hoarse.

I looked into his eyes, and he kissed me—long, wet, and cool. I was drowning, but this time I knew he wouldn't be able to save me.

Chapter Nine: Premonitions

Pacific Grove is famed for its monarch butterflies—big, beautiful brown creatures with yellow spots under their wings. Every year, they flutter from Mexico to California and back again, an incredible 10,000 miles roundtrip. They hang in the pine and eucalyptus trees of Pacific Grove, illuminating the canopy with their golden iridescence. In the early hours of the morning, dew forms on their wings, sparkling like tiny beads of diamonds.

In honor of this incredible journey, the people of Pacific Grove celebrate their return every fall, a festival known as the Butterfly Parade. The local schoolchildren dress up in papier-mâché costumes and parade through a section of the old town. It's a great occasion for families to get together and celebrate one of the most truly marvelous sights of nature.

Saturday morning I helped Sophie make her butterfly wings. Sitting at the kitchen table painting them bright gold and decorating them with large red spots, brought back memories of when Mom and I spent hours working on my school assignments. We loved to paint, and sometimes we even made Christmas crafts or designed greeting cards for friends. I missed those times, but glad I could share such special moments with my little sister. It was tough for her to grow up without a mom, too, but at least we had each other.

"Help me out, Alice," Sophie said, stretching her arms out. "I wanna try them on for size." She twirled, pleased with the gold and black wings she painted.

"Okay," I said. As she stretched her little limbs out as far as she could, I helped her wiggle into her costume. The wings neatly folded back when she put her arms down and spread out when ready for flight as she raised them. Her soft, blond hair framed her oval-shaped face, and she looked happier than I had seen her in a long time.

"How are my girls?" asked Dad, poking his head in through the kitchen door when he heard the peal of laughter.

"Ready to fly," I said.

We all giggled as Sophie started to flap her arms around the kitchen, as if about to take off.

Dad drove us to the school gates of Pacific Grove Elementary School and parked the car. We jostled through the crowd for the best spot to see the parade. Sophie skipped into the classroom to join the other kids, all decorated with colorful designs, iridescent wings, and quivering antennae.

Dad and I proudly watched as Sophie marched by, flapping her wings. We laughed at how happy she seemed and it made us happy. She beamed at us, and at that very moment, from the smile on her face, I just knew all the messy glue and paint had been worthwhile. It also confirmed my original thought—*we are right where we are supposed to be*—*with each other*. I linked my arm in Dad's, happy that he had made the choice to take us there to Pacific Grove. I knew everything would be all right and that things would work out with Henry, one way or another.

After the parade, Dad took us girls to brunch at First Awakenings, a café just up from the aquarium. We sat at one of the bistro tables outside, beneath a big blue umbrella. On such a bright, sunny day, I welcomed the shade—plus being fair-skinned, I tended to burn easily.

A waitress took our drink orders: an iced tea for Dad, a strawberry milkshake for Sophie, and an orange smoothie for me. I ordered a Cobb salad and had barely started eating it when my cell rang. Since Henry and I had started seeing each other, I'd had little time to spend with my new friend Emily. Of course, she wasn't the kind of girl who would let such neglect pass unnoticed.

"Hey, Ali. What are you up to today?" she asked, her sugary sweet voice filling my ear.

"Nothing much," I replied. "Just having lunch at the moment, but I've got no plans for this afternoon." I had an urge to go out, and I knew that if I didn't find something to do, it would just give me an excuse to mope around the house.

"Wanna hang out?"

"Sure. What do you have in mind?"

"Well…I need a dress for homecoming," Emily said. "Will you help me find one?"

I sighed. . . Not the best person to ask, since I hated shopping, but I'd been neglecting my friend for several days, so I decided to join her. Besides, I didn't have a dress of my own, and since I planned to invite

Henry as my date, I wanted to look special. "Sounds good," I said. "How about we meet at three by the dolphin fountain at the mall?"

After I hung up the phone and set it down on the table, Dad looked at me curiously, arching an eyebrow. "The mall? Honey, since when have you been interested in shopping?"

"Homecoming is next week, and I need something to wear." I took a bite of my Cobb salad, ready to change the subject.

Dad, however, still had questions on his mind. "Homecoming, huh? Is there a boy involved? Anyone I should be aware of?"

I shook my head and averted my eyes, crunching noisily on a piece of lettuce. "No," I fibbed. "I'm just going with Emily, but I still want to look nice."

"Sweetheart, you always look nice."

"Aw. Thanks, Dad," I said.

*

Monterey Plaza was the typical American shopping mall experience. In addition to the coffee shops and ice cream parlors, there were big, dependable chain department stores, Mexican and other kinds of restaurants in the food court, and a cinema multiplex. A fun place to get lost in on a Saturday afternoon.

In Macy's, we perused the racks of dresses, with all the new fall fashions on display. Emily had very eclectic taste in clothes, and she normally opted for bohemian clothing in shades of black and green, the colors that complemented her spiky dark hairstyle and gave a slinky quality to her long limbs.

"What color suits me best?" she asked, holding up a blue dress then a green one. "What about this one?"

I had never seen her in an evening gown and was curious to see how she would look in an elegant getup. "That one looks good," I said, pointing. "Green always looks good on you."

"You really think so?" Emily said, looking doubtfully at the dress. "What about you? Which one are you gonna try?"

I selected a purple gown that showed some cleavage and cut low in the back. It was unlike anything I usually wore, but I figured I might be able to pull it off. "How about this?" I asked, hesitantly holding up the sexy garment.

"Oh yeah, that looks great!"

We carried our dresses into the fitting rooms, giggling all the way. Five minutes later—all decked out in evening gowns, messed-up hair, and sneakers—we emerged and looked at ourselves in the full-length mirror.

"Wow. You look beautiful," I said to Emily, naturally pretty, but right now—she was absolutely stunning, almost unrecognizable, in her full-length gown. Such a transformation, and for the first time, I noticed her arms were slender and delicate.

"Thanks. So do you. That color really suits you."

I gazed at myself in the mirror and adjusted my cleavage. I pictured myself standing next to Henry, statuesque like a pine, and I would need heels just to reach his chin; even then, he would still a good head taller. I had deliberately chosen a vintage-looking gown, with a timeless, classic feel to it. Instinctively, I felt that he would like it.

Emily was smoothing the dress in front of the vanity mirror when her face contorted in pain. She brought her hand up to her temples and opened her mouth in anguish.

"What's wrong?" I said, steadying her with my arm, fearing she might keel over right there in Macy's.

"Nothing. I'm fine," she snapped, trying to regain her composure. "I'm all right. It's just—I had a sudden flash of something."

"A flash?" I said. "What? Like a vision?"

Emily nodded and started to breathe deeply. A look of terror swimming in her eyes—a strange, frightening look I've only seen once or twice before, like a terrible thing had possessed her soul and wasn't going to let go. Her brow furrowed.

"Here. Come sit," I said, guiding her to a footstool.

Emily tried to steady her breathing, holding her hand over her chest.

"Level with me, Em. This isn't the first time this has happened, is it?" I asked.

Emily shook her head and glanced at me with wide, truthful eyes. "No," she confessed. She hesitated, then took a deep breath. "Sometimes I—see things."

"What kinds of things?" I asked, my voice growing hoarse.

"Flashes, events. . . Sometimes I can see into the future."

"The future?" I repeated.

"Yeah. It's been going on since I was five. My mom even took me to a shrink once, and I've been told I'm a sensitive - psychic."

Psychic? Emily? How is that possible? Immediately, everything made sense. That had to be why I sometimes felt Emily could peer into my soul, how she knew about my mom's death even before I told her, and so many other seemingly inexplicable incidences.

"How often does it happen?" I asked.

"Every so often, maybe once or twice a month. Sometimes it's just little things."

"Like what?"

"Well, when I'm standing in line at the grocery, I'll flash forward to a point where I'm chopping onions or something, and I'll remember that I forgot the garlic. Other times, it's bigger things. Like I'll think of someone, and they call me on the phone, seemingly out of the blue, as if I knew they were going to call. Once I reached out to an aunt who died, by holding a séance and clutching her handkerchief."

"Like my mom," I said. "You knew about my mom, didn't you? The first time you met me in class?"

Emily nodded. "Yep. You don't think I'm a freak, do you, Alice?"

"Of course not! I would never think that. What did you see just now though?" I asked.

"The homecoming parade," Emily began slowly. "I saw a girl, in great pain. Her head was submerged under this dark, murky, dangerous water. She was trying to get up to catch her breath but couldn't because someone held her there. I saw these big, strong hands."

Strong hands trying to drown someone? I shuddered at the terrible image of who that could be. "Wh-who was the girl?" I asked carefully, not really ready for the answer.

"I don't know," replied Emily. "I only get glimpses, flashes. I couldn't see her face."

"Did you see who was holding her?"

Emily screwed up her forehead then shook her head again. "No. His face was hidden in the shadows. I couldn't see him clearly."

"What happened to the girl? Did she drown?"

Emily closed her eyes, tightly squeezing them hard to remember the details of the dream. Her forehead creased in pain. Suddenly her eyes opened again, and she shook her head. "I can't see anything else. It's just—gone."

I exhaled deeply and suddenly realized how foolish I must have looked standing there in a purple evening gown. The fancy fabric began to make my skin itch—*maybe I'm allergic to glamour*, I thought and decided to take it off. "C'mon. Let's get outta these things. Care to grab a coffee?"

Emily nodded, and we retreated to our changing cubicles to remove our dresses. I left mine hanging in the returns stall, pretty certain that I would never see it again.

In the coffee shop, our mochas sat untouched, growing more tepid by the minute. I observed Emily slowly calm down. Soon, she was cheery again, like nothing out of the ordinary had happened. For me, though, the memory of her watery nightmare, her vision, remained firmly etched in my mind.

"So you're a psychic, huh?" I said to her over sips of mocha.

"Yeah, but it's not really something I like to brag about," Emily said. "I mean, it's kinda...weird."

"No, not that weird. There are other things in the world that are a lot weirder." *Like me falling for a century-old ghost*, I thought but didn't say aloud. "Have you ever predicted anything major? A tsunami or car accident or war or anything?" I asked.

"Yeah, my grandma's death. She lived in Salinas, where we used to live before we moved here. Eighty but very independent. One day, I witnessed her falling down a flight of stairs. I told my mom, and we tried to call Grandma and warn her not to go out that day, to stay away from stairways, but we couldn't reach her. An hour later, the police came by to tell us they'd found Grandma's body at the bottom of a flight of stairs. She had slipped and fallen, broke her neck."

"God, that's awful, Emily. I'm sorry," I replied.

"Yeah, I know. I remember the way my mom looked at me when the police told her, as if she thought I caused it. Since then, she hasn't been the same toward me," Emily said.

"So she blames you?" I asked, incredulous.

Emily nodded slowly, and tears began to form in her eyes. "Yeah. She thinks I'm a freak, that I just think about bad things and cause them to happen."

I clasped Emily's hands in mine. "You're not a freak. You're not!"

Emily sniffed, then smiled at me. "Thank you, Alice."

Still, no matter how hard I tried not to think about it, I just could not get Emily's vision out of my mind. *Who is the girl being held underwater? What monster was holding her, and why would anyone want to drown her?* All those questions filled my head leaving the plaza that afternoon.

Chapter Ten: Homecoming

I returned to Macy's later that week to buy the purple dress. I didn't particularly love it but somehow, it felt like fate, as though not buying the frock might somehow alter my destiny in a bad way. I handed two-hundred dollars to the cashier, shaking my head. I had never spent so much money on a single item of clothing in my entire life. I had been saving my pocket money for the last year and hadn't spent much in the past few months, though, so at least I could cover the hefty price tag. Now, I only hoped it would be worth it, that Henry would like what he saw.

I walked home with the bag tucked under my arm, my thoughts once again consumed with Henry. He had an intoxicating effect on me, and I was quickly becoming obsessed with him. I had just bought an expensive dress, and I'd begun taking an interest in clothes and fussing over the way I looked. What happened to satisfaction through reading Brontë and hanging around the house in comfy sweats?

*

When Thursday night came, the night of the homecoming dance, I spent an hour in front of the mirror, trying on the dress. It showed more cleavage than I normally showed, and it hugged my figure like a glove. I fashioned my hair in several styles and up-do's, trying to find the best look. Ultimately, I tossed the bobby pins, spray, and hairclips aside and settled for the same-old, same-old and let it fall around my shoulders.

As I dangled a silver earring in front of the mirror, I still couldn't believe what a fuss I was making. Henry's and my first official outing as a couple, so deep down, I was eager to show Henry off to my friends— a change for me; I actually care about something and someone.

Henry had promised to pick me up at eight, so I waited nervously to hear a car pulling up outside. Sophie sang out of tune in the bathroom, and Dad went into his cave somewhere downstairs, probably reading a newspaper in the den. I ran to my bedroom window every time I heard the faintest sound.

Finally, I heard a honk. I grabbed my jacket, took one final glance at myself in the mirror, and ran down the stairs, almost tripping on the last few steps. At the bottom, I bumped into Dad.

"Hey! Where's the fire?" he said. The surprised look in his eyes betrayed this thought—one minute, I am his baby daughter, and now I am a young lady on the verge of womanhood.

"Homecoming, Dad. Remember?"

He smiled. "Since when are you so interested in homecomings?" he asked with amusement.

In Chicago, I had never shown any interest in such pretentious things as dances, cheerleading, or pep rallies—nothing that celebrated American high school culture. It wasn't necessary to tell my dad that having a boyfriend had changed all that.

"Who are you going with, anyhow?" Dad asked.

Keen on escaping the interrogation as quickly as possible, I fibbed a little. "Just a few friends from school, like Emily and Christian, that minister's son." I had no problem name-dropping, as long as it would appease my dad and free me to go.

"Oh, okay," said Dad, relenting a little. "Well, have a nice time."

A knock on the front door startled me, and a rock fell to the pit of my stomach when Dad raised his eyebrows and went to open it.

"Yes?" he said to the young man on the doorstep.

Henry stood in the doorway, tall and proud, dressed in a smart brown evening jacket—not a regular cliché black suit or a tux like most of the other guys would rent for the occasion. His clothes were always more unique and far more striking, truly vintage rather than some cheap lackluster reproduction or knockoff. He looked so—aristocratic— with his hair combed back, and clean-shaven. To me, he never looked more handsome.

"Hello, Alice," said Henry when he saw me over my dad's shoulder. He turned to my dad. "Excuse me, Mr. Parker; I'd like to introduce myself."

Dad looked at Henry, at me, then back at Henry again. He seemed a little taken aback by Henry's good manners. "A friend of yours?" Dad asked me.

"My name is Henry Raphael," Henry continued most cordially. He extended his hand out to Dad.

Dad looked back at me in awe, his mouth agape, then dumbly shook Henry's hand. "How do you do, Son?" he finally said when the cat let go of his tongue.

"I plan to take your daughter to homecoming tonight," Henry said, "but I would like to ask your permission, Sir. I know I should have asked earlier, but Alice only just invited me."

"Oh she did, did she?" said Dad, arching his eyebrows at me. "I thought Alice was going to the prom with Christian and Emily."

"I am, Dad," I interrupted. "Henry's just going to drive me there."

"He is? Do you have a license?"

"Of course, Sir. I want you to know that I respect your daughter and would never take advantage of her, or you."

Dad peered at us, again speechless, "Well, that's good to hear." Then he turned to me, wagging his finger, and stated emphatically, "I want you home by midnight, young lady, understand?"

I nodded.

Dad watched me like a protective papa bear as I walked out the door. I sensed his eyes following us as we made our way down the garden path.

The wind cut through my soft denim jacket as I hurried down the path with Henry toward our waiting chariot. The black and battered truck with a brown tarpaulin covering the contents in back. *I wonder what he keeps inside there,* burst into my head as he hustled me to the passenger side.

Henry smiled at me and opened the door for me to climb in. *Ahhh. . .warm and toasty inside;* a nice contrast to take the edge off the chilly October wind. Henry was always considerate and gentlemanly like that.

"Your father seems most gracious," said Henry. "He is also strong and direct. I like that, admirable qualities in a man."

"He is?" While I, too, admired many qualities of my dad's, no guy I'd ever dated before had seemed to take much notice of him.

"I have met many fathers during my years, Alice. Believe me when I tell you he is one of the good ones."

I fell silent, pondering his words. If he had met a lot of fathers, that could only mean he'd dated a lot of daughters. "I guess," I said, trying to mask my curiosity but failing miserably. "So, uh. . .you've dated a lot?"

Henry smiled and looked over at me, with a coy expression on his face. "As we have previously discussed, I have spent many years here,

Alice. A young man has to find a way to kill the time, does he not? Loneliness can be a thing most dreadful."

*

The homecoming parade started on Alvarado Street, in the old town of Monterey, and the procession then weaved through Main Street and ended up at the high school.

Over the last couple days, the school gym had been converted into a dance floor, where the main party would be held.

Henry parked his truck outside the school gates, and we walked to the gym. Inside, the building was decorated with red, white and blue balloons and was about a quarter full, with a few teachers and students already milling around, waiting for the procession of Homecoming King and Queen to arrive from the parade in town. A large table in the corner was topped with a punch bowl, and some of my teachers were chatting there.

"Wow. It's beautiful, but they should have sprayed some Lysol or something. It smells like a locker room in here," I said, turning my nose up at the unmistakable stench of adolescent exertion.

"I have attended quite a few of these affairs over the years. Believe me, this is one of the better ones."

"Oh you have, have you?" I asked. "So I'm not your first date here? And I take it I won't be your last, either," half-teasing, but the remark's truth stung. I was only the latest in a long line of Monterey High School dates for Henry.

"When you've lived in this town for as long as I have, you are often asked out by the local ladies," said Henry, sounding ashamed and defensive all at once.

"Let's try to find Emily," I replied, eager to change the subject. "She's wearing a long green dress."

"Okay," said Henry, slipping his hand in mine.

I loved the idea of him holding my hand, as it drew attention to the fact that we were a couple. Smiling, I spied Emily in the corner, looking glitzy and glamorous.

Over the last several days, I had tried not to give Emily's visions too much thought. After all, even she had admitted that they didn't always come to fruition. For example, she hadn't predicted that I would fall into the bay, that Henry would rescue me, or that I would carry on an affair with a ghost. So, I tried to bury it in a corner of my mind.

"Hey, you," said Emily when she saw me. "I'm glad you went with that dress. It looks so good on you."

"Emily, I'd like you to meet Henry," I said, by way of introduction.

"Pleased to make your acquaintance," said Henry, then offered his hand for a formal and polite shake.

"It's really great to meet you, Henry," said Emily, her eyes glowing as she appraised him. "Alice talks about you a lot—I mean, like, all the time."

"I do not!" I said, glaring at Emily, my cheeks burning with redness.

"Likewise," said Henry. "She says you are one of a kind."

"That's true," Emily said, smiling and taking it for a compliment. "I am. There's no one else quite like me."

"Would either of you ladies care for some punch?" Henry offered. We nodded.

"I shall return shortly," he said, then walked away to the punch table.

"Well? What do you think of him?" I whispered, watching Henry walk away.

"Oh my God, Alice! He's totally hot," said Emily. "I can't believe you're here with him."

"What else?" I demanded. "Do you get any other vibes from him?"

Emily shook her head. "Uh-uh. It's kind of weird. I mean, I don't get any vibes at all, and I usually get something when I meet someone for the first time. You know, like a pet name. . .or their favorite food or. . . if they like baseball—something. But with him, nothing—as though a big wall surrounds him, one even I can't penetrate."

I nodded and spied Henry at the punch bowl. I had a similar sense about him. An enigma, a keeper and protector of deep secrets. *I would love to know those secrets*, I thought then more specifically to see if he was hiding anything from me.

I asked Emily, "Any flashes since the other day?"

"Nope, nothing," she replied.

I was almost disappointed. I thought again of the girl underwater, wondering who she was and what that all meant.

Breaking me free of such grim thoughts, my ghostly boyfriend came back with three glasses brimming with punch. He gave one each to Emily and me.

"To your good health," he said, lifting his glass.

"Bottoms up!" Emily squealed.

We toasted each other and drank the punch.

I smiled, feeling happy and a bit proud. As I looked around the party, I sensed that all the girls were looking at Henry. I knew they were curious about how the incredibly handsome guy ended up the awkward new-girl-who-almost-drowned. It was a different feeling to be the center of attention, and for a moment, I had a sense of what Heather felt like. It also made me feel relieved—Henry isn't only a figment of my imagination, other people see him too. Including my dad.

Without a doubt, Henry was the best-looking guy at the party. Sure, there were quite a few hot jocks, but Henry's well-cultivated qualities and old-fashioned manners made them seem young and small in comparison. There was something elegant about him and it had a little to do with his height since he stood at least six feet. Much more than that, it was his walk—a confident stride, shoulders thrown back, and steady gaze. I felt the buzz of excitement in the air around us, heard the whispers, and I reveled in them.

"Who's that guy?" the senior girls whispered to one another.

"Maybe he's from out of town," one said, "like L.A. or San Francisco or something."

When another couple waltzed into the gym, my balloon was deflated and found myself instantly jerked to earth. Heather—the homecoming queen herself wearing King Channing on her arm. She wore a striking, golden gown with white trimming, her hair braided with yellow and white little flowers, lightly flowing down her back. Completing the ensemble—a silver tiara bringing out her shiny, blonde mane, giving it an even shinier appearance. Something inside me changed when I saw her this time. For the first time since I'd started school, I felt just as pretty and special as she. In Henry's company, I realized how Heather must have felt every day of her life, knowing that everyone envied her. It gave me a tiny glimpse into her world, and I couldn't deny that I liked it.

Emily gaped at Heather's gown with envy as though transfixed by its beauty. Suddenly, she cupped her hands at her mouth. "What's wrong?" I asked, "Don't you think it's gorgeous?"

"It's not that," she stuttered. "It's. . . I don't know," said Emily. "I've seen that dress someplace before."

"Where? At the mall the other day?"

"I-I don't remember. . .," Emily repeated, shaking her head. "Maybe."

The music from the band started, and Heather and Channing were the first to take the dance floor. Of course, looking absolutely stunning, like a wedding cake topper.

Emily continued to stare at Heather, and just as I began to ask if she'd seen a flash or something, Henry interrupted me. . .

"May I have the pleasure of this dance, milady?" He asked, holding his hand out for me to grasp.

"I'd love to," I replied, gazing—smitten—into his eyes.

Henry and I walked out to the dance floor, right beside Heather and Channing. Some of the jocks applauded, which made me smile. Out of the corner of my eye, I saw Christian monitoring us, looking chagrined, but all I cared about at the moment was Henry.

Heather caught my eye and gave me a wink of approval. I smiled back, and for a moment, felt accepted into her circle. This made me supremely happy. Henry had his hands around my waist, with mine over his neck.

At the end of the dance, Henry leaned down and kissed me on the lips.

By the time I surfaced, the music had stopped, and it seemed everyone watched us. We caught a few wolf-whistles from the jocks and Emily smiled broadly. Poor Christian tried to look at everyone else but me.

"Thank you for the dance," he said, his face mere inches from mine.

"You're welcome," I said, flustered. "Boy, it's hot in here," I observed, certain that the actual temperature had nothing to do with it. I started to wave my hand in front of my face, trying to cool myself down.

"Would you like another drink?" said Henry.

I nodded.

"All right. I'll be back in a second," Henry said. Then he made a beeline back to the punch bowl now swarming with thirsty dancers, like a watering hole in a smoldering African savannah.

I went back to stand next to Emily.

"You guys were smokin'," she said, wearing a wide smile. "I mean, off-the-charts hot."

"The kiss was incredible," I replied, touching my lips.

"What was it like?"

"Like—"

"Hey, Alice," interrupted a deep voice.

I turned around and saw Christian, looking very smart in a brown suit, white shirt, and blue tie.

"Great party," he said, looking around semi-awkwardly, trying to strike up a conversation.

"Yeah," I replied. "Nice suit, but have I seen it before?" While it felt a bit cruel and judgmental, I couldn't help but wonder if he owned only one.

Christian laughed. "Probably. I wear it to church a lot. Anyway, who's the guy you were dancing with?"

"Oh, that's Henry, the guy I've been seeing recently."

"Oh, I see," said Christian, with more than a hint of disappointment in his voice.

"And you know Emily," I said, trying to deflect attention from myself onto my friend.

"Yeah. Hi, Emily," said Christian politely.

"Hi," said Emily, smiling broadly. "Christian. Last time I saw you, we all went kayaking together, when Alice decided to take a dunk."

"Did you have to remind me?" I teased.

I caught Emily giving Christian that special smile of hers, the one she usually reserved for special friends, and I began to wonder if it would be feasible to play matchmaker. Needless to say I loved Jane Austen's *Emma*.

Christian smiled but seemed more interested in talking to me. "I'm looking forward to our book club on Saturday," he said. "Have you read Ethan's choice? I had no idea he was such an Alcott fan."

"I've been really busy, but I'm hoping to catch up over the next few days." The truth—I'd only started the opening chapter. I had been so preoccupied with Henry that I had no time to think about the book club or anything else. My own life was becoming so exciting that everyone else's fiction seemed to pale in comparison.

Henry returned with a couple more glasses of punch, one for me and one for himself. As he handed the glass to me, he nodded politely at Christian. I missed the silence between them while awaiting introductions, but I was struck by how different they were, not only in looks but in mannerisms.

"Uh. . . This is Henry," I stammered. "Henry, this is Christian, from my school book club."

Henry and Christian shook hands like a couple of boxers before a match. I quickly downed my punch in one swig, like an old lush.

"Hey! Steady now, girl!" Henry said with a laugh.

"Would you like to dance?" Christian asked me unexpectedly.

"Er, sure. Henry, do you mind?" I asked.

"No, by all means," said Henry cordially, taking the empty glass from my hand.

Still, I hesitated, biting my lower lip with anxiety.

"Don't worry, Alice," said Emily. "I'll take good care of him." She then looped her lanky arm in Henry's as he just stood there impassively.

Christian led me onto the dance floor, quickly filling with other couples. I danced awkwardly with him for a moment, my whole body stiff and my mind on Henry. After a while, I managed to relax a little.

"You're a good dancer," I said, offering him a genuine compliment.

He smiled, showing a perfect set of white teeth. Close up like that, I could see his good-looks and I noticed his healthy complexion, his wonky nose speckled with cute freckles.

"I've been to a lot of church dances in my time. That's the benefit of being the son of a minister," he said. "Some people say religion is just a lot of song and dance. I guess they're right!"

I laughed, but my chuckle was cut short when I caught sight of Henry watching us from the corner. Emily chatted to him amiably, but all the time, I felt Henry's eyes watched me. I didn't mind. I liked that he was so protective.

Christian seemed to pick-up on it and stiffened a little. "So—what's the story between you and this Henry-guy? Where did you meet him? I mean, he doesn't look like he's from around here."

"Henry saved my life when I fell into the bay. Don't you remember?"

"No. I had no idea. So what's that mean? You owe him or something?"

"No. It only means he saved my life," I replied evenly. "Besides, I like being with him. He makes me feel special."

"That's because you are special, Alice. Still, I think you deserve better."

The remark irritated me, especially since Christian didn't know Henry well enough to judge him. "Why would you say that? You don't know anything about Henry."

"Maybe not," replied Christian, "but something about him makes me. . . I don't know—uneasy."

"Uneasy? In what way?"

"He has this weird, dead look in his eyes, for one thing. Surely you've seen it. He looks almost like he's stoned or something."

"Well, he's very much alive, believe me," I replied, still stinging from Christian's remarks.

He offered a halfhearted little laugh. "Well, maybe you're right. I don't really know the guy the way you do. I'm sorry I said anything."

The music stopped, and I thanked him for the dance, anxious to return to Henry. I rushed over to him with a smile on my face.

"Enjoy the dance?" he asked politely.

"It was okay," I said, linking my hands in his.

"I thought I would have to come and rescue you again," he said pointedly.

"I don't need rescuing this time," I said, letting myself slip back into his arms.

The music changed to a slow song.

"Shall we?" he offered.

I nodded. Henry and I stepped back on to the floor and danced to Stevie Wonder's "Woman." I put my arms around his neck, breathed in the scent of his skin, and enjoyed being the luckiest girl in the world.

Henry was an incredible dancer, better than Christian. There was something real old-fashioned about the way he held me and danced. In that embrace, I felt entirely safe—he could dangle me over the Golden Gate Bridge and I wouldn't be afraid. I rested my cheek against his shoulder as we danced.

When the music stopped, we carried on dancing, as if in a trance. Then he kissed me fully on the lips.

I surrendered myself to him, but I eventually had to come up for air. I looked into Henry's eyes, as he smiled broadly. "Okay, Soldier," I said. "I have to go to the bathroom."

Henry nodded. "Hurry back."

I went looking for Emily and found her chatting to Juanita Sanchez, talking about boys. "C'mon," I said. "We need to talk. Come with me to the ladies' room?"

She nodded.

I grabbed her arm, and we hurried across the dance floor and turned left at the end of the corridor that led to the girls' locker room.

"Looked like you were drowning out there," Emily said, referring to our kiss.

"I know, and sometimes I feel I'm in way over my head, and the beach is very far away."

"Well, just keep swimming, honey, and don't stop," said Emily. "That guy is hot...and he's obviously hot for you."

I giggled. "I could use some fresh air. Wanna go up on deck?" I asked.

Emily nodded. "Let's go.

We headed to the balcony that overlooked the outside basketball and tennis courts. As we climbed the stairs, we heard loud, angry voices coming from above. The door to the deck stood open, and through the gap I spied Heather and Channing arguing loudly.

"I just don't want other guys looking at you," said Channing, pacing around Heather, with her elegant arms folded across her chest—*didn't Heather do anything that wasn't glamorous?*

"You're being ridiculous. Guys look at me all the time. You know that, Channing," Heather snapped.

I tugged Emily's sleeve, motioning that we should go back downstairs. I wasn't much into eavesdropping.

Emily, however, pulled back, insisting that we stay. She placed a finger over her lips and whispered, "Shh!"

"I know what you've been doing behind my back!" Channing shouted. "The whole school knows! You think I'm just some dumb jock, but—"

"No, what I think is that you're nuts!" Heather shouted.

"Emily, we should go," I whispered.

Emily reluctantly nodded and followed me as we tiptoed downstairs.

Seconds later, Heather came charging down the steps. We managed to hide behind the stairs at the bottom as she swept past, her gown glittering as she disappeared down the corridor.

"What was *that* about?" I asked Emily.

Emily shrugged. "I dunno, but whatever it is, Channing's sure riled up about something."

"C'mon. Let's get back to the party."

When I returned, I spotted Henry and Christian by the punch bowl—their voices loud, drawing stares from curious onlookers, including some of the teachers.

"I just think Alice should be allowed to make up her own mind without you interfering," Christian said. "She's a decent girl."

"If anyone is interfering, it would be you," replied Henry.

"Who are you, anyway?" Christian asked. "I know I've seen your face before. Where?"

"What's going on here?" I demanded, rushing up to them.

"It seems preacher boy has a problem with me," said Henry, glancing derogatorily at Christian.

"Don't call me that, and don't mock my faith," said Christian. "The devil has taken your soul."

Henry took a swing at Christian and sent him crashing to the floor.

"Henry, stop!" I cried.

Henry stepped back for a moment, stunned.

"You okay?" I asked Christian.

Christian nodded, too surprised and humiliated to do anything but rub his jaw. I helped him to his feet. By that time, some teachers came over to see what was causing all the excitement and the jocks gathered like Romans to the gladiator games, hoping to witness a fight.

I looked around for Henry and saw him rapidly heading for the exit. "Look after Christian," I said to Emily.

She nodded, looking stunned. I quickly followed Henry out the door. "Henry!" I screamed, running after him. "Henry, wait up!"

He turned around, his eyes shining wildly.

"Go back to the party. You belong there, not I."

"Yes you do. What happened in there? You totally lost it."

"I-I have no idea," he said. "The boy drives me mad. Who is he to judge me? He knows nothing about what I've been through."

"Just come back inside with me," I said, rubbing his back and linking my arm in his. "C'mon, Henry. Come with me."

Henry shook his head. "No. This was all a mistake. Ah!" He ran his fingers nervously through his hair. "You drive me mad, Alice."

"Why are you getting so upset?" I said, having no idea what else to say—I wouldn't really understand what went on inside that handsome head of his. "Tell me," I whispered softly.

"It's just…He can be with you in a way I will never be able to," said Henry fiercely. "Do you not understand, Alice?"

I shook my head, not entirely sure I understood any of it. "I don't have any feelings for Christian, at least not that kind. I'm with you, Henry. Isn't that what's important?" I said.

"No, Alice. This is all wrong. I can never have you, not in the way I want, and you can never have me." He looked into my eyes, bearing his tortured soul. "Is it not obvious? If we stay together, we'll only tear ourselves apart."

I shook my head, not understanding a word of it. It sounded like a break-up speech, one of those it's-not-you-it's-me things, and I was not ready for that.

I couldn't convince Henry to go back into the dance, so he drove me home. Not a word was spoken on our commute after our unfortunate evening. He even refused to look at me when he dropped me off.

I walked in just before midnight and everyone had gone to bed. My dad didn't wait up because he trusted I wouldn't break curfew.

Silently and heartbroken, I walked in defeat through the darkened house up to my room and closed the door. Mindlessly, I put my pajamas on, consumed with worry over Henry. *What is happening to me?* For a tiny moment, I wished I were dead. At least then I stood a chance of being with Henry forever…

Chapter Eleven: Disappearance

As soon as I walked into the schoolyard the next morning, I immediately knew something was wrong. Two Monterey County Police cars parked ominously outside the principal's office, their bumpers nudged up against the row of pink rhododendrons lining the school wall. I wondered if there had been some trouble at the homecoming festivities, perhaps some of the jocks and cheerleaders getting drunk and causing trouble in town. When I had left with Henry, the seniors had already been quite restless and rowdy.

The corridors echoed with excited chatter as I made my way to my locker. I strained to hear what they said, but couldn't make it out. I spied Emily walking toward me like a guided missile. As she neared, I saw her green eyes as big as saucers.

She opened her mouth, and a torrent of words came tumbling out. "Oh my God! Did you hear the news?" Emily asked, practically bursting to tell me.

"What news?" I asked, my heart almost skipping a beat.

"Heather Palmer. She's just. . . She disappeared!"

"What do you mean disappeared?" I asked incredulous.

"She didn't return home last night. She had that huge fight with Channing last night, and…"

"I know," I said, nodding. I would never forget that argument we'd overheard on the balcony, the two of them going at it with such intensity.

"Well, she left the school, but no one has seen her since. Her mom called the police early this morning."

"That's terrible," I said and meant it. Poor Heather. I wondered what could have happened to her. *Maybe she just slept over at a friend's house and this is all just a misunderstanding*, I thought, soothing myself.

"The police are questioning, like, everybody."

"So that's why the cars are out there."

"Yup."

"What do you think happened to her?" I asked.

"I don't know," Emily said with a shudder. "The Coast Guard's been out since dawn, but no one's found a body yet."

A thought suddenly crossed my mind. "Wait! That vision of the girl you saw floating with her head held under the water. . . Do you think that could have been Heather?"

Emily scrunched up her forehead, thinking for a moment. The kink appeared in the middle of her forehead as it always did when she thought hard. "I considered that, too. I guess it's possible. I had that premonition about her dress, too. Still, I'm not getting any vibes from her now. Normally, whenever Heather brushed past me, I could sense what she had for breakfast that morning, where she had just been, even when on her period. I could even sense if she'd recently been making out with a guy—which was more often than you'd think—but today, no matter how hard I concentrate on her, there's just—nothing. It's really strange, like she's disappeared from the face of the earth. I felt the same way about my grandma, even before the police showed up to tell us about her fall."

Disappeared from the face of the earth? In the short time we'd lived in Monterey Bay, I'd learned the painful truth—it is common for people to go missing there. Maybe that's what happened to Heather—she drowned. That would explain why Emily could no longer sense her. Maybe she's stuck in the same place Henry is and become unreachable. *Could she be a ghost too?*

All I could imagine was Heather drowning in the bay, her long, yellow hair as fine as seaweed, floating in the water. I saw her face-down, the fish nibbling at her limbs, eating away at her flesh. Then I thought of her emerging onto the beach with the tide, a ghost-like creature, destined to spend her life in the fourth dimension until she atones for harming another.

Squeezing my eyes tightly shut, I tried to vanquish the horrible image from my mind. When I opened them again, I saw Channing standing in the corner by the lockers. He looked haggard, like he hadn't had a wink of sleep the previous night—my guess is that he'd been interrogated fiercely.

I nudged Emily. "Should we go talk to him?"

Emily nodded, and we walked over.

Channing's normally handsome features looked laced with worry lines with puffy eyes and dry mouth. He looked like he'd been run over by a very large truck.

"You okay?" I asked. "We're really sorry to hear about Heather."

He looked at us gloomily and shook his head. "The cops questioned me for three hours this morning, showed up at my house at freaking four in the morning. Those idiots think I'm involved in her disappearance. Can you believe that?"

"That's ridiculous," I said. "I know you wouldn't hurt her."

"Yeah, well, tell that to the boys in blue," Channing said, his eyes hopeless. "When a girl goes missing, it's always the boyfriend who gets canned."

"What do you suppose happened to her?" I asked, probing.

Channing shrugged. "I dunno. One minute, we were dancing, and then she wanted to go up on deck for some air. We had an argument about something, then she ran out on me. I just figured somebody gave her a ride home. I didn't call or anything. With Heather, you've gotta give her space sometimes, just let her cool off, ya know?"

The bell rang, but instead of going to first period, we were all ushered into the hall for a special assembly.

Stone-faced, Principal Philopolis walked up to the podium. "It is with great regret, students, that I call this assembly this morning. It appears that our homecoming queen has gone missing. No one has seen Heather Palmer since last night, and her mother has called the police to investigate. If anyone has any information that may help the authorities to locate Heather, I urge you to please come forward. Any disclosures will be treated with the strictest confidence."

I looked around at the gawking faces of the students in the assembly hall, *did any of them know anything? And if they do, would they care enough to step forward?*

"What about Channing?" Emily whispered to me. "That fight he had with Heather. . . Should we say something?"

"Say what?" I said. "It was just a lovers' quarrel. That doesn't prove anything. We can't go around accusing people. We don't really know anything about what happened to Heather."

None of the students accomplished much that morning, even though the teachers tried to carry on as though nothing had happened. We were all already tired from the night before, and Heather's disappearance only made it more difficult to focus.

At lunchtime, the only topic of conversation around all the cafeteria tables was Heather. As I helped myself to the salad bar, I couldn't believe some of the petty, cruel things the other girls were saying, like Heather being dead made her a prime target for bitchy barbs.

"Ya know, my mom always says people get what they deserve," said Melissa. "I guess that's true of Heather."

"Yeah, well, I shoulda won homecoming queen, anyway," said Juanita. "That girl sure didn't deserve her tiara. She practically slept her way to the top."

I felt like opening my mouth and saying something; I'd always been one to speak out against injustice. I couldn't believe how catty my classmates became. Only the day before, they had been part of Heather's entourage, pretending to be her friend. At Homecoming, the whole school had practically worshipped her like some golden-gowned goddess and now—everyone from jocks to geeks continuously badmouthed her.

By mid-afternoon, as I tried to get through trigonometry, we received more sensational news: The Coast Guard found some of the golden flowers in Heather's braid floating in the bay. They had been fished out by one of the trawlers returning from an overnight catch.

"She's dead. I know she is," said Emily dramatically when we heard the news. "I mean, where else would she be?"

"You can't know that," I tried to reassure her, even though I wasn't entirely convinced myself.

"Then where is she? People just don't disappear," Emily said.

"They seem to in Pacific Grove," I said, remembering the surfer who also vanished off Carmel without a trace. Dad told me there was still no sign of him and his car remained abandoned in the parking lot so long it had to be towed away. Mysterious swimmers disappearing, lights in the bay, vanishing homecoming queens: They all seemed to be routine happenings in our sleepy little town.

I wondered what would happen if Heather had drowned in the bay. *Will she suffer the same fate as Henry and be confined to the fourth dimension forever? Will I see her again, maybe walking along the costal path at night, lost and tearful like poor White Dove?* I thought about asking Henry the next time I saw him.

The bell finally rang at the end of the last period, and there was a flurry of excitement among the students.

I slowly walked the coastal road home after school. I needed time to think. Mostly about Henry, but thoughts of Heather kept creeping in.

I made myself a cup of coffee and settled down with some home-work at the kitchen table. I tried to read *Little Women*. Our book club was scheduled to meet the next day, and I hadn't read a word of it. I knew Ethan would quiz me, and I didn't want him to get the better of me. I quickly skimmed through the chapters, making my own mental Cliff's notes. Luckily as a fast reader, I can absorb a lot of information quickly.

The front door opened just after six, and Dad and Sophie came in. He tossed the evening edition of local newspaper onto the kitchen table and shook his head.

I looked up from my book and read the headline: "Local Home-coming Queen Disappears."

"Did you know this girl?" he asked, pointing to the picture of Heather wearing her movie star smile. She looked every inch the home-coming queen with her blonde braid and all-American, beach-babe grin. On the surface, she appeared like a young woman who had everything going for her, but the one thing she didn't have was good luck.

"Sure. She was in some of my classes. She was. . ." I said then stopped. I had a hard time talking about Heather in the past tense.

"Tragic. Such a pretty girl, too," said Dad.

"Yeah, she sure was," I conceded. Heather's beauty hadn't gone unnoticed by anyone, not even my dad, who didn't ever seem to notice women after my mom died. He was so oblivious, I began to doubt he'd ever find someone again.

"Anyway, how was your evening with what's-his-name?" said Dad, opening the refrigerator.

"Henry," I clarified, sipping my coffee.

"Yeah, that's right - Henry," replied Dad, pulling out a carton of juice. "Well, how was it?" he asked loftily.

"Fine, Dad."

"He didn't try to, uh—?"

"No, he didn't. He's not like that. Henry is always a gentleman."

"A gentleman, huh? Well, that's a first. Don't get too many like that anymore."

"He's not like other boys," I said, and I meant it.

Sophie came skipping down the stairs carrying her crayons, eager to get started on the coloring book that Dad had bought for her in the aquarium gift shop. "Alice has a boyfriend," she said in a singsong voice as she smirked at me.

I didn't say anything. It was the first time my family expressed any interest in my love life. Not that I minded; I actually found it cute—I just wasn't used to it.

That evening, we ate mushroom risotto that I cooked. After dinner, I was absolutely exhausted. The events of the past twenty-four hours had caught up with me. So after doing the dishes, I excused myself and went up to my room.

I wedged my window open with my copy of *Little Women* and looked out toward the bay. Heather's disappearance had really affected me. Where is she? I asked over and over again, imagining her horrible fate and hoping she hadn't been sentenced to death, or worse, sentenced to the fourth dimension.

That evening, her image really began to haunt me. Wherever I looked, I saw her: in the bathroom mirror, in the window reflection, and in the small mirror atop my vanity. Finally, I could stand it no longer. After brushing my teeth, I slipped into my PJs and went to bed. Closing my eyes, I hoped Heather's ghost would go away, along with my all-consuming thoughts of Henry.

*

The next day, I went through the Saturday morning ritual of going to the market with Sophie. The winter vegetables started to make an appearance, and we browsed through the butternut squash, the zucchini, and the ripe avocadoes. When we got home, I made a simple salad of lettuce, tomatoes, cucumbers, and avocado then covered the bowl with plastic wrap and stored it in the refrigerator for later.

It was a sunny October day, so when Dad came home, we enjoyed lunch on the back terrace. In spite of the grim undercurrent in our community, we managed to squeeze in a few laughs as we ate.

After dinner, I headed to our book club meeting at Starbucks. When I got there, I spied Christian and Rachel sitting in the far corner. As I approached, I heard Heather's name; she was still the topic of conversation. I hadn't had a chance to speak to Christian since the dance and his fight with Henry, not confidant in how he would react to me.

Much to my surprise, he looked at me with a friendly smile on his face. "Hey! Guess what we're talking about."

"Heather?" I replied.

"What do you think happened to her?" asked Rachel.

I shrugged. "The police are still looking." I glanced around the table and noticed the empty seat. "Where's Ethan?" I asked, surprised he would be late, since he chose the book for discussion.

"I dunno, but I'm sure he'll turn up," Christian replied. He looked at me shyly. "Hey, I wanna apologize for the other night."

I shook my head. "No, I'm the one who should apologize. It was inexcusable what Henry did, attacking you like that and calling you names. I'm sorry."

Christian smiled at me gratefully.

Thirty seconds later, Ethan arrived. He sat down without a word, opened his copy of Little Women, and went to the counter to order a latte.

"Hey, bud. We thought you might be a no-show," said Christian good-naturedly.

Ethan avoided our eyes, and sat down his latte. "Let's get started," he said. "The central character is confused and alone, repressed beyond belief."

"I disagree with that," I said.

Ethan and I dove into a literary debate, something I immensely enjoyed. We had only been debating for two minutes, when he picked up his books and stormed out of the coffee shop, abandoning us and the high-priced drink—shocked, I just watched him go.

"What was all that about?" Rachel said in astonishment.

I wondered, too. I could recall a time I'd seen him and Heather talking together at the lockers, and I wondered about their connection. They seemed an unlikely pair.

When I returned home, I almost collided with Dad, who rushed out the front door with a pained expression.

"Alice! Thank God you're home, honey," he said, obviously flustered.

"What's wrong?".

"Uh—just a little crisis in the bay. A few sea otters have washed up onshore, some mysterious disease. I have to go to the aquarium."

"Now?"

"Yes, and I need you to stay home and look after your sister."

"Sure, Dad. Of course."

"Thanks, Sweetheart. I'll be back as soon as I can," he said, disappearing down the path.

"Do you want me to leave some food for you?" I shouted after him. "I can make you a plate to warm up."

"Nah," said Dad. "I'll get something on the Row." Then, just like that, he jumped into the car and was gone.

Since it would only be the two of us girls for dinner, I decided to make some tortillas to go with the salad I'd made earlier.

Sophie sat at the kitchen table scribbling away and singing. She sounded happy, and for a moment, her child-like glee helped me forget about all my distractions.

Halfway through rolling out a third tortilla, the doorbell rang. Wiping flour on my jeans, I walked over to the front door.

There stood Henry his eyes unwavering and wearing a fiercely intense expression.

"Wh-what are you doing here?" I whispered. "My dad's gonna be home any minute now, and if he finds you here—"

"—You cannot keep me away," said Henry, cutting me off. "I have been thinking of nothing else for the last few evenings."

I glanced over my shoulder and saw that Sophie still played in the kitchen. I knew she would tell Dad if I asked Henry in, even though it wouldn't be out of spite. The twelve-year-old mind doesn't allow for much discretion.

"I can't invite you in, but we can talk outside."

"Alright."

I closed the front door quietly then stepped out to join Henry on the front porch. It was twilight, and the lights on the neighboring front porches were just beginning to turn on.

Henry stood there with his hands in his pockets, as if he had rehearsed his speech a thousand times and was eager to get on with it. "I am unsure what hold you have on me, Alice Parker, but somehow you have managed to corrupt my soul. I cannot get you out of my mind, no matter how hard I try."

"I thought it was you who corrupted mine," I whispered, looking down.

He reached out to caress my neck with his strong hand.

I shivered at his powerful touch and leaned my forehead against his. "What have you done to me?" I breathed.

"I apologize for how I acted at the dance. I just cannot bear to see you with another man. Something in me just snapped."

"It's okay. I overreacted, too. I'm just not used to guys fighting over me." Never before had I felt like a heroine penned by Jane Austen.

"I find that hard to believe," said Henry, smiling.

"It's true," I said. A strong sense of relief suddenly washed over me, and I knew in that moment that we were good, everything was going to be okay.

"Would you like to go for a drive along the coast?" said Henry. "It is very romantic, almost mystical this time of the night, with the moon over the bay."

"I can't. I have to look after Sophie."

Henry jerked his head back, and his eyes seemed to penetrate the front door. "Sophie!"

"What? What's wrong?"

Without a word of explanation, Henry brushed past me and opened the door. At the speed of light, he ran into the kitchen as I hurried in behind him. I looked over his tall frame and lying on the floor struggling to breathe and convulsing wildly—my precious little sister, with her colorful crayons scattered all around her.

"Oh my God!" I shouted, my heart missing a beat. "She's having an asthma attack."

It had happened once before, when Sophie was littler. Even though we were with Mom at the time, it had scared the hell out of me. She had stopped breathing, and we had to give her CPR.

"We've gotta get her to the hospital," I cried.

Henry picked up her limp body and carried her to his truck.

I grabbed the front door keys and followed, my heart racing wildly.

Henry drove through the streets like a maniac, honking his horn loudly as he snaked through the congested traffic trying to get to Monterey County Hospital, only two miles away.

"Get out of the way," I said, waving like a crazy person at the cars in the road. "Move!"

On the way, I called Dad on his cell phone and told him, in a panic, to meet us at the emergency room.

Five minutes later, we arrived at the hospital. Henry pulled his truck up to the emergency ward, opened the door, and ran in with Sophie in his arms.

I ran ahead to open the double-doors. When I spotted a paramedic walking out, I shouted to get his attention. "Help us! Please! My little sister is having an asthma attack."

"Okay, Miss. Calm down, and follow me."

The paramedic ran to get a stretcher from the corridor and wheeled it to the front door. Henry placed Sophie on top, and they wheeled her in.

"You'll have to wait in reception," said the paramedic, holding his hand out to stop me from going any farther.

Helplessly and terrified, I stood back and watched Sophie disappear down the corridor, surrounded by doctors and nurses.

In the waiting room, Henry did his best to console me. Memories of being in the hospital with my mother came flooding back, this was equally terrifying.

"She can't die. She just can't," I said to Henry. Despite my best efforts to conceal them, huge tears began to form in my eyes. I prayed that Dad would get here soon and hugged Henry, laying my head on his chest.

Henry gripped my shoulders with his strong, comforting hands. "She won't die. Alice, look at me."

I looked into his gorgeous blue eyes.

"She will be fine," he said, in the most certain, reassuring voice I'd ever heard.

Nodding, I sobbed in his arms. I wanted to believe him, but I couldn't be sure—especially not after what had happened with our mother. I knew through experience that hope can be a fickle friend.

"How did you know?" I asked between tears. "That she was going to have an asthma attack?"

Henry shrugged. "Sometimes I see things. All part of being in the fourth dimension."

Twenty minutes later, Dad came rushing into the waiting room, smelling like the ocean. "What happened?" he demanded, half-angry, half in shock. He glared at me—then at Henry, and back at me again.

"Asthma attack," I said. "One minute, she was coloring, and the next. . . Well, I was talking to Henry, and—"

"—Talking to Henry, huh?" Dad said, cutting me off. I hated the look in his eyes, as though I'd done something terribly wrong. "It seems to me you've been talking to Henry a lot lately, even when you are supposed to be looking after your sister. What's gotten into you, Alice?"

"Mr. Parker, Sir, with all due respect, it wasn't Alice's fault," began Henry. "She was just—"

"—Was I talking to you?" snapped my dad. "What have you done to my daughter? Alice is always so responsible, so focused—until you came along!"

I had never seen Dad so angry, and it frightened me. Speechless, I said nothing to either of them.

"I am sorry about what happened to your daughter, Sir," said Henry politely.

"You don't have to tell me how sorry you are, young man!"

"Dad, you're being unreasonable. Henry drove us here; he brought Sophie to the hospital to get the help she needs. If it wasn't for him—"

"—I'm being unreasonable? I don't know what's been going on with you lately, Alice. You mope around all day, and when you're not home, you're off with this boy who I know nothing about. You've been neglecting your chores, and the housework is behind."

My chores? The words stung, really needled me. All I had been doing lately was shopping, cooking, and housework, filling the role of a mother when I wasn't even out of high school.

"Just admit it, Dad. You want me to be just like Mom! Well, she's gone, and you've left me to deal with all the cooking and cleaning while you're off fooling around with sick sea animals! I get tired, too, you know!" I shouted, shocked by the venom in my own voice. I couldn't help it, though. All those suppressed feelings came boiling to the surface, and I had to let them out, even in a hospital waiting room.

Dad, equally caught off guard, took a step back and wiped his mouth.

Our vicious spat was interrupted by one of the doctors coming out of Sophie's room. "Mr. Parker, your daughter is no longer in critical condition, but we'd like to keep her overnight for observation," the doctor announced.

Dad's shoulders relaxed, and he almost broke into a smile, relieved as I was. "Thank you," he said, nodding to the doctor. "Can I see her now?"

"In a few minutes, but only you. We need her to get some rest."

"Honey," Dad said, turning to me, "I didn't mean to come on so heavy with you. You and Sophie are my life. If anything ever happened to either of you—"

"—I know that, Dad, and I'm sorry I worried you."

We hugged each other tightly, both glad to learn Sophie would be okay.

"Well, I'm sorry I yelled at you. There's no need for you to stay here tonight," Dad said to me. "Go on home, and I'll call you with any news."

I shook my head. "No way. I'm staying here where I belong, with my family."

"You know, you are like your mother," Dad said, nodding, "at least when it comes to the stubborn department." He offered a sheepish half-smile and followed the doctor to Sophie's room.

"Your father is a fine man," said Henry as he watched him walk away.

"Yes, he is." I nodded, thinking it very gracious for Henry to say that after Dad had just yelled at him. I was lucky to have both men in my life, and I wanted to hang on to both of them for as long as I could. Choices are never easy, but choosing between the two of them—that would have been nearly impossible.

Chapter Twelve: Heather

We took Sophie home from the hospital in the morning. Henry had stayed with me until Dad ordered him to go home. Sophie sat in the back seat, chirpy as ever, singing along with the show tunes blaring over the radio, so bright and cheery. *Must have loved all the fuss and attention in the hospital*—I thought, then immediately felt ashamed for such a thought.

Dad said little to me in the car. Once or twice, I glanced over at him, hoping to catch his eye, but he remained stone-faced, his eyes fixed on the road ahead and his hands gripped on the wheel. I hated it when he gave me the silent treatment. I would much rather have heard him shouting, but he had never been good at expressing his emotions.

When we arrived home, I opened the front door.

Dad carried Sophie up to her room. "Off to bed, Princess," Dad said, dropping Sophie on her bed. "Doc said you have to rest."

"But, Dad, I wanna play with Sally-Anne," said Sophie, referring to her favorite toy, a porcelain doll Mom and I had bought for Sophie's sixth birthday. Since our mother's death, Sophie and Sally-Anne had been inseparable.

"You can play with Sally-Anne after the two of you have a rest. She looks kind of sleepy, too," Dad emphasized, tucking her in bed.

I lingered at the door as Dad brushed past me. When he left, I turned to Sophie, all snuggled up under her covers. "I just want you to know that I'm glad you're okay."

"I'm always okay, Alice," Sophie said, smiling up at me.

"No jokes. You really scared me. You mean more to me than anything."

Sophie smiled. "I know, Alice. I just wish you were happier, that you would smile more. Your teeth look pretty when you smile."

From the mouths of babes, I thought, nodding to confirm I'd listened and turned to head downstairs.

Dad was making coffee in the kitchen. When I walked in, he had his back turned to me, the air thick with tension.

"How's the research going? Any news about what's causing the otter plague?"

"No," he said, stirring creamer into his coffee. "It's got us all baffled."

"Maybe there'll be a breakthrough soon," I said, putting my hands in my jean pockets.

"Alice, I don't want you to see that boy anymore," Dad blurted out, placing his mug down firmly on the table.

"What? But I thought you said—"

"—I just don't like him, and I don't want you to spend time with him."

"How can you say that, Dad? You don't know anything about him."

"That's precisely it. Neither do you, not really."

"I do, too!"

"Tell me, then, Alice. What is it you *do* know about him?"

"I know that I care for him and that he makes me happier than I've ever been before."

"Great. He makes you happy."

"And I don't deserve that? Don't you want me to be happy, Dad?"

"Of course you deserve that! Like I told you, you and Sophie mean everything to me. I think about that girl from your school, that Heather, and I… God, what if that was one of my girls?"

"What has that got to do with me and Henry?" I countered.

"I just want you to be careful," Dad said with a scary finality in his voice before he walked out of the kitchen.

The more I thought about Dad's words, the more I wondered if he might be right. I didn't know much about Henry, apart from the little he told me. He was from San Francisco and a bit bohemian, sailing down to Monterey on one of the fishing boats. In a nutshell, that's all I had. . . Aside from the fact he isn't even alive—really.

I also considered Heather and her disappearance. *How is her mom feeling?* How anxious the poor woman must be, not knowing what happened to her daughter. Then I remembered Mrs. Prescott, who lost her son in the bay, and how crazy she had become. *Will Heather's mom end up like that, too?* I couldn't even fathom how my dad would end up if anything happened to Sophie or me.

*

That night, I dreamt of Heather. She wore her gold homecoming dress and called out to me. Then, Henry appeared at her side. He held her in his arms and kissed her passionately, all the while slyly looking at me.

I woke up confused and covered in a thick coating of sweat from head to toe. Henry and Heather were becoming a bit of a problem, consuming my head day and night.

*

The following Sunday morning, Dad and Sophie went to Mass. I suggested that I meet them outside the church afterward so we could go for brunch. I longed for us to be back together again, happy and getting along. I also had another agenda; I wanted to visit Heather's mother. Dad nodded and said they would look for me once Mass was over.

Sitting outside on the church steps, I watched a flock of black crows circle and dance in the sky above. Inside, the congregation sang the final hymn, their voices rising and falling with the verses. I knew when Mass had come to end because I heard the shuffling of dress shoes against the floor as the crowd eased up the aisle to exit.

When the throng of parishioners came out, I searched for Mrs. Palmer among them. I saw her walking down the steps, with the minister. She looked surprisingly well, considering that there'd been no sign of her daughter. I studied her face, but it was composed and inscrutable, her gray-blonde hair immaculately tied up in a bun.

Christian stood among some young students, chatting amiably, dressed this time in a navy-blue sweater and chinos. When he glimpsed me, his face lit up, and he sauntered over. "Loitering outside the church again? This is becoming a regular habit of yours."

I smiled at his attempt at humor. "Oh, maybe the devil will drag me inside one day. How was Mass?"

"It was great. Dad said a prayer for Heather."

"That's nice. I'm sure her mom appreciated it."

We chatted a little while longer before I started to walk away from the church. The germ of an idea began to form in my mind, and I whipped out my cell phone. "Hey, Ems, it's me," I said when she picked up. "Can you meet me in an hour?"

*

"Are you sure this is a good idea?" I asked Emily, suddenly having second thoughts, as we stood outside the blue Victorian house on the borders of Pacific Grove and Monterey.

"Of course! If it means putting an end to your bad dreams and my visions, it has to be good, doesn't it?" said Emily.

The first thing that caught my attention was the manicured lawn with purple and white flowers leading up to the front porch. All the gardens in Pacific Grove were tidy, but this one seemed obsessively so.

I cast my eyes over the clapboard house and wondered who hid behind those lace curtains. "Okay. Let's go," I said and walked up the garden path with Emily. I took a deep breath and knocked on the door.

A few seconds later, Mrs. Palmer appeared, still looking as calm and relaxed as she had that morning. I expected her to have red, puffy eyes, instead they were clear and lively.

"Mrs. Palmer?" I asked, then introduced myself, "I'm Alice Parker."

"And I'm Emily Kline."

The woman seemed surprised to see us. "Pleased to make your acquaintance. What can I do for you young ladies?"

"We're from Monterey High, we were, uh—*are* friends of Heather's," I said, even though it wasn't exactly true.

Mrs. Palmer seemed to stiffen at the mention of her daughter's name. She glanced from Emily to me and back again. After a moment, she relaxed a little and smiled at us. "I see. Well, you'd better come in."

I glanced at Emily, and she nodded, so we both went inside.

Lace seemed the predominant motif in the Palmer house as it lined the curtains, doilies, and acted as bordering for the linen cushions. The scent of a sweet antiseptic filled the house, something like wood polish. Everything appeared prim and orderly.

A framed picture with the words "Lord, Bless This House" stood in prominent display on the mantelpiece. *Did Heather's mother know she was the most popular girl in school—especially with the male students?* There was no evidence in the house to suggest it; in fact, it felt like we'd traveled back in time.

Mrs. Palmer led us into her front room and motioned to a white couch. "Please sit," she said.

Emily and I sat down, only inches away from each other for solidarity, our knees almost touching.

"We're just so worried about Heather and wondered if there's anything we can do to help. . ." Emily began.

"That's very kind, but Heather's in the Lord's hands now. He will take care of her."

I couldn't believe what I heard. The woman's daughter is missing, yet here she is—calmly sitting in her armchair—saying the good Lord would take care of everything. I just could not relate to her perception and almost found it offensive.

"Aren't you worried about your daughter?" I asked bluntly.

"Of course I am," Mrs. Palmer replied, "but what can I, a mere mortal, do? It's out of my hands."

"Have the police come up with any leads?" I queried.

"Yes. They came around and asked me all kinds of questions about Heather, about any boys she's been seeing, who her friends are, and where she likes to go after school. I told them Heather isn't seeing anyone special. She's just not that kind of girl. She's never shown much interest in boys."

Emily and I looked at each other, incredulous. This didn't even sound like we spoke of the same girl—the girl every boy wanted and every girl wanted to be. It was hard to believe that her mother could be that clueless as to her daughter's more accurate reputation.

"What about Channing Myers?" Emily asked. "He was the homecoming king."

"Heather said he is only a close friend," Mrs. Palmer said.

I studied the picture of Heather on the mantel—next to a display of religious icons. She smiled with those pearly white teeth, blond hair highlighted and eyes radiant. Not a hint of the troubled teen, the girl with dark secrets lurking beneath her sunny disposition.

"Have any other boys taken an interest in her, besides Channing?" I asked.

"Well, now that you mention it, there was one," said Mrs. Palmer, fiddling with the hem of her dress.

Emily and I leaned forward.

"Who?" I asked. "Can you tell us his name?"

"No, but he sent little gifts to my little girl—notes and flowers, that sort of thing. I thought it was rather sweet. He was kind of...old-fashioned."

"Old-fashioned?" I repeated out loud.

"Yes, old-fashioned," said Mrs. Palmer. "He used lilac paper and envelopes to write to her, something I've not seen for a long while, not like all these emails and texts and whatnot that kids use today."

"Lilac paper?" I repeated, a sinking feeling in my chest as I remembered the note on the purple paper Henry had given to me in the Poe book.

Mrs. Palmer nodded. "When I was a young girl, boys wrote to me on that kind of stationery. They took the time to pour their hearts out on paper, to pen these long, ardent love letters. Of course, the boys today will do no such thing."

"Can we see one of the letters?" I asked, my voice trembling.

Mrs. Palmer looked at us for a moment, then stood up. "Of course. I'll be right back."

I glanced at Emily but said nothing. Mrs. Palmer returned shortly, holding a folded letter in her hands. She offered it to me, and I took it in my hand and silently studied the ornate handwriting.

"It's rather lovely, isn't it? Old-fashioned, as I said," said Mrs. Palmer as I turned the paper in my hands.

While Heather's mom continued to chat away, all I could concentrate on was the lilac paper. No! It's not possible... Is it? He couldn't have anything to do with Heather's disappearance. Then again, the more I thought about it, the less I could really say when it came to Henry knowing so little about him or his past.

Mrs. Palmer continued to talk, rambling on and on about what growing up in Monterey fifty years ago. I remembered Henry saying he had been to many dances and on many dates in Monterey, and I assumed many teenagers went missing over the years. *Is there a connection?* I asked no one in particular, the thought making me shudder.

I silently handed the letter to Emily, who took it calmly. Then she closed her eyes. Her forehead started to wrinkle up, and she began to tremble and shake.

"Are you okay? Do you sense something?" I asked.

Emily shook her head and kept her eyes shut. Her long eyelashes began to twitch, and the telling kink appeared in her forehead.

Mrs. Palmer just stared at her, silenced and bewildered. "Are you all right, Dear?" she finally asked.

Eventually, Emily opened her eyes and looked around the room in a stupor, blinking. In her fingers, she still clutched the lilac paper, and she rested her eyes firmly on Mrs. Palmer. "Yes, I'm fine. Alice, I think we should go though. We've taken up enough of Mrs. Palmer's time," Emily suddenly said, bolting up from the couch.

"Okay," I said, confused. I thanked Mrs. Palmer for her time and followed Emily as she rapidly walked away from Heather's house, with her mother standing in the doorway, watching us go. "What happened in there? What did you see?" I asked.

"Something terrible. There was all this coldness, this—fear and this swirling fog. . . I could hear Heather's voice calling—I don't believe she's dead."

"Not dead? Then where is she?" I asked.

Emily just shrugged, unable to give me the answers I sought. Even worse, I could not pull my questioning mind off the lilac paper—I had to know the author of those love letters. More importantly, I worried her mysterious suitor had something to do with her disappearance, and what if that suitor has beautiful, blue-eyes? The blue eyes I pursued myself.

*

On Monday, we headed back to school. I dreaded the thought of another two months, with only Thanksgiving break to look forward to. I knew I would have to knuckle down and work hard for the remainder of my schooling, especially if I wanted to go to Berkeley or NYU.

It had been a week since Heather Palmer went missing, and she remained the talk of the school as if her spirit had settled over Monterey High with an icy grip that refused to let go. Her empty chair loomed large in biology, a strange aura surrounding it, and no one else would sit in that makeshift shrine.

Heather's absence even affected gym volleyball. Jessica replaced her as the team captain, but she had neither the charisma nor the athletic prowess of her predecessor. We played a few games against the opposition and lost dismally.

In the locker room, I shivered after a lukewarm shower, wondering when the school would ever fix the water heater. My locker stood a couple away from Heather's. I remember secretly watching her, admiring her beautiful fair hair and her sensuous femininity.

Heather's locker was open, and in the semidarkness, I glimpsed an item of clothing—one of her scarves with the blue and purple stripes, one she wore often. I was surprised the police hadn't taken it as evidence for their investigation, but there it hung, left behind.

Furtively, I glanced around the locker room. All the girls were pre-occupied, drying their hair and toweling off their bodies, slathering their legs with lotion, spraying perfume and hairspray, and chitchatting about boys. When I could be sure no one watched, I reached into Heather's locker and pulled out the scarf. I wrapped it quickly around my knuckles a few times and sneakily slipped it into my gym bag.

Why did I take this? I'm not a kleptomaniac or petty thief, I thought as I walked the hall trying to appear normal. Strange, but I just want a piece of Heather with me as sort of a keepsake. Truthfully, I hoped the scarf would come in handy for my own investigation— with Emily's help of course.

When Emily and I left the locker room to go to our last class of the day, I pulled her into a corner. "I've got something to show you," I said. I reached into my bag and retrieved the pilfered scarf. "It belonged to Heather. I took it from her locker."

Emily's eyes widened like saucers. "You did? Why?"

"Because I need to find the truth about what happened to her. Will you help me? You said you're psychic and clairvoyant, right? I'm hoping we can use this to help us find her."

"I don't know, Ali," Emily said, shaking her head. "We were in her house, around her things and her mother—although I felt a strange sensation around, I didn't get an idea of where she stands. It's like she's completely vanished, leaving no trace—not even a vibrational presence."

"But you said you're not sure she's dead. Even if she is, you might be able to communicate with her, right? I remember you told me that when your aunt died, you had that séance so you could contact her spirit. You used a piece of her clothing. Maybe that will work with Heather's scarf. She wore it all the time."

Emily hesitated but finally nodded. "Okay," she agreed, "but we need to do it somewhere private. The last thing I need is our classmates trying to hire me for palm readings, throwing crystal balls at my locker, or asking me to predict who's gonna win the next football game."

I smiled. "Thanks, Em. Why don't we use the old study room next to biology? No one goes there after school," I suggested.

"All right, but we've gotta be careful. We can't get caught."

Chapter Thirteen: The Séance

When final bell rang, Emily and I hurried to the old study room and quietly shut the door. I walked over to the blinds and pulled them firmly down, shrouding the room in relative darkness. A table sat in the middle of the room, encircled by a few chairs.

Emily had brought a small glass and twenty-six pieces of square paper, on which she had written the alphabet. "I would normally use an Ouija board, but I think this will be okay," said Emily. She placed Heather's scarf in the middle of the table and arranged the letters of the alphabet around it in a circle. The small glass went in the middle. "You ready?" she asked.

I nodded, and we took our seats.

Emily closed her eyes and sat still for a few minutes, then she put her fingertips on the glass. "Is anybody here?" she asked in a solemn voice.

I tried to suppress a smile and did my best not to giggle while Emily's eyes remained closed and the familiar kink rippled her forehead. I knew if I laughed, she would be offended, so I bit my lip hard to stave off the laughter. Even though I respected Emily and her abilities, I wasn't exactly accustomed to a séance so she would have to be tolerant.

"Is anybody here?" Emily asked again. "Please speak to us."

At once, the glass began to move, gliding slowly across the table toward her.

"I don't believe it!" I exclaimed.

"Shh!" Emily whispered harshly. "I feel a presence." She closed her eyes, in deep concentration. "I'm beginning to get an image."

"What? What is it?" I asked with urgency while at the same time not wanting to break the mood or concentration.

"I see—a buoy," Emily said.

"A boy? What boy?" I repeated.

Emily shook her head and was about to speak, but the glass started moving again.

I held my breath and watched it glide toward the letters. "Is it Heather?" I asked, despite myself.

"I'm not sure, but I think it's a female. I feel a solidarity and kinship with her."

The glass continued moving and stopped on one of the paper slips.

"S," I repeated.

Seconds passed, and the glass moved to the next.

"T," I said, frowning. "Who's S.T.?"

"Shh. We're not finished," said Emily.

Within the next few minutes, the glass had indicated five letters: S, T, E, L, L, and A.

S-T-E-L-L-A? I froze and stared at the letters in disbelief. *This can't be possible*, I thought—can't be.

"Stella?" Emily said. "Who's Stella?" she asked then turned to me. "Stella has a message for you, Alice."

I looked at Emily, wild with fright, "Is this some kind of joke?" I asked. "If so, it's not a funny one."

"No," Emily said adamantly, shaking her head. "No joke. Stella has a message for you."

"For me? Are you s-sure?" I asked, my voice trembling.

"Yes. She says she cares for you and that she will see you very soon."

She'll see me soon? Suddenly, my heart leapt into my throat.

"She says you must follow the light. You hear me? It is imperative that you follow that light, Alice."

I nodded, indicating that I heard her—paralyzed with fear, I couldn't verbally acknowledge her past the lump in my throat.

Right at that moment we heard a loud bang on the door, and a shadow appeared through the glass pane. The knob of the door started rattling violently since we took the precaution of locking it from the inside.

"Hey! What are you doing in there?" the custodian demanded.

"Uh—nothing! We're just finishing up," Emily called and hurriedly cleared the table. She put the glass and letters in her bag and handed me Heather's scarf.

I opened the door and rushed past the startled janitor, Emily trailing in my wake.

"Hey, Alice, wait up!" my friend said once we were outside.

I continued walking furiously toward the school gates, not looking back. Finally, I stopped and turned back to look at my friend, my eyes flashing angrily. "That's some kind of sick joke, Emily!" I said.

"What do you mean? You know who Stella is?"

"Yes! Stella was my mom's name."

Emily raised her hands to her mouth. "Oh my God. I had no idea."

I studied Emily for a moment and realized that she was telling the truth. I took her hands in mine and sighed deeply. "I'm sorry. It just freaked me out in there." I hesitated, wondering if I should tell her the rest. "Do you remember when I told you, after I fell into the bay, that I saw something in the water?"

"Yes, of course," said Emily, "but you never told me *what* you saw."

"Her. . . " I said.

"Her? Who——Heather?"

"No! My mom."

"What!?"

"I saw her, Emily. It was very clear, her reflection in the water, smiling at me as if beckoning me to join her."

"Oh, Alice, I had no idea."

"I think Mom wants me to be with her. She must be very lonely, wherever she is."

"Your mom loves you, Alice. Even then, she must have been trying to tell you something."

"Right. To follow the light. But what's that supposed to mean?" I asked. "Before the glass started moving, you said you saw a boy. Who was it? Channing?"

Emily shook her head. "Not a boy—a buoy. You know, those things out at sea—only this one had a light attached."

I looked at Emily, and my mouth fell open. "A buoy? There are some a couple miles out in Monterey Bay. I maneuvered around them when we were kayaking. Do you suppose they have anything to do with Heather? I mean, we had her scarf during the séance."

"I dunno, Alice."

"What do you mean, you don't know?"

"I just don't know. It's not like you can buy a copy of *Psychic Visions for Dummies* or something. I get many images, and I don't always know what they mean. I'm sorry, Ali."

"I know, and I'm sorry, too."

When we reached the coastal path, I said goodbye to Emily and walked home alone. I couldn't believe my mom could be talking to me from beyond the grave. I had expected to contact Heather, but instead, my mother had sent me some cryptic, scary-sounding message from the afterlife.

*

Dad was at home when I returned. He was working at the kitchen table, with maps and data scattered all over the place. The mystery plague killing the sea otters was really disturbing him, and he looked exhausted from nights of worry. "Where have you been, Alice?" he immediately asked when I walked in.

"With Emily."

"You look pale. Everything all right?"

"Yes, Dad." I nodded, not quite looking him in the eye. "Where's Sophie?"

"With a friend. I've been at this all day." He stretched, looked down at the maps and data spread across the table then rubbed his eyes. "I need some fresh air. Want to go for a walk?"

I nodded, knowing a walk with my father might do me some good.

We took the coastal path down to the sandy beach by Lovers Point. The wind had picked up and was blowing the fine grains of sand along the beach like golden veils.

In the far distance, I spied something in the sand. "What's that over there?" I asked, pointing at the mysterious object.

We trudged up to it, only to discover it was the corpse of another unfortunate sea otter, In death, they looked so different from their usual demeanor—that cute, cuddly fur-ball having once swum on its back in the bay. The smell was rank, and I plugged my nose in disgust.

"Been dead for several days," Dad surmised, turning the rotting body over with a large piece of driftwood

"What do you think is causing it?"

"Maybe some kind of virus," Dad said. "Well, it's a real mystery, I plan to visit the lab so I can perform an autopsy."

I shuddered, wondering what evil plague had attacked the helpless little sea creatures, condemning them to death. I also wondered if it could be an omen. Is there a deadly plague in the water? If so, could it have anything to do with that ancient curse?

I looked out over the sea and caught a light shining in the darkness, coming from one of the buoys. *Follow the light*, I thought to myself. Perhaps the clues to solving Heather's disappearance lay out to sea.

Chapter Fourteen: The Storm

A number of buoys floated out in the bay, and a trio of them bobbed up and down about three miles off Point Pinos. I had first noticed their lights flashing when out kayaking. The hypnotic glow from the red beacons was both rhythmic and calming, and I thought maybe they were the lights I was to follow. In fact, I felt I *needed* to sail out to them as though my mom guided me. Maybe out there lay the key to removing the shroud of mystery around Heather's disappearance.

I would need a boat. I thought about asking Connor and decided to drop by his surf shop over the weekend. I didn't want to ask Henry. Ever since I had seen the lilac paper, I'd been harboring some dark suspicions, and to be honest, a little fear.

Dad had offered me some work at the aquarium, and much to his surprise, I accepted—only because I needed the pocket money for a boat rental.

When Saturday came, I left for the aquarium at the crack of dawn and walked along the coastal path, past John Hopkins Marine Lab, to Cannery Row. I'd always liked the aquarium where Dad worked. Housed in a converted cannery; the inside was huge and cavernous, like the mouth of a gigantic whale. Large tanks, pumped full of seawater, acted as home to exotic sea life from the Pacific, like jellyfish, sharks, and rays.

A friendly girl named Katy showed me to the staff quarters, gave me a pair of overalls, and took me to the back rooms. I was expected to do some cleaning in the storage area behind the main exhibit. Stacks of glass tanks in all shapes and sizes were piled up. Some had green algae so thick that I couldn't see through the glass. I wiped the algae off the glass, moving the cloth in a circular motion. I must have been there for hours, as I lost all track of time.

Suddenly, a reflection appeared in the glass, a familiar face.

I screamed. "Holy Crap! You scared me!" I cried, as my heart missed a beat.

"You have been avoiding me," said Henry, staring straight into my eyes, a smile never crossing his lips.

I tried to avert his gaze, but could find nowhere to hide. I was embarrassed for him to see me like this—in those ill-fitting overalls, covered with dirt and algae, and my hair all disheveled.

"It's this business about Heather," I confessed. "It's freaking me out, and I haven't been able to concentrate on anything else. I haven't been sleeping well. I keep seeing these visions of Heather in the water, crying out to me."

Henry looked at me steadily; he didn't seem convinced. "There's something else. Something you're not telling me."

The image of lilac paper floated into my mind but I held my tongue. I didn't have any real proof, and as far as I really knew, it could be a coincidence. I didn't want Henry to pick up on my paranoia. Besides, seeing him again softened me a little. He looked so handsome in his crumpled brown jacket, standing among the tanks of kelp and glass walls of the aquarium. He was dead all right, but in a strange way, there was still something corporeal about him.

I looked at the tanks I had cleaned and felt satisfied I'd done a good job. Dad would be pleased. He and Sophie wouldn't be back from Santa Cruz until the evening. Glancing at my watch, I saw there would still be time to go out on the bay.

"Do you have any plans this afternoon?" I asked tentatively.

Henry shook his head slowly. "No. Why?"

Not sure why I asked, but it was too late to take it back. "Can we sail out to the buoys in Monterey Bay? I'm looking for something."

Henry's forehead wrinkled. "Looking for what?"

I shook my head. "I'm not sure myself, but something tells me I need to go to the buoys and investigate something. It's for my own peace of mind. Will you take me out there this afternoon?"

"I am not certain that is a good idea, Alice. The sea looks rather rough and unfriendly today. There's a storm brewing, and it looks to be an ugly one."

I peered out the window that overlooked the bay. "What are you talking about? It's as calm as a pond," I said.

"Now, perhaps, but look at those storm petrels," Henry said, pointing up at a couple of seabirds that were wheeling in the sky. "When they fly inland, it is a sure sign that a storm is on its way."

"We won't be very long, a couple hours at the most," I persisted.

"Alice, we cannot afford to be caught in a wicked storm."

"Fine. If you won't help me, I'll go on my own," I said, determined to reach the buoys, with or without his help.

Henry sighed. "All right, but if we are going, we must go now."

Elated, I threw off my slimy overalls, tossed aside the thick gloves, smoothed down my hair, and left the aquarium and followed Henry down to his waiting boat.

I felt a tremendous sense of adventure when out on the water. The wind had picked up, and with Henry at the helm, *Evening Tide* skimmed over the choppy waves, the bow making a determined line toward the horizon.

"Any idea what we'll find out there?" I asked Henry.

He was strangely silent, one hand gripping the tiller and his eyes fixed firmly ahead. "I have no idea," he finally said with a shrug, the wind whipping his shiny hair. "Are you sure Emily saw a buoy? Maybe it was something else, like a lighthouse."

"No, she saw it pretty clearly floating in the sea."

I contemplated his question for a moment. I got the sense Henry doubted Emily's truth. Not knowing much about her, myself, I couldn't counter. She was eccentric, and everyone in the school thought her odd, but she always appeared sweet and sincere in my eyes. She predicted Heather's claiming of the homecoming queen tiara, and she'd had visions of a girl floating in a gold dress. Crazy or not, she'd been right about a number of things.

Most intriguing, though, was the séance. If it was some cruel practical joke, she would have had to find out my mother's name, and I'm pretty sure it would have been difficult on the spur of the moment. I suppose she could have gone to the web some time before and easily looked up Mom's funeral details in Chicago on that endless mine of information. Why she would do that? This conclusion led me to believe Mom was trying to contact me. All things considered, I had to believe in Emily and that she told the truth about what she'd seen, sensed, and heard.

I glanced back over at Henry. *Is he just trying to create a rift between Emily and me? Did he write those letters to Heather?* My thoughts troubled, my brow started to furrow as the boat sailed out to sea. I hoped the buoy would hold the answers. *Everything will become clear in an hour,* I told myself. The buoy was only about a mile away, and I could see it bobbing in the murky water.

"Another ten minutes," Henry said. "We're almost there."

My heart raced with anticipation. The buoy loomed nearer and nearer, its steeple bobbing in the water, the beacon light luring us with its flash. I listened to its mournful clang as we floated closer and closer. The bell continued to clang sorrowfully, like the wail of an unhappy maiden.

Henry expertly maneuvered his boat alongside it.

I gazed down at the midnight blue of the water, wondering what I would see beneath the glass-like surface.

Henry scanned the side of the buoy. "There's something down there," he said, peering into the murky depths.

"Look!" I pointed. "There!"

A long length of rope was tied to the buoy, its knotted coil draped with dark green seaweed that floated in the water like a troupe of dainty ballerinas.

Henry reached over the side of the boat and began to tug at the rope.

I squinted, straining to peer into the dark water. Eventually, I saw an object rising out of the water. "What is it?"

Henry frowned. "Something is attached to the rope. It looks like a polymer bag." Henry then tugged hard and heaved the bag up onto the deck off the boat. "It's knotted at both ends," he said, "to keep the insides dry. Shall we open it?" he asked, looking at my ecstatic face.

"Of course!" I replied, trembling in anticipation.

Henry reached inside the plastic and pulled out a small box, about the size of my palm, fashioned of a pale wood. He handed it to me.

"What is it?" I asked, puzzled. I turned the box over in my hand, wondering where it had come from. On the top, markings were engraved in the yellow wood. Studying them, I could make-out the depiction of a rose with its stem wound around to almost a complete circle, it's delicate leaves spread from the coiled stem. "What do you think this emblem means?" I asked Henry.

He shook his head slowly. "I cannot say," he said. "It appears to be a symbol of some kind."

"Thanks, Captain Obvious," I said with a smile. I examined the side of the box, but it was securely locked with no visible means to unlock it.

Immediately, I got a terrible chill and the wind picked up. I gazed fearfully at the sky, which suddenly darkened from sunny blue to a menacing gray.

"We have to return to shore now!" Henry shouted and ran back to the tiller, starting to steer the bow of the boat back toward the coastline.

I tucked the box inside one of the upper compartments, away from the main deck, just as a huge wave came over the bow, drenching me in salt spray.

"Come back to the stern!" shouted Henry.

I obeyed his command. The deck was already slippery as I made my way to join him, the boat beginning to dip and sway fiercely from the wind's force. The waves danced like angry demons on both sides of the boat, slapping against us, and the sail flapped so violently that I was afraid they'd be ripped to shreds. The wind howled, mocking our measly efforts and began to push us back out to sea, away from the coastline.

Henry tried his best to maintain a grip on the steering, but still the boat edged toward the fathomless horizon. "We must take the sail down!" he wailed. "Otherwise, the wind will carry us miles off course." He then set to work to bring down the billowing main sail.

I ran to the sail and tried to help, all the while trying not to slip and fall overboard. Another wave came over the side and drenched me in cold, salty water. I screamed, fearing that I would drown—again.

"I never should have brought you out here!" Henry shouted through the white salt spray.

"We can still make it back to the shore," I said, my hair drenched through.

"No, it's too far," Henry replied. "We'll never make it." He then ran back to the stern and tried to turn the boat around.

"What are you doing?" I asked in amazement, since he seemed to be heading directly into the eye of the storm.

"It's our only chance," said Henry, jutting his jaw out in a determined fashion and continuing his course.

Violent waves surrounded our small boat as Henry maneuvered it directly into the storm. Suddenly we heard a cracking sound, followed by a groan, and the boat sounded like it might split in two. The sea gushed into the boat from a small hole below.

"There's water coming in!" I shouted. "We're gonna sink!"

Henry ran to the side and peered over to have a look at the crack.

Soaked, I watched helplessly as the lower compartment of the boat flooded. The water was icy cold and with the boat already tilting, I knew we would sink within a matter of minutes.

Henry remained strangely calm while my hysteria grew. We were surrounded by dense fog, and for a moment, I experienced the same panic as when I'd been lost at sea during my fateful kayaking trip.

The boat skimmed through the bank of mist and thick cloud cover. For a few seconds that seemed to stretch into an eternity, we couldn't see anything. Finally, the boat broke through the curtain and there, before my very eyes, the most beautiful sight I have ever seen.

"The island!" I screeched in awe. *I didn't imagine it! It is really there, silhouetted against a brilliant blue sky.* I marveled at the twin peaks rising high into the air.

"This is our only chance of safety," said Henry, steering the damaged boat toward the shore.

The island grew nearer and I glimpsed faint clouds above the mountain peaks. When I looked high above, I thought I saw an albatross.

Suddenly, the boat rammed the shoreline jarring me out of my fascination—then nothing at all as a sudden blackness came over me and I passed out.

Chapter Fifteen:

Island of Lost Souls

When I woke up, I thought I was in heaven. All I could see above me were white, dense clouds. Slowly, the fogginess in my head lifted, and I became aware of my surroundings. My head felt stiff, and my mouth full of salty sand. I heard a rhythmic pounding sound, like the crash of waves, but—another sound, too—tap-tap-tap, the sound of hammering.

"Hey," I said meekly.

The tapping stopped, and I heard footsteps in the sand trudging toward me. A shadow loomed over me, and a dark, silhouetted face appeared, looking down at my drenched body.

I looked up into the eyes of Henry.

"Welcome back," he said in a warm, soft voice. "You've been unconscious for a while. Are you all right?"

"What happened?" I asked, sitting up in the sand. My clothes were wet, and the sand stuck to them like glue. My tongue felt as thick as sandpaper.

"You bumped your head when we landed," Henry said, squinting at the back of my head, "but I think you will be all right."

Gingerly, I touched the swollen egg forming at the back of my skull. There was a slight throbbing pain as I turned to glance across the sand at Henry's boat, on the shoreline, tilted on its side. The hole in her portside was small, but Henry patched it up with boards.

"What's the damage?" I asked him, rubbing the back of my head.

"It's okay. Luckily I have a tool box in the boat," Henry said. "And there's plenty of driftwood for me to patch her up."

I turned my gaze from the sea to the towering mountains behind me. The sandy beach led to a forest, which, in turn, climbed up to the pointed peaks. "Where are we?" I asked, gazing up the side of the mountains, wondering what lay beyond them. They seemed to reach for the clouds, but an eerie mist obscured the peaks.

"This is the island," Henry said.

The island! Memories came flooding back, and I knew it was the island I had seen before—the island I had been searching for—real after all, and here I stood on the same sandy beach I saw from afar all those weeks ago. I felt a mixture of elation, apprehension, and fear. *What is on the island*, I wondered, and *what secrets does it hold? Why can I see it when no one else believes it exists?*

"Are you strong enough to help me gather wood?" asked Henry, cautiously scanning the beach.

I nodded, eager for a little exploration. I stood up in the sand, wiped off my backside, brushed the knotted seaweed and sand off my trousers, and followed Henry down the beach.

Along the tideline, I spotted several shells in unusual shapes, and there was plenty of driftwood to choose from. I gathered some of the gnarled pieces and followed Henry in his pursuit of more suitable timber. Some of the dry, old pieces would make a nice bandage for the boat.

I picked up a large pink conch and placed the lip to my ear. The sound of the sea came flooding in. It reminded me of my childhood beach-combing excursions with my mom, when we spent our holidays on Cape Cod.

"I think we have enough," said Henry, his arms full of wood.

We trudged along the tideline, back to the boat. As we walked, he seemed uneasy and kept glancing back to the edge of the forest. I wondered what he could be looking for, but I didn't bother to ask.

When we reached the boat, we immediately began patching up the hole. Henry took some nails from his tool box and started to hammer the longer pieces of driftwood into place. In a matter of ten minutes, the hole had been boarded over.

"Will it hold?" I asked, wondering if the pounding waves would knock the boards loose. I didn't relish the idea of sinking in the middle of the Pacific. "How far are we from Monterey?"

"We are but a few miles out to sea," said Henry. He squinted at the patched boat, but he didn't seem completely satisfied it would be sea worthy.

"We need something to plug the gaps between the timber. I know a plant that sticks like glue when wet. It grows by the island's waterfall."

I had never heard of a plant that got sticky when wet, but the mention of a waterfall sounded good.

"Are you thirsty?" Henry asked, looking at me as though doing a medical exam with his eyes.

I swallowed, realizing for the first time that I indeed was thirsty. My mouth feeling dry as parchment, and the beach rubbing against my skin like sandpaper, I nodded.

"The waterfall is a few hundred feet from here. We can get a drink before we set off and collect the plant at the same time. Come. But we must be quick about it," he said, again darting his eyes around the deserted beach. "'Tis not safe to be on the island for too long."

Why is he scoping the beach so much—not safe? I asked in my mind, *What is that supposed to mean?*

Before I could ask aloud, Henry strode up the beach toward the tree line, and I had to quicken my pace to catch up with him.

We clambered up the beach, and for a while I forgot about my troubles at home. Being here was like being lost in paradise. Sounds of the birds high in the sky, and some of the most brightly colored flowers I have ever seen painted my vision in every direction.

"It's beautiful," I said as we reached the forest line where the ground immediately started to ascend from the beach.

Henry nodded slowly. "Indeed. I thought that very thing when I first came here."

"When was that?"

"A long time ago, after the shipwreck."

I thought for a moment, realizing it had to have been a century ago. I gazed up at the craggy cliffs, which seemed a long way up.

"The trek is a bit slippery from here," said Henry, "You must watch your step."

My sandals were not exactly suitable for hill climbing, so I stepped carefully, watching my footing and reaching out for the sticky vines and low hanging branches to haul myself up.

"How far away is the waterfall?" I asked, straining my ear to catch a sound of rushing water. All I could hear was the hush of the forest and the faint chirp of birdsong.

"Just a few hundred feet," Henry said as he nimbly traversed the slope.

His footsteps were steady as he easily navigated the uneven terrain of the forest. I, on the other hand, had to focus all my concentration to prevent myself from slipping, falling in a hole, or twisting my ankle.

Suddenly, we heard a crack in the distance, like the sound of a snapping twig.

Like a startled deer, Henry instantly paused to listen.

"What?" I asked, excitedly, trying to whisper.

"Shh!" he answered fiercely.

I strained to listen for any sounds in the forest—nothing but silence. Henry continued to hold his hand up, motionless. After what seemed an eternity, he motioned his hand forward, and I silently followed him up the path.

We soon glimpsed the ocean through a break in the trees. I marveled at the sight of the radiant blue water stretching from the beach and ending in a thick cloud that seemed to circle the island.

I turned to Henry, who still looked pensive after the climb. "Breathtaking!" I said as I motioned to the crystal-blue waters that formed the shallows surrounding the island.

Henry nodded slowly, but he didn't allow us to linger for too long. "The waterfall is around the bend. We must continue."

Our last scramble came through a thick patch of bushes, speckled with sweet purple flowers that gave off the most divine aroma. Some white and blue butterflies danced along the hedgerow as we scrambled along the rocky path. The Island felt eerie but mesmerizing at the same time. I felt strangely at peace.

When we turned the corner, I saw the cascade, a spectacle of nature at about twenty feet high with the waterfall pouring over a rocky lip into a turquoise pool below. It was one of the prettiest sights I had ever seen.

"Come on," Henry urged. "Drink!"

I followed him to the edge, cupped my hands, and dipped them into the sparkling pool. Then I brought my hands to my lips to savor the cool water. I gulped greedily, and then I started to splutter.

"Not so fast," Henry joked. He drank leisurely, in slow, long gulps, and then he lazily rested on his back to enjoy the sun.

After a few more swallows, I settled back and started to take in the surroundings. "Does anyone live on this island?" I asked.

"Yes, which is why we must keep it a secret."

"A secret? From whom? I don't understand why ships can't find this place," I said, trying to make logical sense of it. "How it can just appear and disappear?"

"There are some things that simply cannot be explained, like apparitions."

I looked at him and cracked a smile. "Yeah, I guess you're right. You sure can't explain ghosts."

"Follow me," Henry said as he stood up.

He marched to the side of the waterfall, where an overhanging branch jutted out of the rocks. The leaves were green, plump, and succulent. Henry tore some generous strips off and offered them in his palm for me to smell.

"This is the plant that sticks like glue," he said. "We'll need it for the boat."

"Mmm. It smells like eucalyptus," I said, savoring the aroma.

I had never seen such a plant before, but I figured Emily would know about it, as she grew herbs, so I tore off a few leaves and put them in my own pocket as a souvenir and a bit of proof.

"Okay, let's go", Henry said.

He quickened his pace and headed back into the forested slope. It was much easier going down, but I still had to watch my step because I knew just one misplaced foot could send me tumbling.

Halfway down, a strong breeze raced in from the ocean shivering the leaves on the trees with a restless sigh. My still-damp hair caught the breeze; it covered my face and adhered to my skin.

Then a loud cry from the forest burst into my peaceful awareness. "What is that?" I asked fearfully. It sounded half-human, too human to be any kind of animal as far as I knew.

Henry froze. "We must go now, Alice," he announced, pulling me roughly by the arm.

"What! "Why?"

He pulled my arm so hard that it almost popped out of the socket.

"What's wrong?" I muttered.

"Alice, we have to leave right now," he repeated urgently. "I follow the rules in your world, you must follow the rules in mine," he added sternly.

It was too late; from over the crest of the hill, a large tribe of men appeared. About a dozen of them—looking like young warriors, some with beards but most unshaven. All wore ragged, weather-beaten clothes—gray slacks and flannel shirts. Even from a distance, I saw they were barefoot. I heard the loud cry they howled when they caught sight of us.

"Run!" shouted Henry.

My heart beat rapidly as I followed his orders. He sprinted down the hill, back to the beach. The men were in hot pursuit, jumping over the bushes and rocks, as agile as mountain lions, crunching the branches underfoot.

"Who are they?" I asked, panting heavily as I tried to keep up with Henry.

"No time to explain. Just keep running," Henry commanded.

We reached the end section of forest, where the trees met the beach. I looked back and saw the men catching up with us, leaping and hollering like warlords. One of them, a fierce, strong-looking bearded man broke free from the main group and charged toward us, looking dangerously determined.

Henry's head shook as he ran. "I never should have brought you here," he repeated. "I-I broke the rules," he muttered.

"What rules?" I asked, panting. Curious to uncover the island's secrets—even in fright.

"No mortals are allowed on the island," Henry answer, slowing a bit so I could catch up to him.

My heart raced and my mind tried to keep up with my legs. *If no mortals are allowed, who are those men chasing us?* My legs burned, and I was sure I would collapse as soon as we reached the sun-drenched sand.

"Do not stop," urged Henry. "We must get to the boat." He tore down the beach like a track star, pulling my hand, urging me to run faster.

I looked back and saw that the leader of the group had broken through the tree line and quickly closed the distance between us, running and shouting at us to "Stop!". Again, I found myself wondering who these men were and what we had done to incur their wrath.

Henry had reached the boat and, without hesitating, began to push the bow into the water. Waist high in the shallows, he quickly steered the boat out to sea, pointing the bow resolutely toward the horizon. Then he turned back to face me. "Make haste!" he urged. "Don't stop, Alice. You can do it."

I quickened my pace, but every step became pure agony. I could almost feel the leader's hot breath at the back of my neck. I heard him exhaling, kicking up the sand under his bare feet as he tried to catch me.

In seconds, I had reached the boat. Henry quickly hauled me over the wooden side, where I floundered on the deck like a seal. My lungs felt as though they would burst while I writhed in agony, my mouth pressing against the hard wooden boards. I prayed the boat was sea worthy.

Henry pushed the boat a few more feet out to sea, then acrobatically leapt onto the deck and hoisted the sail.

I struggled to get up to peer over the stern of the boat. The lead man reached the tideline, and there were a dozen men not far behind him. Now about fifty feet out to sea, our boat quickly gained distance from the shoreline.

The lead man didn't stop; he leapt into the water. In a fury, he started to swim after our disappearing boat, making strong, rapid strokes.

I screamed, convinced he was going to catch us, but a gust of wind picked up in our favor, moving the boat out of reach just in time.

The man stopped swimming about thirty feet from the shore and, realizing his efforts were futile, started treading water. He raised his fist and cursed at us.

"Who are they?" I said, finally resting on the deck.

Henry's pale face seemed even paler than usual. "They are the immortals," he said solemnly, "the undead."

"The undead," I repeated in a hushed voice, shivering.

"I fear a terrible curse will come," said Henry.

He reached into his pocket and started to plug the patchwork of timber with the leaves we had collected. Just like he said, when wet the leaves acted as glue, sealing the holes between the wood.

I stole a final glimpse of the island as it disappeared, becoming shrouded in mist once again, and then it was gone.

"Will I ever see it again?" I asked no one in particular, a hint of sadness swimming in my heart.

Chapter Sixteen: Ghost Maven

Henry was silent for the remainder of the trip back to Monterey. He was an expert navigator—following a combination of the sun position, the wind, and tides—and knew exactly where we were headed. I tried to get him to talk, in my constant quest for answers about what had happened and the island inhabitants, but he refused.

When the boat docked on the small beach by Lovers Point, I reached into the compartment to retrieve the wooden box found in the buoy. Surprisingly, it was still there and seemed to be intact. I imagined opening the box to find mysterious contents and the meaning behind the inscription.

"Thank you," I mumbled to Henry, not knowing quite what to say as I jumped onto dry land.

He nodded, took a deep breath, and finally spoke. "I think we should lay low and not see each other for a few days," he said. "It will be better—safer."

"Why?" I asked. "Henry, I need to understand what happened. Who were those men?"

"Undead like me. Some of them are grigoris."

"What's a grigori? You mean they're undead too?" I asked hesitantly.

Henry just looked at me, probably deciding whether or not to tell me.

"Well . . .," I prompted.

"They are the island's watchers. Not dead because they were never alive. Created only to guard the island—no emotion, they follow the directions they've been given and that is all they will do."

An island of ghosts and grigoris? I expected mystery but it seemed to go beyond mystery into realms completely unknown to me. I couldn't fathom what Henry told me. On the surface, the place seemed so idyllic and beautiful. I couldn't believe—didn't want to believe—it harbored such terrible secrets. . . Nightmare stuff.

"Where did the island suddenly appear from?" I asked, trying to fathom the mystery.

"At certain times, because of how the moon regulates our tides, the two worlds collide, yours and mine, and the island appears, giving access to the fourth dimension."

My mind felt so overwhelmed and confused by Henry's explanation, I just jumped onto the dock and without speaking another word to Henry, I carried the box up the path and headed home.

I turned to look at him, to see if he would meet my eyes—instead, he already set sail—away from Lovers Point and his boat soon disappeared. Henry not even looking back disappointed me, I was hurt he kept his gaze fixed on the horizon. *Can't he understand how this must feel for me? I'm not dead—am I supposed to be familiar with his world when I've never even been exposed to it before? How incredibly insensitive!*

When I arrived home, Dad was still out with Sophie. The empty house gave me a chance to ponder all that had happened. I trudged up the stairs to my bedroom, placed the mysterious wooden box on my windowsill, and sat down to do a mental review of the day's adventures.

*

"Well? What did you find?" asked Emily excitedly when we met for coffee at Magnolia Bakery the next day.

"This plant?" I said, showing Emily the resin leaves from my pocket.

She lifted them to her nose, inhaling the scent to help with identification. As she was an herbalist and made funny-tasting tea out of local plants, I knew she was the most logical person to ask. Even though our classmates often ridiculed Emily for bringing in strange concoctions to drink.

"Where did you find these?" she asked in surprise. "They look and smell like Acantholyptys, only found on tropical islands, they definitely don't grow here around the bay."

I reached into my backpack and pulled the wooden box gingerly out of the flannel wrapping.

"And that's not all. Look" I said, placing it on the table for Emily to see.

"Whoa," exclaimed Emily, looking curiously at it as I carefully unwrapped it. "You found that at the buoy?"

I nodded. "Yep. Tethered at the end of a rope, sealed in a watertight bag. Look at this inscription," I said, motioning to the lid.

Emily examined the rose inside the circle and narrowed her eyes.
"What? Have you seen something like that before?" I asked.

Emily nodded. "It looks like the symbol for necromancy."

"Necromancy?" I repeated slowly.

"Yes. A rose inside the circle is the symbol of a Maven, someone who has command over evil spirits."

Evil spirits? I gulped. "Wait. You mean, like, werewolves and vampires, that kind of thing?"

"Yes—and ghosts," Emily said. She shook the box lightly. "What's inside?"

"That's the thing," I said. "It's locked, and I can't figure out how to open it without damaging it."

"Have you even really tried?"

"Not really. Truth be told, I'm a little afraid of what I might find inside."

"Your mom wanted you to find this, Alice. I think we should open it."

"Did she? Did she really?"

"I'm not lying. She told me."

"I'm sorry. I know. I-I just don't understand what all of this means. Have you ever heard the word grigoris?" I asked, hoping with all of her metaphysical knowledge, Emily would be able to explain since Henry assumed I should already know.

"Well, I've read about them. Grigoris from an ancient Greek word meaning 'watchers'. They were protective spirits created by the village sorceress. They didn't have law enforcement and the police for protection so the grigoris would act as sentries. If someone tried to enter with ill-intentions, they would suffer weird accidents and illnesses. You know, there's this place near Salinas where we can get more specific answers." Emily, rose from the table and said, "Let's go."

I had no choice but to follow.

*

"What is this place?" I questioned, darting my eyes around the crumpled, dilapidated sandstone building on the edge of Salinas.

We'd driven twenty miles in Emily's Volkswagen Beetle from Monterey. A clapped-up old thing with lots of character and personality of its own. As eccentric as its driver with a colorful interior and a Native American talisman hanging from the rearview mirror.

"It's an old Spanish mission. I spent much of my time here when growing up," said Emily, turning off the ignition. "Mom had to drag me away when I was a kid. C'mon. There's someone that I think will be able to help you."

With a peaked curiosity, I followed Emily down the broken footpath to the front door of the mission. The grounds were overgrown: the place obviously hadn't employed a gardener for a long time, if ever.

We paused at the door, but instead of knocking, Emily called loudly, "Adriana! Adriana, it's Emily."

"Who's Adriana?" I whispered, but before she could answer, someone opened the door. I wasn't at all prepared for who stood there.

A tiny woman, about eighty-years, with gray, wispy hair and leathery skin greeted us. Her eyes were sunken, and her head seemed to be shriveled, atop a slender neck. She appeared extremely frail and incredibly strong all at the same time. "Emily?" she said, and the two embraced warmly.

"Adriana is my psychic mentor," explained Emily. "She taught me how to meditate, how to predict the future, and how to harness my clairvoyance. I wouldn't know the things I do if not for her help."

"And you are even more beautiful than I remember." Adriana chuckled and brought her hand up to Emily's face to caress her cheek.

At that moment, I realized the old woman was blind. Still, when she turned to me, her white eyes studying my face, I sensed that she could see me.

"And you are Alice," she said.

What? Did Emily tell her about me or something? Amazed and a bit uneasy the old woman knew my name, I hoped a reasonable, logical explanation existed. Maybe Emily phoned ahead and told her about our plans. "Yes, I'm Alice," I said, "How did you hear about me?"

"I've been expecting you," she said, ignoring my question. She smiled and invited us in.

We sat in a shady corner of the mission, under two weeping orange trees. Adriana had made us some mint tea, which we sipped from dainty porcelain teacups. It was almost as if she weren't blind at all; so agile as she went about her business of hospitality.

"Now, I believe you have something to show me," she said, her white eyes peering directly at me.

I glanced at Emily, and she nodded. As if on cue, I took out the box and placed it in Adriana's wrinkled, frail hands.

Her gnarled, old fingers traced the lid of the box and ended their journey on the rose inside the circle. "Ah, yes, the rose within a circle. . . This is the symbol of a necromancer or as I've been taught—a Ghost Maven."

"A Ghost Maven?" I repeated. "What is that?"

"A ghost-keeper, the sacred keeper of righteousness and justice over the fourth dimension—Ghost Maven for short."

"A Ghost Maven. . .fourth dimension. . ." I repeated to myself with a shiver, *how can anyone govern ghosts and where is this fourth dimension supposed to be?* Instead of asking what I really wanted to, I blurted, "You mean, like, a ghostbuster?" *That must have sounded absurd.*

Adriana chuckled, releasing a drawn-out laugh. "That's what they called me for many years, the county ghostbuster." She looked at me intently with bulbous, white eyes. "But there is more to it than that." She settled back in her seat as she began an epic tale.

"Go on, Adriana," Emily coaxed.

"Ghost Mavens were once the guardians of peace along this coast-line for many centuries. Gatekeepers—protecting the sacred lands from evil through magic. Incredibly strong, they could harness the power of the sun and earth to help them ward off wayward spirits, demons and other bad omens. They kept evil at bay and could detect and track ghosts then banish them to a place where they could do no harm to beings on earth. But a thousand years ago, a terrible uprising occurred. . . The lost souls rose up, and many Ghost Mavens were killed in the fierce battle. A few of us survived, but our legacy was lost, powers weakened. We had to take sanctuary, knowing we'd been sorely defeated."

"Ghost Maven," I repeated slowly to myself, loud enough that Adrianna and Emily could hear.

Adriana looked at me with frightening consternation, "Yes, my dear, and one day you may bear that title, too."

"Me?" I asked incredulously, looking from the blind woman to Emily. "What has any of this got to do with me? I'm—just a girl."

"You will know when the time is right," said the old woman.

I shrank back in my seat. Adrianna made me feel very uncomfortable, with her gnarled hands and faint smell of eucalyptus that engulfed her. "How will I know when to use what's in the box?" I added, still shocked and confused, questioning my reality.

Adriana's face became solemn. "You will know, Alice. You must listen only to your heart. The box cannot be destroyed by fire. Only fanning the flames will unlock its secrets."

"How did she become blind?" I asked when back in the car, driving home. Dust flared up from either side as we drove the Bug through the arid agricultural land that separates Salinas from Monterey.

"She fought a ghost," said Emily, not taking her eyes off the road, "and lost her eyes in battle."

Chapter Seventeen:

A Real Date

I hadn't seen Henry for a few days, not since our visit to the island. I'd been preoccupied with the wooden box, as well as suffering from more nightmares about Heather. I desperately wanted to learn more about her disappearance, and all the questions had me tossing and turning through many sleepless nights.

When Henry called me on my cell phone, I almost didn't know what to say. . . "How did you get my number?" I asked, stumbling over the words.

"I have my ways," said Henry, sounding playful. "I just rang to make sure you are all right."

"I'm good," I replied flatly.

"And Sophie?"

"She's good, too. Much better, thanks. She's really grateful to you for taking her to the hospital, for being there."

"Aw. That's nice. And how's your dad?"

"He's okay, though he's really worried about this mystery plague that's affecting the sea otters."

Silence on the other end of the phone.

"Have you heard about that? The otters?" I prompted.

"Yes. It seems to come in cycles," Henry answered. "Tell your father he mustn't worry. The animals will be fine."

"Okay, Dr. Doolittle," I said, frowning and more than a little puzzled.

"I beg your pardon?"

"Never mind. Anyway, when will I get to see you again?" I prompted.

After an uncomfortable silence, he answered, "How about Saturday afternoon? There's someplace I wish to take you."

"I'll be ready," I replied with some excitement.

*

Saturday afternoon came, and Henry waited for me down the street, in his battered truck. His vehicle always looked incongruous among the shiny family cars, all those newer-model Fords and Jettas that lined Forest Avenue. I hurriedly put on my purple sweater, tied my shoes, and ran down the stairs.

Heather Palmer's disappearance had put every parent in Pacific Grove on edge, so I had told Henry to park at the end of the street so as not to worry my dad. Armed with some schoolbooks to help bolster my lie, I told Dad I was just going to the library to do some homework.

Despite myself, I kept thinking about the lilac paper and what Heather's mom said about a mysterious boy writing to her. *Surely her secret admirer couldn't be Henry—could it?* I wondered as I ran down the street and hopped into Henry's waiting truck.

Wearing a plaid shirt and faded jeans, he smiled thinly at me, knowing something troubled me. "What's wrong?"

"It's Heather. Emily and I paid her mother a little visit last Sunday."

Henry studied me but said nothing.

I hesitated before I spoke again. "She said a boy wrote love letters to her—on lilac paper."

"And you think it was me?"

"No, no," I said, everything within me became conflicted and confused. Troubled, I broke away from his gaze.

"Yes, you do. That is what you think. I know you, Alice. But look, simply because I wrote you a poem on lilac paper, does not mean I have anything to do with her disappearance. I am offended that you would think that of me."

I sensed anger rising within him. "No, I don't. . . I honestly don't know what to think about any of this, Henry." I turned my head away. "I just had to tell you, though. It's hard for me to keep secrets from you and you shouldn't expect so much from me."

"Look at me, Alice," Henry said, turning my face toward him with his hand on my chin. "I had nothing to do with Heather's disappearance—nothing," he said sternly, his eyes sincere and unblinking.

"Okay," I replied. "I'm sorry. It's partly because of my dad. He makes me a little jumpy when I'm with you. As you might have noticed, he's not exactly your biggest fan."

Henry gave an adorable smile. "That's understandable. I am accustomed to fathers disliking me. I'll win him over in time," he said confidently then turned on the engine.

We drove out of town, along the Pacific Coast Highway, toward Big Sur. I'd only been as far as Carmel with my family, so I felt a surge of excitement and freedom as we drove farther south. The windows down, I relished the caress of the cool sea breeze that rolled in from the bay.

"Where are we going?" I asked, watching Henry's thick blonde hair shine in the afternoon sunlight, making him look even more Adonis-like than usual.

"To a special place," he replied enigmatically. "I often go there when I want to be alone."

"I thought you couldn't leave Monterey Bay."

Henry smiled. "Well, technically, we're still in the bay area."

We drove for another couple miles, and the coastline of Big Sur stretched before us. A stunning view, with crashing waves, thunderous cliffs, and stately redwoods teetering down to the sea. Far below, the rocks met the majestic sea, a collision of land and water.

"I used to drive this road with Jack Kerouac," Henry mentioned as he skillfully navigated the winding corners.

"You knew Jack Kerouac?!" I exclaimed. He is one of my favorite authors and epitomized the Beatnik generation. "I've read *On the Road*, like, a hundred times."

Henry nodded and smiled. "Yeah, he was a great guy who knew how to live—one hell of a man."

"What was he like?"

"Well, he drank a lot. I made his acquaintance just before he died, when he came down here to write Big Sur in the early sixties. He thought I was a high school dropout, and he essentially took me under his wing."

"Wow! That's so cool," I exclaimed, looking at Henry with new-found admiration. It was then that I realized immortality had its advantages. "Who else have you met?"

"Hmm... John Steinbeck, for one, and Steve McQueen used to come here a lot with the Hells Angels."

"No way!" I said, shocked that he'd met some of my heroes.

When we reached a section of cliff populated with a dense stand of redwoods, Henry turned his truck down a dirt path leading straight to the ocean. It would have easily been missed if he didn't already know about it. We drove for half a mile through the dark forest, the truck bouncing along the pot-holed track. As we drove, we startled a deer, and the creature bounded into the woods with a white flash of its tail. At the end of the dirt road, a cabin loomed into view.

"What is this place?" I asked, casting my eye over the dwelling, rustic and almost hidden from view by the surrounding trees. The roof was triangular in shape, a corrugated chimney pipe poking out of the corner. Ivy covered some of the log walls, blending perfectly with the forest.

"My secret hideaway," said Henry. "I wanted you to see it."

We jumped out of the truck and walked along the path to the cabin on the edge of a cliff. Just past the trees behind it, I caught a glimpse of the ocean, sparkling like a diamond blanket in the far distance.

Henry turned the key and opened the door to let me in. The inside of the cabin was just as rustic as the outside in some ways, but also surprisingly modern. Neat and orderly—not at all the sort of place I would have expected a century-old ghost to hang out.

"It's nice," I said, taking in the interior. "Cozy. Do you own it?"

"I am a caretaker of sorts. The last owner bequeathed it to me when he died," Henry said.

A collection of records stood in the corner. I walked over and flipped through the album covers, mostly rock and pop from the sixties and seventies: Jerry Lee Lewis, Elvis Presley, Abba, and Pink Floyd.

"You have a great collection." I had a few of the same CDs at home, but nothing to rival his stack of vinyl.

"I loved the seventies," said Henry. "A great decade for music— Rolling Stones, Beatles, Pink Floyd. What would you like to listen to?" he asked.

"You choose," I suggested. "I trust your taste."

He thumbed through the record collection with his long pale fingers. Finally, he selected an album and placed it on the old record player. When he turned it on, the needle slowly lifted from its setting, moved sideways, and dropped onto the vinyl groove, filling the air with the sounds of John Lennon and Paul McCartney.

"Beatles, huh?" I said, recognizing the tune instantly because my dad was also a big fan. He had been quite the music listener before my mom's death, but since then, the house had been devoid of any such melodies.

"Yes. This is one of my favorites," Henry replied and started to hum.

Rhythmically, I started to move my feet to the sound of The Beatles. Being in the cabin with Henry, I felt like I'd been transported back to the sixties, the hippie era of free love. After all, we were very near Big Sur.

Henry opened the sliding-glass doors that led to a balcony overlooking the cliff. I followed him onto the wooden deck, surrounded by a protective railing. The view of the coastline was spectacular, with the granite pink cliffs receding into the distance and the waves crashing against the shore, restless and majestic. The raw power and beauty of nature stirred something within me as Henry took me in his arms.

We danced slowly on the balcony, with my head resting on his shoulder. I heard a lone seagull cry in the distance, but my mind blocked out all noise other than the crooning Beatles and the sound of my heart beating so close to Henry's silent one. .   "I wish it could always be like this between us," I murmured, "no fear, no worries, no weird little boxes or mysterious men on some disappearing island."

He nodded, burying his head in my neck and breathing in my scent. "Me, as well. I have never been happier than I am with you, Alice."

I felt the same. For the first time in many months in that spectacular place, I enjoyed calm, happiness, and peace of mind.

When the song came to an end, Henry bent his head down to my lips and kissed me. It was such a sweet kiss that I didn't want it to stop. Finally, we came up for air. I looked into his blue-gray eyes and felt I could swim in them without a life vest.

He smiled. "Are you hungry?"

Only then did I remember that I hadn't eaten since breakfast. It was past lunchtime, and my stomach growled heartily, but all the excitement of being with Henry made me forget about food. "Sure." I nodded. "What have you got?"

"Would you like me to make you some pancakes?" Henry offered.

"You cook?" I asked in surprise.

"Of course I do…and I rather like it," he replied matter-of-factly.

"Wow. This, I've gotta see," I replied. Smiling at the novelty that a guy was about to cook for me, I followed him into the kitchen.

The kitchen looked surprisingly modern, with a small gas stove, an espresso machine, and a blender. A pile of cookbooks lined the shelf, including a few from some well-known local authors. A wooden shelf above the cookbooks, was home to an extensive collection of spices and condiments.

Henry opened the small bag he had been carrying and brought out some food.

"Let's see. We've got eggs, milk, flour. . ."

Then he pulled a bowl out of the top cupboard and placed it on the table. He whisked the eggs and flour with the milk, until he had a thick, bubbly batter. He fetched a frying pan, placed it on the small gas stove, waited for it to get hot, and poured the pancake mixture into the pan.

"What would you like on your pancakes? Maple syrup, chocolate, or just plain?"

"Maple syrup, of course," I said with a smile.

"Good choice," he answered and poured a generous puddle of it on the pancakes he had tossed on a couple of plates. "Maple is my favorite, also."

I took my plate and walked over to one of the stools. "Mmm. These are great," I mumbled, munching on the pancake.

"I don't have many visitors," Henry said. "But when I do, I like to cook."

Afterward, we went into the living room, and I noticed some of the fine drawings hanging on the walls. Etchings of old San Francisco, including a portrait of a beautiful girl, about my age. I peered at the charcoal portrait and examined the signature. To my surprise, the name of the artist belonged to Henry.

"You can draw, too?"

"Another thing I enjoy. It all started as a young boy in San Francisco. I went down to the docks where my father worked and sketched some of the workers. When I got older, some of the madams in the more respectable houses on Nob Hill let me draw them."

"Uh-huh," I said, grinning at him and trying my best not to blush. "Who is this girl?" I asked, pointing to the drawing of the pretty young girl with the wide eyes.

Henry's eyes grew reflective as he studied his handiwork. "Marie-Rose. A girl I knew in San Francisco."

"She's beautiful," I said, admiring the mane of red hair.

Henry nodded. "She was."

I continued to gaze at the portrait. Marie-Rose smiled back at me, her eyes looking into mine, as if she had a secret to tell and wanted to talk to me. *What was she thinking when she posed for this drawing?*

"Will you sit for me?" Henry asked when he observed my admiration over the portrait of Marie-Rose.

I had never posed for a portrait before, and the thought of Henry sketching me—caressing my curves onto paper with his pencil—charged me with an erotic energy I'd never experienced before. So enticing the idea that it filled my skin with goose bumps.

"Sure," I said. "I'd be honored. Where do I sit?"

"Over there, on the settee," he said, pointing to a green sofa with a blanket thrown over the top.

Henry took out a large sketchpad and pencil from one of the cupboards. He pulled one of the chairs across the room and sat down, with the back of the chair toward me. Adopting the artist's position, he straddled the back of the chair, resting his pad on the back, and started to sketch.

I watched his fingers as he quickly drew—feeling his eyes on my body as he appraised my arms. . .my legs. . . hesitating on my breasts before caressing every nook and cranny of my form with his pencil. I giggled like a silly schoolgirl, not knowing how to handle such intense, passionate desire.

"Shh…stay still."

"I'm not used to staying still," I protested, squirming in my seat. "I've always been a bit of a fidget."

"Well, then at least stay quiet. I'm sketching your face at the moment."

That made it harder to stay quiet than to sit still, but I agreed to do so and pursed my lips—smiling only with my eyes.

Henry showed me the portrait when he finished, and I was amazed by the likeness of it to the reflection I saw in the mirror. He had captured a side of me no one saw: Alice, the blossoming woman.

"You're very talented," I said. "Can I keep it?"

He nodded, but he stopped me as I began to roll it up for safekeeping. "Wait! Let me sign it first." I handed it to him, and he signed *Henry Raphael* in the bottom corner. Then he looked at his watch. "Look at the time—I must take you back. Your father will be worried, and we mustn't incur his wrath further."

Slightly disappointed since I hoped to stay the night with him in the cabin. I was still a virgin, and had no concept of making love at all, let alone to a ghost. I wondered how experienced he was, how many muses he'd caressed with more than his pencil. Even though Henry's heart didn't beat, he seemed very much alive. *I wonder if he knows what I am thinking.*

Henry rolled up the drawing, reached for a rubber band and rolled it onto the sketch, handing it back to me. "A keepsake for you."

I clasped the rolled sketch in my hand and thought about where I would put it. I certainly didn't want my dad asking questions.

*

We drove along the coastal road back toward Pacific Grove. The sun was setting above the ocean, casting golden light upon the rippling blue waters—a truly magnificent sight.

Henry parked the truck a couple blocks down the street from my house. "Here we are, milady," he said.

"Thank you for a memorable day," I said and when I looked into his blue eyes, I felt as though going into a trance. *Maybe no one will rescue me this time.*

"Someone's waiting for you in the kitchen," Dad said as I walked through the front door.

"Who is it?" I peered past him and saw Emily sitting at the kitchen table, her already pale face a bit whiter.

"Where have you been, Alice?" asked Dad.

"Uh. . . I went to the local library, like I said. I had some studying to do."

Dad looked at me with unwavering eyes. "Okay. Well, I'll leave you girls to it. Nice talking to you, Emily."

"Nice talking to you, Mr. Parker."

When Dad left the room and out of earshot, I turned to Emily. "What are you doing here?" I whispered.

"I had another vision," she said, staring at me intently, her green eyes wide like a cat's, her hair sticking up wildly in all directions.

"About me?" I guessed.

Emily nodded.

"What did you see?"

"It was clearer this time, so much clearer. You were running up some steps, a tall flight of stairs, trying to escape from someone or something. All around you swirled this fog—"

"—Fog? What else?"

"I saw a light shining at the top of the stairs, really intense and almost blinding. You ran toward the light."

"The light?" I repeated, remembering my mother's words from the séance: "*Follow the light.*"

"What happened when I reached the top?" I urged.

"I don't know. I couldn't see past there. Alice, I'm scared for you. It was a really horrible vision. I'm sorry. I don't mean to frighten you, but I had to tell you."

"No, I'm glad you told me," I soothed while wondering what the vision could mean and the terrible forces at work.

Chapter Eighteen: Twelve Sailors

While I was trying to deal with Emily's frightening premonitions, Henry was confronted by some terrible force of his own. He later told me about the horrifying chain of events that seemed unstoppable.

After he dropped me off at home that day, Henry sailed his boat back to the island. Once again, it appeared out of a bank of mists and clouds. In the late evening light, the mountains took on an ominous presence, and the birds in the trees had fallen silent.

He threw the towline onto the sand and then jumped out of the boat, into the crashing waves. He hauled the coiled rope over his shoulders and pulled the boat in, then tied the rope to the pole and trudged up the beach, toward the forest.

Out of the darkness, twelve men stepped in front of him. They were dressed in old sailor uniforms, just like Henry, and the scent of death lingered on them. He turned back toward the boat but saw that the men had formed a tight semicircle around him.

One of the men, the leader of the group, walked forward. He was a tall, thickly set man with a bruised face and dark, curly hair. There was not a shred of kindness or mercy lurking in his eyes as he said, in a heavy Irish brogue, "We've been waiting for thee, Henry. 'Tis not polite to keep company waiting."

"What do you want, O'Reilly?" Henry asked, looking the Irishman straight in the eye. He sensed the men tightly closing in around him, and he watched them all out of the corner of his eyes.

"Lad, is that any way to greet thy ol' captain?" said O'Reilly.

"For a century now, O'Reilly, you have not been my captain, and I no longer take orders from you," Henry snapped defiantly. He squared his shoulders, prepared to fight if necessary.

O'Reilly smirked. "Still insolent, just as you were on the boat. That stubbornness will be the death of thee, it will."

"I asked you what you want," Henry repeated, his voice firm and steady.

"Some might call it—poetic justice," said O'Reilly. "Thou brought company hither to our nice little island—a lass, in fact. That is forbidden, is it not?"

Henry's eyes narrowed, and he cast his gaze from one unfriendly face to the next, all of them loyal followers of O'Reilly.

"The boys and myself have been talkin'. We've been stuck on this island for over a hundred years now, all because of thy. . . What shall we call it? Indiscretion? The way we see it, thou art indebted to us. Wouldn't thou agree?"

"I owe nothing to you or anyone else," Henry growled.

"If my memory serves correctly, we are solely here because of thee, lad," said O'Reilly, all evidence of his Irish charm melting into a sinister voice.

"Tell me who among you didn't get yourselves here—some of our lot went into the light. We—this means you too, O'Reilly—have rules and breaking them will mean more than an everlasting existence between the third and fourth dimension," stated Henry.

"Oh, but we're all sinners, Henry," O'Reilly said, "and as the good Lord says, we shall repent and offer service or sacrifice. We choose a sacrifice instead. We are all weary of this place, none more so than I. Thou inquired as to what we desire. We wish to move on, and this is where you come in, my boy."

"Has it ever occurred to you that I'd like to move on, too?" Henry said. "I know the misery of this existence, and trust me when I say I would help all of you if I could. Do you not believe that I regret what happened?"

"Ah, touching, but thy weak apology will not suffice. Thy words do nothing to aid us, but we think there may be—another way."

"How?"

"I've been doing a little research, a bit of an investigation, and I've happened upon a clause, a loophole in the curse, if you will."

"What kind of loophole?"

"He who is on the fourth dimension can atone by giving up the thing he loves.'"

Henry frowned, trying to comprehend the meaning behind O'Reilly's words.

"Use your imagination, boy," O'Reilly snapped. "What is it thou loves most in the world?"

Henry was silent. If he was unsettled by O'Reilly's evil grin, he didn't let on.

"That girl you brought here. Thou have been keeping much company with her as of late," O'Reilly finally blurted out, wearing a maniacal grin on his face.

Alice? So that's what this is all about. Henry swallowed, trying to control his rage. "Leave her out of this. This is between you and me."

"Anything that concerns thee, concerns me, Henry. We're all in this together."

"I swear, O'Reilly, if you so much as touch a hair on her head."

"You'll what? Kill me?" O'Reilly's laugh was long, cruel, and hard. "Thou cannot kill one who is already dead. My heart is already stilled, but hers is not."

"No! Not that," said Henry, shaking his head. "Alice is innocent in all of this."

"The bay wants her," O'Reilly said, "and thou wilt surrender her to it."

"She is not mine to surrender," Henry said, trying to control his rage.

"We demand justice, Henry, a life for a life. Thou knowest the rules."

"If a life is what you require, take mine in her place."

O'Reilly's laugh was maniacal this time, his face darkened and turned uglier. "If I could, I would. Truth be told, nothing would give me greater pleasure, but it works not that way."

Henry was silent for a moment and bowed his head. His brow furrowed, he looked up. "What am I supposed to do?"

"Have I not been clear? You must sacrifice her life to the bay."

Despite his usual bravery, Henry began to tremble.

"You have until the next evening tide to surrender her," O'Reilly said. "If you fail, we will come to do it ourselves."

Chapter Nineteen: Point Pinos

On Sunday morning, Henry parked his truck a couple of blocks down the street, where we had agreed to meet at noon. Dad and Sophie had already left for church, and I spent the morning doing housework and laundry. I was anxious to see Henry again; the memory of our time in his cabin, the dance, and our kisses were still vivid. When he called, I practically flew out the door.

I jumped into his waiting truck and immediately felt revived, a charge of electricity coursing through my veins. I glanced across at Henry in the driver's seat, remembering our sweet time together the previous day. I leaned forward to embrace him, but when I did, his body stiffened. "What's up?" I asked, aware of his anxiety.

"Nothing," he replied, not looking me in the eye. His brow creased, and for a moment, he appeared to look his true age.

Something bothered him, and I didn't need to be clairvoyant to sense it. "What's the matter?" I probed. "Just tell me."

"I am simply—not comfortable deceiving your father, that's all," Henry said. "I was brought up under the rule that children should respect their parents."

"That's easy for you to say. You've been without parents for a very long time." As soon as I the words left my lips, I regretted them.

"Correct, but their absence only makes me value them all the more, and I try to adhere to the values they taught me," said Henry, his voice softening. "I wish I had my parents even now."

I was silent for a moment, missing my own mother. I completely understood his feelings and I felt foolish for saying something so cruel.

Henry started the truck, the rev of the engine breaking up our melancholy.

"Where are we going?" I asked.

"A place where we can talk," he said.

I hoped he would take me back to his lovely cabin near Big Sur, but he turned left. Instead of going up the hill, toward Carmel, he turned right, heading down the coast, toward Asilomar. It was low tide, and the water slowly lapped up over the rock pools, which shone like jagged black diamonds on the beach.

We passed a lush green golf course that stretched all the way to Point Pinos, a rugged headland that jutted out into the bay. Henry swung the car into the parking lot and stopped near some small sand dunes. He gestured for me to jump out, and we walked along the golf course, toward the sea.

"Why are we here?" I asked, full of curiosity.

"We're heading for that lighthouse over there." He pointed to the tall building in the far distance.

Point Pinos Lighthouse stood over the rocky point of a headland. It was built in the 19th century as part of a house; its tower stuck up from the top like a very tall chimney. It was in a great location to warn ships of the treacherous, slippery rocks, and I read in a tourist brochure that the lighthouse is the first and last one operating on the West Coast.

As we approached it, I craned my neck to look up at the lighthouse. It stood almost one-hundred-feet tall, majestic with white brick reflecting the sun. I had never been there before, though I had glimpsed the building from offshore while kayaking. I had also seen its light shining like a beacon on some of the dark, stormy nights outside my bedroom window—a strangely comforting sight.

"So, why are we here, exactly?" I asked again, puzzled.

"Follow me," Henry coaxed. "I want to show you something."

He opened the black, rusty door to the lighthouse, and we took a quick look around.

"No one's here?" I asked.

"The keeper is away," Henry said. "The light operates automatically. It has for a few years now, although it used to be manned."

The inside of the lighthouse was furnished with solid wooden furniture, an antique clock in the corner, and the bookshelves held volumes about birds. On the walls hung old maps and prints of the bay.

A black, winding staircase led up the tower. I followed Henry up the stairs; there must have been over two-hundred of them leading up to the observation deck at the top of the tower.

As I climbed the steps, I remembered Emily's words. She'd had a vision of me climbing stairs, almost stumbling in the darkness, though a light shined at the top. She did not see what happened next and that frightened her. An eerie sense of foreboding fell upon me while remembering her strange vision. Still, there was no going back, and I certainly did not want Henry to see my fear or to think I did not trust him, so I continued following him up the tower.

When we emerged on the observation deck, the panoramic view of the bay was breathtaking. To the south—the beaches and cliffs of Carmel; to the north—the Monterey peninsula; and beyond a glimpse of the historic village, Moss Landing.

The deck was about twenty square feet, and a rail ran around the top, protecting visitors from what would be a fatal plummet to the rocks below. I peered over the edge and shuddered. We stood almost a hundred feet above sea level. I had never really suffered from a fear of heights, but the view from the top dizzied me. Down below, waves crashed against the rocky shore in a rhythmic explosion of foamy blue and white.

"Amazing, isn't it?" Henry asked, squinting, mesmerized by the ocean.

I nodded.

"They say this lighthouse is one of the most haunted in all of America," Henry said, gazing at me strangely. "If you listen carefully, you can hear piano music from the former lighthouse keeper. She died falling down the stairs." He paused to listen.

I strained my ears, but all I could hear was the sound of the crashing waves far below. "Why are you telling me this?" I asked, looking around nervously. "And why did you bring me here?"

"Because there is something I must do," replied Henry.

"What is it, Henry?"

Henry's face became tormented, and he opened his mouth with great pain. Gripping the side of the lighthouse rails, he turned his anguished face toward the sea.

"Ah!" he screamed. "No! I-I cannot do this. I shall not, damn it!" He gripped his hair tightly, white knuckles clenching it as he continued to bellow at the sea.

I stared at him in amazement and confusion as his contorted features took on the face of a madman.

"Henry? Henry! What's wrong with you?"

"I should never have brought you here. I'm sorry, I'm so sorry," he said, gripping his head in pain. It looked as though demons tormented him. Clasping his head in the palm of his hands, he sunk to the landing as though very ill all of a sudden.

"Tell me, Henry!" I couldn't help but run to him. Clearly, he was in torture over something and I knew I could help—would help no matter what. "You must tell me what it is that tortures you so! You would demand I tell you, so I demand you tell me!"

Then, as suddenly as it had come on, his fit seemed to subside.

"Why did you bring me here and why do you now regret it?"

"To kill you, Alice," he said, the terrible confession tumbling out of him in an almost inaudible tone. "To give you to the bay," he whispered then looked at me, searching my eyes.

"What!?" This, I did not expect. *Henry planned to murder me? Was he going to push me over the railing?* Maybe that's what Emily saw that made her so afraid.

"I have avoided telling you about the shipwreck. There are some facts you must know."

"I'm listening." I said, shaking uncontrollably and putting a little distance between us.

"That terrible, fateful night, we—the boat was lost at sea. . . I never told you the whole story, Alice, but now I must."

"So tell me then!" I blurted out, now more angry than afraid.

"We set sail from San Francisco, on *Evening Tide*," Henry began, "We left port with thirteen crew members, including myself. O'Reilly, he was the skipper. a big, brawny guy from Ireland, handy in a fistfight. I met him at a poker match in one of the old gambling houses. He traveled west from New York to make his fortune. San Francisco, with all its saloons and pioneer spirit, attracted men like O'Reilly, men who longed for quick riches.

"O'Reilly won our fishing boat during a lucky hand of poker in a saloon, the Stars and Bars Inn, on North Beach. I visited the place on Friday nights, as I enjoyed the atmosphere, the girls, and the gambling. The night I met him, he said he was putting together a crew and needed twelve hard-working men, and he invited me along. A glut of squid was sighted off Monterey Bay, and many fishermen tried to take advantage of the algae bloom the squid fed on. It sounded like a grand opportunity to me.

"They were decent, dedicated, and brave shipmen, most with young families to feed. O'Reilly promised that we would earn at least a hundred dollars apiece on the trip. That may not sound like much now, but a century ago, it was akin to a fortune, and we were all desperate for money. Many lost their homes in the great San Francisco fire of 1906, and when their houses burned to a crisp, people had to find work to get back on their feet, to put a new roof over their and their children's heads."

"But you didn't have a wife or children, right? So why did you join them?" I asked.

"Because of a girl I met."

"Marie-Rose?" I guessed. "The girl in the portrait?" I said, vividly remembering the woman's beautiful face etched by Henry.

Henry nodded. "Yes. At that time, she was the most beautiful girl I had ever seen with hair as red as claret wine, and her laughter could charm a thousand Irish rogues."

"Go on," I said with irritation when he obviously paused in recollection.

"We set sail on November 13, 1915. No one had predicted the fog that floated down the coast as we sailed that night. It shrouded everything in a thick blanket. Our plan was to sail down to Monterey, fish in the bay for a whole week, then return home, our nets bursting with catch. I couldn't help thinking about beautiful Marie-Rose when we set sail, dreaming of how I could shower her with gifts when I returned with a small fortune. We planned to elope—we were desperately in love."

I swallowed. Despite the circumstances, I felt a tinge of envy creeping in. I wondered if Henry loved me as much as he had loved Marie-Rose.

"Marie-Rose came from a well-to-do family in San Francisco. Her father was a merchant banker, and her mother a bit of a philanthropist—one of the first suffragists busying herself assisting charities and orphanages in the city. Marie-Rose and I met on New Year's Eve at one of her fundraising balls in the city."

"That evening, she stole my breath away. I could not take my eyes off her, her lacy black dress, skin like porcelain, and wide china-blue eyes. After that night, she agreed to our courting."

"Despite her parents' objections, we started a clandestine romance. I often took her sailing in San Francisco Bay in my dinghy. One day, her father returned home and caught us together. He threatened to kill me and exile Marie-Rose from the family. Madly in love, I wasn't willing to give up so easily. I hoped to save enough money to elope as I knew her father would never approve of me as a husband. He was a very wealthy, prominent man, and I just a fisherman. We were so in love, neither of us considered the truth that I would not be able to keep her in the manner she had grown accustomed to living, so instead, I enlisted to be part of O'Reilly's crew."

As I listened, it occurred to me everything that had happened to Henry happened because of love. He had truly fallen for Marie-Rose. I thought back to the curse of Monterey Bay and the tale of White Dove with her lieutenant lover and their tragic ending.

"Marie-Rose was at the docks when we set sail, waving me off. When I returned, we would catch a wagon train and head east, maybe to Chicago or New York after eloping. We had to escape San Francisco because we knew her father would forever haunt us if we stayed. Marie-Rose promised to be waiting for me when our boat returned to San Francisco Bay.

"As we sailed, we took watch shifts. The fog rolled in quickly, and by the time we reached Monterey, it was so thick it blinded us. When it was my turn to watch, my mind drifted to my darling Marie-Rose, and I stopped being as watchful, not paying enough attention to the sea. I had been awake all night the evening before, sorting out our plans for when I returned: train tickets, wagon fares—all the details. Then my eyelids grew heavy, and I fell asleep while on my watch.

"That night, I dreamt of Marie-Rose. I must have been asleep for only a short time but that was all the sea needed. I awoke to a sudden jolt when our bow crashed into some rocks just off Monterey Bay, and the boat instantly split in half. Seawater began to gush inside. Being split in half left no hope of salvaging the boat. Soon, we were all up to our waists in freezing, salty water. O'Reilly gave the order to abandon ship, and we jumped into the icy bay."

Henry then closed his eyes and said no more. He kept his eyes shut for several seconds.

I could tell it was very painful for him to relive the torment. I shuddered, imagining the horror he must have gone through since drowning is my own worst nightmare.

"But it was an accident," I tried to protest, "It wasn't your fault." Even as I said the words, I knew they wouldn't be enough to appease his regret and guilt he had carried for so many decades.

"I killed those men, Alice," said Henry, "and now they want retribution and regrettably, they have discovered a way to get it."

"What can they do?"

"They demand your life as atonement for my failure. O'Reilly ordered me to kill you and give you to the bay. Now that I have disobeyed, he will seek vengeance for himself—on you—and this town."

I turned to Henry and gazed into his fearful blue eyes. "I'm not afraid." *What?!* I heard myself say it, but I was lying for certain. Inside I was terrified, and a tight knot formed in my stomach, one that refused to relent.

"Darling Alice, I love you for that, but the only way we can be together is—to go away."

"Go away?" I said, my voice touched with a tinge of excitement. "You mean…leave Monterey?"

Henry nodded. "O'Reilly will never rest so long as you are alive. Our only chance is to leave town."

"But I can't. What about Dad and Sophie?"

"They will manage. I fear for your life if you stay."

"But what about you, Henry? I thought you couldn't leave this place."

"It is worth risking a try," said Henry stoically. "I will do it for you."

I turned my head away and gazed out over the sea. I loved Henry, but wasn't sure I could leave Dad and Sophie behind. Also, I was fearful for Henry if we left and what the consequences would be. *There must be another way*, I thought, desperately hoping one actually existed.

"We can fight O'Reilly and his men!" I announced confidently. "We can get help."

A couple of faces floated through my mind, and I knew they would do their best to help—whatever that ended up to be. The more I thought about it, the calmer I felt, and I shared this with Henry.

"Very well," he said, hope returning to his eyes. "We will give it a try." He then pulled me in for a reassuring and passionate kiss, melting some of my fear away.

"I love you," I said, words I never said to anyone but my family before now. I waited for him to parrot the words back to me, the words I wanted to hear. I desperately wanted him to love me, too.

Instead, he remained quiet, and turned and looked out toward the horizon. For a moment, I detected a pained expression and a hint of melancholy—and fear. Whatever happened next, and whether he could say the words or not, I knew I would love him forever.

Chapter Twenty:

The Untouchables

Later that afternoon, Christian and Emily were waiting for us at Magnolia Bakery. I had called each of them, my voice so desperate and urgent that they had agreed to come at once. Since arriving in Monterey all those weeks ago, I hadn't had a chance to make many friends, but I trusted the two of them and valued their opinion.

They were sitting in a far corner of the yard when we walked in. Emily had told me that she had gone out with Christian once or twice since homecoming. I had encouraged it, partly to shake off Christian's infatuation with me, but also because I thought they might make a good couple. Besides, Emily deserved someone like Christian, someone kind and considerate with a good head on his shoulders. I wasn't sure I could appreciate a guy like that. Maybe there's something wrong with me, I sometimes thought. Maybe I'm only attracted to guys who come with pain and danger.

When Emily saw me, she immediately stood up and ran over to give me a hug. "Are you okay?" she asked, looking at me with her questioning green eyes.

I nodded and glanced across at Christian.

"Hey, Alice," he said. "We're real worried about you. Everything all right? You sounded weird on the phone." He greeted me with warmth, but when he noticed Henry standing behind me, his tone hardened, and the smile melted away. "What's he doing here?"

"Henry and I need your help," I said, getting right to the point. "Something bad has happened."

Christian looked from me to Henry, then back at me again. "Has he got anything to do with the trouble you're in?" Christian asked. "I wouldn't be surprised if he does."

"I knew this was a bad idea," Henry said and started to walk out.

"No! Stop!" I said, tugging Henry's jacket sleeve. I turned to Christian and Emily. "Look, what I'm about to tell you will require your patience and understanding—also your forgiveness."

Christian and Emily glanced at each other, then at me.

"Sure. Go ahead and tell us, Alice," said Emily.

"Okay, but we'd better sit down."

The four of us sat down uneasily at the table. I took a deep breath and began to tell them the whole sordid tale. I related the main points, skipping most of the details, but ended with the fact that O'Reilly and his eleven men were planning to attack Pacific Grove.

All the while, they listened in silence, like little kids hearing a ghost story around a campfire. Their faces seemed to grow whiter with each word. Afterward, I waited, searching their eyes for any signs of resentment, anger, disbelief, or disapproval, but I found none.

Then Christian cleared his throat. "How many of them did you say are coming?"

"Twelve."

"Like twelve jurors, huh?" Christian said snidely, turning to Henry. "Kind of fitting, isn't it?"

Henry remained silent, so I spoke up in his defense, "We didn't come here for a lecture, Christian. Henry has paid the price for what he did, and he has been a huge help to me and looked after me all this time."

"Yes, it's quite gentlemanly of him not to throw you in the bay!" Christian snapped. "But his actions have put us all in danger, especially you, Alice," Christian pointed out.

"I've had enough of his sermons. I told you it was a mistake to come here," Henry said sternly, standing up to leave.

"No! Wait!" I shouted pulling him back down. "Henry is very apologetic for what has happened. Don't you think he's been punished enough? We all make mistakes in life, Christian, even you. What does the Bible says about throwing the first stone? You, of all people, should know better than that."

Christian was silent for a moment, and then he nodded. "Yes, I suppose I have made mistakes."

"So you'll help us?" I pleaded.

Christian and Emily looked at each other and then nodded.

"Fine," said Christian. "What do you want us to do?"

"Thank you," I said and breathed a sigh of relief. I had assumed they would help, but for a moment there, the minister's son had managed to shake my faith a little. "Well, Henry has a plan."

"Imagine that," Christian muttered, summoning a slap from Emily on his arm.

Henry turned to Emily. "Alice says you can sometimes see the future and speak to the dead."

Emily nodded. "Yes, but it only works with some people. For example, with you, I can read nothing. If you are in some kind of spiritual limbo or exist on a different vibratory level, I won't feel your energy—vibrations. The same is probably true for O'Reilly and his men. They are the untouchables for any with psychic talents—except maybe for a Maven."

"A Maven? Where would we find one of those?" I asked incredulously. "Wait a minute! You saw a vision of me climbing up the lighthouse stairs, and that came true. You also predicted Heather's disappearance. Maybe you are able to in some circumstances. . . Can you at least try to see where O'Reilly and his men might strike first?"

Emily closed her eyes.

The silence was tangible, and we waited expectantly, wondering what terrible visions she imagined.

Finally, she opened her eyes again and shook her head. "Nothing. I'm sorry. All I see is fog."

"Fog?" I replied blankly, my mind taking off when she spoke about the fog.

"Yes. A great fog descended over Pacific Grove, shrouding everything in gray. I can't see past it. I'm sorry."

Henry did not seem all that surprised. "O'Reilly and his men are using the fog to hide. They will plan their attack from within it."

I swallowed nervously, knowing they were going to attack Pacific Grove and all its residents in order to get to me. It was like some hellish nightmare waiting to happen.

"What can we do?" asked Christian fearfully.

"We must fight them," said Henry. "And for that we will need assistance, for we are no match for a dozen vengeful seamen on our own."

"Who can help us?" I wondered aloud. "I mean, it's like fighting an army of ghosts right? How can we kill them if they're already dead?"

"I know where we can get help," Henry said. "Alice, we must try to persuade them. Christian, take Emily and meet us back at your house. It's our only hope to fight O'Reilly and his men."

Chapter Twenty-one:

Bay of Souls

It was twilight when Henry drove me in his truck to a patch of woodland a few miles south of Carmel. The Point Lobos Nature Reserve overlooked the bay. Ancient cypress trees cast long shadows on the grass. The forest was deathly silent; not even the birds could be heard settling into their night roosts, which would have been normal for that hour of the evening. But somehow, the ominous silence spoke volumes.

Point Lobos had been described as the greatest meeting between land and water. We walked to a spot known as Devil's Cauldron, a granite outcrop overlooking the sea. When I peered out, I could see the beginning of a thick haze. *Could this be the fog Emily witnessed in her nightmarish visions?*

"Why are we here?" I asked Henry, shifting my feet uneasily on the damp ground.

The forest grew dark with shadows, and I found it spooky to be there at night. I heard something rustling in the trees, and I tried to convince myself it was just a raccoon or some other curious wild animal.

"If we are to defeat O'Reilly and his men, we need help," Henry said, very solemn during the drive to Point Lobos, keeping his eyes fixed on the winding road and not even bothering to look at me. *So insensitive sometimes.*

I wondered what kind of help he referred to— it sounded as though an army would be required and apart from the Monterey Naval Academy, who could possibly offer us any feasible assistance? *What can we possibly do against an army of ghosts?*

Then Henry let out a long, drawn-out whistle, piercingly shrill and hollow. The tone was eerie as the sound echoed around the woods like the call of a distressed animal.

A deathly silence followed as I waited to see what would happen and whom or what would emerge from the undergrowth. Seconds passed, though, and nothing happened.

Then slowly, I could see something emerging from the darkness. At first, I thought they were just shadows, tricks of the dimming light of the evening, but as they approached, I realized that they were all too real. About a dozen men and women of all ages entered the clearing, single file. They wore plain, simple clothing, mostly muted colors of gray, black, and brown. They blended into the landscape like the brown and green lichens that grew on the bark of the trees.

"Who are they?" I whispered to Henry.

"Drowned souls, like me—victims of the bay," Henry explained.

I gasped at the realization that all those people walking toward me were actually dead. They drowned in the bay and now walk among us as the living dead, confined to wander aimlessly along the coast of Monterey until they find a way to atone for past deeds. Not one of them had human blood pumping through their veins—*I am the only one here with a beating heart*, I thought as I observed the procession.

Their eyes gave them away, all appearing lost and confused. A chill crept over me as I watched them advance like a silent army. They made no sound as they trekked through the wood, not even the snapping of a twig underfoot.

When they reached the middle of the clearing, they formed a semicircle around us, waiting for Henry to speak, their faces motionless with dark eyes filled with hate. None of them seemed to be interested in me, and I almost felt invisible. In a way, that was a good thing.

"Thank you for coming," said Henry in a loud, commanding voice. "I know some of you don't want to be here."

"Why did you call us?" demanded a woman who stood at the front. Thin, with straight dirty-blond hair, she looked to be in her mid-forties, but was most likely a century or so older. She was so thin that she reminded me of my mother's chemo days. The look in her eyes frightened me the most; a dull, lifeless look, devoid of hope, the unmistakable face of the undead.

"Because I am in need of your aid," said Henry. "Long ago, I drowned in the bay, just like you. I made a terrible mistake and have spent a century trying to atone. Like you, I have been cut off from all others, unable to visit my family or loved ones as I atone for my deeds, but then I met Alice," Henry continued, turning to me.

I felt all eyes on me, and I shivered. It was as though a dark blanket enveloped me.

"I saved her from the same miserable fate we all share, and in return, Alice has shown me compassion like no one ever before. She has shown me what real love is."

"You broke the rules!" the woman spoke her accusation with a scowl. "We are prohibited from being involved with humans. This is the fourth dimension and the rules cannot be broken without paying the consequences."

My heart sank as I realized they did not want to help after all.

"We do not need rules," Henry bravely said. "Do you not see? All of us have the power to move on. It is within us, each one of us, but the bay will hold us back using our fear as the bonds. If we release the fear, we can be free to atone for our deeds through service to humans—the fastest way out of our predicament."

A murmur spread through the crowd, and included noticeable confusion and hesitation displayed in their dull eyes. One or two glanced sideways at each other, seeking guidance. Henry's words had thrown them into turmoil.

"Why should we help you?" asked a heavyset man near the back, dressed in a black t-shirt and dark trousers with an ugly knife scar across his face.

"Because all of us are joined by the same predicament–the bay's curse," Henry encouraged, "We all share the same fate. We drowned and tried to atone, but sorrow is our common bond. If we stand united, we can beat this curse."

"What do you expect us to do?" shouted a younger Latino man.

"I need your help to fight O'Reilly and his men. They are coming on the evening tide. I cannot fight a dozen men alone, and I need your help."

"Why should we help you?" asked the blond woman, who appeared to be the spokesperson for the group.

Henry turned to face her. "Because I made a mistake and have paid the price for the last century. We must show compassion for those we left behind and the human race. If we show that compassion, it will be proof we are ready to atone through service and only then will we be truly free."

I studied the group, wondering if Henry's words made any impact on their position. Many just stood motionless, as still as granite, impossible to discern. I saw no flicker of sympathy in their undead eyes.

Some of the ghosts, though, began to whisper to each other in the enveloping darkness, and the wind carried the sound through the trees reminding me of the time I'd heard those whispers before on the day I came to search for Henry along the coastal path. *Were they watching me then?*

One boy standing in the back of the group, slightly apart from the others, walked into the clearing. A handsome boy, around fifteen or sixteen, with sandy hair and a cleft chin—features like a Greek statue. He listened intently to the other ghosts, but would not speak, and I found myself wondering about him.

"We do not get involved with the living," the woman said with finality. "Our answer is no. It is not our fight to lose."

My heart sank, and I glanced sideways at Henry. I expected him to look thoroughly disheartened, but he didn't seem too fazed by the news. Instead, he slowly nodded his head in acceptance.

"As you wish. I respect your decision, and thank you for coming."

One by one, the ghosts turned their heads and slowly started to disappear back into the forest, as silently as they had come. I watched the boy in the back hesitating—torn by the decision to go or to follow Henry. Just as he was about to leave, I remembered Mrs. Prescott's son—*Is that him?* His clothes were a bit more modern than the rest.

"Johnny?" I called. "Are you Johnny Prescott?"

The boy turned to me with contemptuous, unfriendly eyes. "Why do you want to know?" he asked with unconcealed hostility.

"Because I know your mother, Mrs. Prescott. She often talks about you."

Johnny's eyes showed no trace of emotion. "I have no mother. I left that life behind a long time ago."

"Well, she has never left you behind. She still misses you very much. I know if she were here now, she would tell you she loves you."

Johnny's eyes flickered, and for a moment, I thought I detected some recognition, some glimmer of interest.

"She would tell you how sorry she is for all the things she said to you when you were alive. She never thought of you as a failure. In fact, she thought quite the opposite. Your mother was proud of you, Johnny, and she has always loved you." I told him before starting to walk away.

"Wait!" Johnny called. "If you see my mother again, will you pass on a message to her?"

"Of course."

"Tell her I hope—that she's okay. That she needn't worry about me."

"Sure," I said. "I will do that."

When the last of the ghosts left, Henry and I walked away from the clearing.

"I'm sorry. They should have listened to you," I said.

Henry shook his head. "We have very little time, now. We must leave."

Chapter Twenty-two:

The Church

Henry drove his truck like a NASCAR driver down the winding road back to Pacific Grove. We had hardly exchanged words since the meeting at the clearing. Once or twice, I glanced across at him. He just looked focused, solemn at the wheel—gripping it tightly as he navigated the curves and bends on our way back to town. I glanced at the speedometer, and it showed we were traveling more than fifty miles an hour.

It was becoming more and more difficult to see our surroundings through the window. A thick fog covered the whole town with a dense blanket making visibility nearly impossible. So often before, the mist rolled in from the sea, but I had never seen it so thick and impenetrable before.

"Where did all this fog come from?" I asked. "I've never seen it so dense."

"It rolled in from the bay," said Henry. "It is unnatural. It is menacing, and an evil lurks inside."

I shuddered, wondering what he meant by that. Are O'Reilly's men inside the fog?

We drove for a few more miles, but as we approached Pacific Grove, the fog grew thicker still. Henry turned right onto Route 68 and headed away from town.

"Where are we going?" I asked.

"I have to get you out of Monterey and Pacific Grove," Henry replied seriously. "If we take Route 68, it will join 101, and we can go north, towards San Francisco. I have to get you as far away from Monterey Bay as possible."

San Francisco? What will we do once we get there? And how will I explain my disappearance to Dad and Sophie? I was sure they were already worrying about me, glancing at my cell phone confirmed my thoughts. Missed calls from Dad. I considered calling him back, but had no clue what I would tell him, how do I explain my bizarre absence, or why I ran away from home. I was relatively certain he would not buy a story about ghostly sailors coming after me in the fog.

As he had done so many times before, Henry seemed to sense my thoughts. "Do not fret, Alice. I shall take care of everything. There is a place you can stay in San Francisco, and O'Reilly will not find you there. As I told you, my family lived there."

His words puzzled me. I couldn't imagine that any of Henry's immediate family were still alive. And what about my school, my family, and Henry's curse? He was forbidden to leave the bay. I knew he was trying to comfort me and rescue me, but I was still full of unanswered questions, and more seemed to be popping up all the time. "I thought you couldn't leave Monterey Bay," I repeated, fearing the dreaded consequences for Henry.

Before he could answer, we were distracted by flashing lights up ahead, red and blue lights from a police car. Beyond that, two cars jammed together, bumper to bumper blocking traffic.

"What's going on?"

"A roadblock," answered Henry, slowing the truck.

A police officer walked up the road toward us and motioned for Henry to roll his window down. A burly man dressed in a black military uniform with a gun around his belt made him very intimidating.

"Something happen up ahead, Officer?" Henry asked in his most polite voice.

The officer inspected us curiously, staring at us with a scowl. He said nothing for a moment and just clenched his thickset jaw, giving me a once-over. "Traffic accident," he finally said. "We got ourselves a nasty four-car pileup because of this fog. It's gonna take at least a couple hours to clear the road, so I suggest you kids head back the way you came."

"A couple of hours?" Henry repeated then turned to me.

I knew what he was thinking; O'Reilly and his men would be there by then.

"Is there another road out of Monterey?" he asked the policeman.

"No. Just turn around and head back the way you came," said the cop.

"Yes, Sir," said Henry and wheeled his truck around.

"That was close," I said, finally breathing.

We headed back toward Pacific Grove through fog so thick we could see only a few feet in front of us. Because of the conditions, a long line of slow-moving traffic backed up, heading into town.

"What now?" I asked, as Henry was forced to slow his truck to a crawl.

"I plan to take you somewhere I know you will be safe," Henry replied.

When we reached Pacific Grove, I expected him to go left, onto Forest Avenue, back toward my house. Instead, he turned right, toward the center of town.

"Where are we going?" I asked, dumbfounded. I was anxious to see Dad and Sophie and be sure they were safe.

"You cannot go home," he said. "That is the first place O'Reilly will look for you."

"But what about my family? I have to be with them. I need to know they're all right. I don't want O'Reilly to hurt them."

"I understand you are concerned about them," Henry said, "but I must consider your safety first. O'Reilly wants you, not them. The moment he realizes you are not there, he will not waste time sticking around."

"Where are you taking me?"

"To the only safe place in Pacific Grove," Henry replied.

Henry pulled his truck to a stop outside Our Lady of the Cross. The church was shrouded with a thick bank of fog and looked like someone had draped it with gray velvet veils. The tall branches of the Monterey pines grew in symmetry on both sides of the church, their pointed needles standing like skeletons.

"The church?" I asked, confused.

"This is the safest place I know of in town," said Henry.

I shook my head in disbelief. "A church is just a building, Henry. It isn't gonna save me. Do you really believe prayers will help?"

"No, but it is the only building O'Reilly and his men cannot step foot into, while it is intact. We must keep the doors and windows sealed. You will have sanctuary here."

"What about you?" I asked, desperately wanting him to stay with me because with him I felt safe.

"I will join you later," Henry promised. "I must face O'Reilly. This is my fight. I started it, and I will end it."

He opened the door, and I reluctantly hopped out of his truck. There was a light on in Christian's house, and I could see shadows behind the curtains. The door opened, and Christian and Emily came rushing out.

"Are you all right?" asked Christian.

"Yes, but we must make adjustments," Henry said.

"Plan B?" I chimed in. "Fill us in, Henry."

"Alice must stay in the church, Christian and Emily, while I face O'Reilly and his men—alone."

"Alone!?" I protested. "There are twelve of them and only one of you. The lost souls won't help you, and you can't be a one-man army, Henry."

"I will prevail, Alice. Trust me. O'Reilly and his men cannot kill me."

"But what about your soul?" I said. "That's what O'Reilly wants. Without that, you have no chance of moving on. You said yourself that you'll be stuck here if—"

"I will find a way," Henry interrupted. "Alice, these days with you have been my happiest. I want you to know that."

I nodded. "Mine, too," I said earnestly, tears welling in my eyes.

"Take good care of her," Henry said to Christian.

"You don't need to worry about Alice being safe with me," Christian said. "I'm not the one who got her in trouble." Despite the uneasy alliance between them, there was still a strong feeling of animosity.

Henry looked into my eyes, and I gazed longingly back at him. Our lips touched as I closed my eyes and wished we were a million miles away. The kiss was long and cool, and in that mesmerizing moment, I vanished—completely forgetting about the fact that Christian and Emily stood there. Christian, of course, averted his gaze as we kissed.

"Be careful—and hurry back," I said, resting my palms on his chest.

He nodded and started walking back to his truck.

"Henry, wait!" Emily called. She ran like a gazelle and gripped Henry's and my arms. "While you were gone, I had another vision."

"What did you see, Emily?" I asked.

"The marina, boats, and the Coast Guard."

"Pickard?" I asked. "You saw Pickard?"

"Yes! He was calling out to someone on his radio, and it sounded like he was in trouble. I think that is where O'Reilly and his men plan to attack."

"Then I will go there right away," Henry said.

"Be safe," I replied.

Henry nodded, jumped into his truck, and drove off. We watched him disappear into the fog.

Christian put his arm around my shoulder and gave it a little squeeze. "C'mon," he said. "We better start preparing for their arrival."

I nodded and sniffled, following Christian and Emily into the church. I couldn't help the disturbing thought lurking in the back of my mind—*will I ever get to see Henry again?* Mist swirled around the building, but I could still see the cross at the top of the spire. Together, we walked up the steps to the oak doors. Remembering the first time I saw the church—its sturdy design impressed me, with heavy double-doors and a thick timber frame. It looked like it could withstand a hurricane—hopefully it will live up to its façade on that fateful night.

I ran up the steps with Christian, just as the last visibility left Pacific Grove. At the double-doors I paused, even though I briefly attended church a few weeks ago, it still brought back bitter memories of Mom's funeral. The white coffin being carried up the aisle, the pain of grief throbbing in my chest, the clutch of my little sister's cold fingers and my dad's tears—it all came flooding back to me, and again at that moment I felt grief's overwhelming ache. As I walked up the aisle, I wondered if God would forgive me for abandoning Him, now that I was coming back in search of His help. Will He even accept me? Will He let me live, or will He let O'Reilly and his men take me?

A statue of the Virgin Mary stood at the side of the altar. She was dressed in a white and blue robe, her palms outstretched. I had always found her to be beautiful, and I hoped she would not fail me now.

As I sat on the bench, I cast my eyes over the Stations of the Cross. Feeling guilty sitting in church, a sinner who turned her back on God—blamed Him—lacking all compassion and forgiveness.

In my backpack, I still carried the box I found. As I pulled it out, it gave me comfort to hold it in my hands—yet I still didn't know what it meant or what power it had. I put it in a compartment of the altar for safekeeping.

I returned to the bench and silently prayed that God would forgive me. My biggest sin of all was Henry. I had fallen in love with a ghost, but in my heart, he was the best mistake I'd ever made.

Chapter Twenty-three:

Monterey under Siege

They came on the evening tide as promised, all twelve of the vengeful specters—their hard, muscled bodies dripping wet, ice-cold skin smelling of the sea under dark uniforms clinging to their frames. When their heads surfaced, their eyes were fixed on the shore, like predators locked onto their prey. Not one pair of eyes showed any trace of regret; all were set and ready for the kill.

O'Reilly, the tallest and meanest of the sailors came ashore first, water dripping from his tight black shirt. He stood on the beach with muscles flexed, scoping the area. With the wave of his large hand, he commanded the others forward. They marched in step like an army, stones crunching underfoot as they headed up the shingle shore.

When O'Reilly reached the edge of Monterey Beach, he leaned back and sniffed the air, like a bloodhound trying to catch a scent of something in the air. "This way!" he ordered, urging the others on.

The eleven sailors followed O'Reilly up the beach like disciples.

Among them was Jack, a seventeen-year-old sailor from Mendocino, with short-cropped blond hair and unusually thick eyebrows. His face bore an expression of perpetual dread, as though constantly brooding about something.

Then came Blake, a handsome, pale-faced guy with curly hair, angular features, and thin lips. He walked with a slight limp in his right leg from being violently slashed by a knife during a brawl in San Francisco.

The last ashore was Monroe, the youngest. He had curly blond hair, pink eyes, and deathly pale skin—he looked to be an albino, especially in the silvery moonlight trying to work its way through the horrendous fog. Not a flicker of warmth coursed through his veins, and he bitterly hated everything and everyone around him.

The twelve men walked toward the hamlet of Pacific Grove. The boats in the marina stood like skeletons, their tall masts reaching up toward the sky. In the harbor, the sound of the foghorn blared loudly, reverberating through the bay.

*

Captain Pickard was confused by the strange weather. In all of his thirty years in Monterey Bay, he had never seen a fog so dense.

Already, there had been several grim reports from fishing boats and sailing vessels adrift at sea with hazard lights on. They were cast motionless in the ocean, afraid to come near the shore for fear of smashing blindly against the rocks. There had already been one horrible incident—a trawler hit a jetty at Moss Landing and ran aground.

Pickard picked up the radio. "Coast Guard station to Alpha One. Do you read me? Over."

Crackling on the line was the response.

Damn it, thought Pickard, *all the circuits appear dead.* "How the hell am I supposed to deal with all the maritime disasters in this mess with no communication?" he muttered, fearing there had already been casualties—*how long before help can arrive through this fog?*

Pickard snapped his head toward a noise in the marina, the strange murmur of unfamiliar voices. *Maybe they are from the naval academy, sent to help in the crisis.* "Thank God," he said aloud, glad for reinforcements. He fumbled for his flashlight then unlocked the front door of his cabin and went outside.

Instantly, fog swirled around him.

"Who's there?" shouted Pickard. He squinted, trying to see through the gray murkiness. "Captain Mainwaring? Is that you?" Pickard shouted again, still hoping the naval academy had sent help.

Through the mist, he saw the silhouettes of about a dozen men walking down the jetty toward him, and Pickard released a sigh of relief that someone had heard his distress call after all.

"Finally!" cried Pickard. "I thought I was gonna have to deal with this on my own."

The men did not reply, just kept walking.

"Is Mainwaring among you?" Pickard cried out again, trying to discern the captain among the shadows.

Again— no reply. The men continued marching along the jetty, coming his way.

When they got within visual distance, Pickard realized they were not from the academy. They resembled nineteenth-century sailors, and not one of them looked friendly. In fact, their eyes were filled with contempt.

"Wh-who are you?" Pickard whispered with apprehension.

O'Reilly marched up to the old man and with a flick of his hand, struck Pickard down.

The old man's groaning sounded like a tire that had just been punctured and deflated to the walkway in a heap. With a long sigh, he let out his final breath.

Looking contemptuously at Pickard's fallen form, O'Reilly urged the men forward. "C'mon," O'Reilly said, stepping over the lifeless body. "This way."

*

The thick haze continued to roll into the town smothering everything in its path—trees, houses, cars, and telephone poles. People ran for cover, as if being chased by angry demons. They locked themselves in their cars and ran into the closest houses or shops seeking safety. The fog had already caused a number of pile-ups and traffic accidents and now moved toward total chaos.

In the distance, I heard sirens in the bay, warning any ships of the treacherous hazards. Inside the church, I huddled to keep warm. I had tried several times to ring Dad on his cell, but I'd been unable to get through; all the circuits seemed to be busy.

Emily sat quietly in front of the altar, her head bowed in prayer. Her hair unruly and her mascara-clad eyelashes drooped—I didn't want to interrupt her in case she experienced more visions that might be helpful to the situation. We depended on her psychic talents—now more than ever.

"Why doesn't my dad answer?" I asked Christian for the hundredth time, feeling a little scared for Dad and Sophie and hoping they hadn't gotten involved in one of the many car accidents.

"I'm sure he's fine," said Christian, doing his best to reassure me, "and your little sister, too. They're probably at your house, wondering where you are."

I dialed Dad's cell again, and someone finally picked up.

"Hello?" said a voice from the other end.

"Dad!" I breathed a huge sigh of relief. "Thank God. Where are you?"

"I'm with Sophie, at the aquarium. We're sort of stuck here because of the freaky weather. Where are you, Alice? Are you okay?"

"I'm fine, Dad. I'm with Christian," I said. I didn't want to tell him I was inside the church, because I knew that would make him wonder.

"Well, stay put. It's dangerous to go out," Dad said. "The entire bay and town is thick with it. There've already been a number of accidents around town."

"Dad, you must listen to me. Don't go home!"

"What?" he asked. "Why not?"

"Just don't go home! Please stay where you are. It's much safer at the aquarium," I pleaded.

"What are you talking about? You're not making any sense. What's going on?"

"Listen, Dad, it's really important that you don't take Sophie home. Even if the fog clears, please stay where you are."

Then, before he could continue arguing with me, the phone went dead.

"Dad? Dad!"

Quickly, I redialed the number, but the call wouldn't go through. I prayed that he would listen to my advice and not go home. Henry had said that would be the first place O'Reilly and his men would search for me. I shuddered to think what would happen if they found Dad and Sophie at home.

I looked at Christian fearfully. "They can't go home. They just can't."

Christian caressed my hair lightly. "Shh. Have you seen how thick the fog is? My bet is they're not going anywhere for a while. Your dad's a smart guy, and Sophie will be fine as long as she's with him."

I prayed that Christian was right, and a blanket of guilt swept over me. This is all my fault. If I hadn't met Henry and hadn't gotten involved with him, maybe things would be all right. And if there is a God, is He just punishing me? Can I even trust His protection in His supposed house? As I sat inside the church, I desperately wanted him to forgive me for being so angry and take care of my family and me.

I shuddered, feeling the chill in the air that cut through me like a sharp blade and it wasn't just the temperature making me shiver. All the windows in the church were closed, so I couldn't figure out where the draft came from. *Probably the chill of death—the Grim Reaper wrapping his threatening, skeletal hands around me.*

Through the windows, I saw thick vapor rolling, tapping on the panes like ghostly fingers. It spread out and wrapped the church in an ice-cold embrace. We had no escape so it looked as though we would be trapped inside for the long haul.

I wondered how Henry was doing and if he was safe. I didn't believe he could fight off a dozen enemies. I tried not to imagine what they would do if and when they caught him.

Christian sat beside me on the bench and noticed that I shivered uncontrollably. "Are you all right?" he asked. "You're shivering."

"Just a little," I said.

"Here." He took off his jacket and offered it to me.

I took it and nodded my thanks, then wrapped it around my shoulders.

Christian walked to the altar and started lighting some small candles, one after the other, until the entire row burned brightly, giving off a yellow glow. "These should give us a little light and warmth," he said, applying the flame to the last wick.

I watched the burning flames and thought of my mother again. As a kid, I used to go to church and light the candles with her. We would say a prayer for each of the members of our family—Dad, Mom, Sophie, Aunt Bess, Grandma, and me. It was comforting to see those flickering flames, all of them attached to my loved ones. Now, as I watched the flames dance, I realized it would take a miracle to save me.

We huddled together for warmth, Christian's shoulders brushing against mine.

"You're a great friend, Christian," I said. "Thank you."

"For what?"

"For helping Henry and me and for, uh…putting your own personal feelings aside."

Christian nodded slowly. "Sure, Alice. It's the least I can do. That's what a good Christian is for."

I laughed at the irony of his name. "Can I ask you something?"

"Of course. Always."

"Are you afraid of dying?"

Christian thought on my question briefly then said "Nope." He answered quickly as though pondering the question for so long, he felt confident in the answer.

194 Tony Lee Moral

"Neither am I," I replied. "It's living that frightens me."

"What have you got to be afraid of?" Christian asked. "You're young, bright, and beautiful. You have an incredible future ahead of you."

"Oh, if only that were true! I'm scared about a lot of things."

"Like what?"

"Well, that my life won't amount to much and that I'll be a failure. I don't want to be a disappointment to my dad and my mom."

"I don't see any chance of that, Alice. In fact, I know there isn't."

"Really? And how do you know?"

"Oh, I just know. You're gonna have an amazing life. Just wait and see."

Sharp voices from outside interrupted us.

Only then did Emily break from her reverie, opening her eyes, and gazing fearfully at the door.

"What's that noise?" I whispered, convinced O'Reilly and his men found me.

A loud banging on the solid oak door, assured me that my time had come.

Chapter Twenty-four:

Blazing Vengeance

The banging on the church door grew louder, like terrible demons banging on the very gates of hell. Every bang struck my soul, and I quaked.

"Open up!" shouted a hoarse voice, harsh and desperate.

Christian ran to the door and peered through the keyhole. "It's my dad!" he shouted and started to unbolt the latch.

The heavy doors swung open, and Reverend O'Neill ran into the church, followed by about ten parishioners. I was startled to see Mrs. Prescott and Ethan among them. All had the same fearful look in their eyes, as if having confronted the devil himself. They huddled in a corner like frightened mice behind the minister, looking as though he just performed an exorcism.

"Thank mercy you are safe," the minister said, looking from me to Christian. He was normally a composed, very elegant man, but on that fateful evening, fear had caught him in its ugly grip and wouldn't let go. Sweat glistened across his forehead, and bile choked his lungs.

"What's wrong?" I asked.

"There's a terrible evil outside," he answered. "It hides itself in the fog and stalks its prey. It is not of this earth. We are here seeking solace and safety from God. Shut that door, for goodness sake!"

Some of the men pushed the double-doors shut just as the heavy fog began to roll inside the church. I was relieved to hear the heavy thump confirming the doors were closed.

The crowd seemed to calm down a little once inside. A few clustered around the minister, waiting for him to tell them what to do next.

Mrs. Prescott, on the other hand, turned to face me with wrath and hate in her eyes. "I warned you that this day would come, but you wouldn't listen to me! You have toyed with the devil, and now we are all to pay for your sins!"

I shrunk back in disgust at the sight of the old woman. She had jaundiced skin, her eyes bloodshot and bulbous. I had never encountered anyone so hateful and full of spite.

"How dare you even step foot in the house of the Lord, you vile thing! You are responsible for this," she accused, looking me directly in the eye as she walked slowly toward me.

The crowd hushed as they watched her approach. I felt naked and exposed, *what 'sins' is she referring to?* Even though I didn't know the answer, I still felt guilty—laid bare before the old woman and the others, looking on like jurors.

"You're an evil girl! Evil!" she shrieked in a loud voice.

I said nothing and just stared at her, horrified. She looked like she wanted to strangle me like when she assaulted me outside my house.

Christian stepped between us when she was just inches away blocking my view. "This is no time for blame!" Christian shouted. "Alice is welcome here, and all are welcome in the house of God. If you can't accept this, Mrs. Prescott, I must ask you to leave."

The harshness of his words silenced her, but didn't stop her from looking at me with contempt.

I couldn't bear to meet her eyes—too consumed with guilt. I wondered if my unexpected romance with Henry had really brought about all the turmoil and unleashed havoc on the townspeople of Pacific Grove. If I had heeded the old hag's advice and stayed away from the water, could we really have avoided this?

I slowly walked up the aisle toward the altar, away from the crowd, so they wouldn't see my shame. Just in front of the altar, kneeling down on one of the pews, I saw a lone figure, praying. The closer I got, I could see his shoulders tremble. I put my hand on his shoulder and tried to calm him. "Ethan? What's the matter?"

"Forgive me, Father. Forgive me," he said over and over, a desperate plea begging God's forgiveness for something he'd done.

I leaned in closer, "What's wrong?" I asked again trying to console him, "Why are you in so much turmoil?"

He looked at me with wide, terrified eyes— eyes of a boy frightened for his life. I had never seen so much fear in a person before, not even in my mother while on her deathbed. "I-I was walking home from the store when I got caught in the fog. It was all around me, and I was instantly lost. Then I heard footsteps following me. I saw something, Alice—something terrible."

"What Ethan?" I urged, realizing that whatever it was scared the life out of him.

He swallowed and in an almost inaudible sob, he uttered the words, "I saw Heather."

*

While having that terrifying conversation with Ethan in the church, across town O'Reilly and his men found my house. Their shadows loomed large and monstrous as they stood outside the white Victorian clapboard, pausing a moment to look up at my bedroom window. None of the lights were on, since no one was in, but that didn't deter the hellbent sailors.

O'Reilly motioned forward, and a couple sailors followed him up the path, carelessly trampling the flowers that bordered our cobblestone walkway—flowers Sophie helped me plant. When they reached the door, they found it locked and without a second thought, O'Reilly kicked the door down with a brute force then he and his wet crewmen marched inside.

He contemptuously glanced around at our possessions; Mom's china and silver plates then at Sophie's dolls. O'Reilly paused at the bottom of the stairway and looked up, sniffing the air, nostrils again flaring like a bloodhound's.

"Empty! There's no one here," he said, not bothering to climb the stairs. "Come on." As he walked out, he stepped right on Sally-Anne—Sophie's doll, breaking her limbs and squashing her head.

*

Meanwhile, Henry had run to the Coast Guard hut, hoping to intercept O'Reilly and his men. Per Emily's vision, the dirty dozen would strike there first. When Henry reached the jetty that skirted the hut, he could hardly see due to the fog's density. While running through the mist, he almost tripped over something. Bending down to investigate, he found himself staring into the lifeless eyes of Captain Pickard.

"Dear God!" said Henry, "They are merciless!" On instinct, he whirled around in the darkness and spotted several figures looming behind him and that meant he was outnumbered.

*

"You saw Heather. . .?" I asked, struck by Ethan's strange confession.

"On my way back from working at the grocery store, I took the coastal path home, thinking it would be quicker, then the fog rolled in from across the bay. I couldn't see a thing, so I took a wrong turn that led me down to the sea. That was where I saw her, standing right there in the fog only feet away."

"Are you sure it was her? Did she look like she was ok?"

"She looked—terrible—her hair was wet and dirty, with tiny crabs crawling around. It was disgusting. Not only that, but something about her face. . ."

"What?"

"Her eyes, Alice, full of hate. As if she wanted me to die," he said before breaking into an inconsolable sob. "God is punishing me. I know He is."

"Why would he want to punish you, Ethan?"

Ethan sniffed, looking up at me with eyes black as coal. His empty stare said nothing mattered to him anymore, that he gave up all hope of living. "It was me, Alice. I-I pushed her into the bay, and she must have drowned."

"You pushed her?" I said in disbelief, the puzzle pieces slowly falling into place.

He nodded.

"After she had that row with Channing, I gave her a ride home, but I took a detour to the coast. I just wanted to be alone with her. She looked so pretty in that gold dress, in the moonlight. I've always thought her beautiful, but she had never looked lovelier. I just wanted to go for a walk with her, but—"

"—But what, Ethan?" I prodded, getting impatient.

"Well, when I suggested it, she started shouting, saying hideous things to me. She was freaking out, yelling at me, demanding to know where I was taking her. I told her she owed me a favor."

"Owed you a favor? For what?"

"She hated doing her homework, so I always helped her with math and well, it sort of developed from there."

"What developed?"

"Favors. I did her homework in return for…certain kinds of favors. Heather hated studying. She didn't like school, except the socializing part. She wanted to be popular, but she had to hide all that from her super-religious mom, so we made a kind of deal. I did her homework, and in exchange, she let me, uh…touch her."

I sat back on the wooden bench, stunned. It was hard to imagine Heather with geeky Ethan. The homecoming queen, the most popular girl in school, and he is not a popular guy. Doesn't excuse his unspeakable crime—now he was desperate to be absolved. By God and—us.

Would I be absolved if I did the same?

*

All that time, since the others had gathered in the church, Emily had remained silent, with her eyes closed. She sat on one of the benches, as if in prayer. Her breathing remained calm and rhythmic, as if sitting in meditation. I knew she was concentrating so she might be able to predict the movements of O'Reilly and his men. She kept very still and quiet, hoping to pick up any flashes or vibrations. Suddenly, she opened her eyes and cried out, "They're coming!"

"How do you know?" Christian asked, a question echoed by the crowd around her.

"I saw a flash of all of us huddled here, inside the church. A strong voice calling to us. . . They will be here soon."

We waited with apprehension, everyone so quiet I could hear Christian's rhythmic breathing, falling in line with the rise and fall of his chest. The fog outside continued to swirl around the church as we silently, helplessly waited to hear any telling noises whispering of our imminent doom.

The bang on the door sounded sharp and hollow, startling everyone in the church. A strong voice with what sounded like an Irish brogue called out, "Come out! It will be easier for ye if ye surrender. There is no escaping Judgment Day."

I glanced at Christian and said, "O'Reilly," my voice trembling.

He shook his head. "Don't say anything," he whispered. "We must not speak to such evil."

"It is universal law!" O'Reilly continued. "There is no escaping accountability."

"What do you want of us?" Reverend O'Neill shouted through the thick oak door. Despite his position of authority over evil, his voice trembled, and his knees shook.

"We want only the girl—Alice Parker," demanded O'Reilly.

I shuddered at the mention of my name, and all eyes focused on me instantly. I knew they blamed me for what was happening.

"If you don't surrender her, we will burn the church down, and ye will burn with it," O'Reilly threatened.

The other parishioners began to cry out in fear. I gasped—*This is a nightmare where I won't be able to escape through waking-up.* O'Reilly was prepared to destroy the church and everyone in it just to seek revenge on Henry—hard to believe such hate exists in the afterlife.

Silently, I did something I hadn't done for a long, long time: I said a full prayer. I prayed my mom would survive every night while she was ill, and became so angry that God did not see fit to answer my prayers. He took her from me anyway and after that, I gave up hope that God heard and answered prayer.

"Heavenly Father, deliver us from evil," began the minister, his voice reverberating around the church.

"Come out!" O'Reilly bellowed. "We vow not to hurt you. We simply want the girl."

"Must we trade all our lives for hers?" Mrs. Prescott asked, pointing a gnarled finger at me.

Christian shook his head. "If we surrender Alice, they'll burn this place down anyway. We mustn't listen to him."

I sensed some of the parishioners staring questioningly at me, sure they would willingly trade my life to save their own.

Most of all, I wondered about Henry, and prayed he was safe. For all I knew, he had already confronted O'Reilly and lost. Twelve against one is an odd that doesn't stand a chance—even a ghostly boyfriend.

"Let me go, Christian," I finally said. "It's me they want; I had no idea my relationship with Henry would end up involving the entire town."

"If she wants to go, you should let her," said a man I recognized from the grocery store.

"I'm not sacrificing myself for some lovesick teenager. I'm the mother of two, for God's sake," one of the women said.

"If it's the girl they want, they should take her. Why should we get involved?"

"What have we done to deserve this? Let the girl go."

"Over my dead body," said Christian, bravely facing the crowd. "What kind of people are you? You go to church, yet your faith is so weak that you are willing to sacrifice Alice to those evil things out there?"

"She will only be getting what she deserves," Mrs. Prescott hissed.

"And who are you to say what Alice deserves?" Christian argued, casting his eyes on each one of them. "Who among you has never sinned? Because if there is one perfect among you, perhaps that statue at the front of this church should be a statue of you!"

"This is thy last chance," O'Reilly's voice bellowed through the door. "Surrender, or ye will all burn in hell!"

The parishioners cried out in anguish.

Reverend O'Neill looked at me, and I sensed that even his resolve wavered.

Mrs. Prescott stepped up from her pew. "This is all your fault. You will burn in hell for this!" She shouted at me, her eyes glaring furiously. "Why are we still even debating this? She would not listen to me, and now we will all pay for her sins."

The other parishioners began to murmur. Some of them looked at me with hateful glares, and I sensed a mob beginning to form.

"Why should we die because of her?" another woman said. "Give her up! My children need me!"

Mrs. Prescott seemed to enjoy stirring up the others. She pointed an accusing finger at me again and declared, "If we release her, they will not harm us. All they want is her."

Christian jumped up and shook her wrinkly, liver-spotted shoulders violently. "Shut up, you silly old woman."

"Christian!" shouted Reverend O'Neil, shocked. "Let her go."

"I'm sorry, Father, but she's been on Alice's back since the very first day she moved to Pacific Grove, scaring her with her ghost stories, filling her head with nonsense."

"Because I saw what was coming! This evil tempest is upon us because of her!" Mrs. Prescott shouted.

I remembered Johnny—from the gathering in the woods. "Mrs. Prescott," I broke in, "I have a message for you. Before I came here tonight, I met your son. Johnny asked me about you and wanted me to tell you that he misses you."

Speechless, Mrs. Prescott stared at me for a long moment. My quiet words and honesty seemed to have the desired effect—silencing her vile and accusing tongue.

"Look!" cried Emily, pointing through one of the windows.

We glanced out and flames flickered and crawled up one side of the church, smoke billowing out over the once peaceful church grounds. A flaming torch came sailing through the church window shattering glass all over everyone in the vicinity. The torch landed on the tabernacle, and the tablecloth burst into flames.

"Put that out!" shouted the minister.

Christian leapt into the aisle and tried to douse the flames with a tablecloth from a side table.

Another torch came flying through the window, and I immediately ran to put it out. I knew we wouldn't be able to control the inferno if O'Reilly and his men continued throwing flaming torches into the church. A smash, and a third torch sailed into the sanctuary, hitting the altar this time.

While we doused the flames, we could hear loud voices sounding gruff—more like growls. *O'Reilly and his men must be yelling at someone,* I thought and looked out the broken windows into the haze but couldn't see who was involved. "Emily, what's going on?" I asked hoping she could give us something—anything akin to information.

Emily closed her eyes and screwed her forehead up tightly, in deep concentration. "The men. They're not alone. Another group has joined them."

Sounds of a struggle could be heard outdoors—shouts and cries of pain.

"It's the lost souls! They've decided to join Henry!" Emily said with sheer elation.

I could hear O'Reilly arguing, trying desperately to persuade the others to abandon Henry and stay with him.

"Why must you side with him?" O'Reilly said. "He has brought nothing but trouble. We are cursed because of him!" he said, pointing accusingly at Henry. "Henry killed us. It's his fault we are here, and now he must pay—with the life of the one he loves."

"Don't listen to him!" Henry shouted. "He will sacrifice you all to save his own soul. O'Reilly is only capable of loving himself."

"We must listen to Henry!" said another voice, one that I recognized as Johnny Prescott's.

O'Reilly roared, and a battle ensued outside the church. They were evenly matched, Henry and the lost souls against O'Reilly and his eleven men.

Suddenly, more glass shattered as the church window above the altar broke. A flaming stick flew through the window, and the carpet around the altar ignited. This time, the fire was too big to put out. One of O'Reilly's men lifted another called Jackson, and shoved him through the broken window. *Within seconds, he will be among us, and we'll be easy prey, trapped inside this so-called sanctuary.*

All seemed lost for a moment, but then I remembered the wooden box I'd left on the altar. I'd been told the symbol was one of protection and power over the fourth dimension. I gazed at the circled rose with the strange inscription and with a burst of light—an idea was emblazoned on my mind's canvas. "Everyone grab a candle from the altar!" I instructed, motioning to the candles lit by Christian earlier.

"What? Why?" the others protested, their eyes full of panic.

"Make a circle around the altar with the candles."

The minister nodded, understanding my idea. "Yes! Do as she says to. We must make a protective circle."

Reverend O'Neill ran to the altar, picked up one of the small votives, and handed it to a parishioner. Following my inspiration—we placed the lit candles in a large circle.

"Does anyone have a rose clip, flower, something with a rose. . ." I asked them looking around for volunteers.

Mrs. Harmon walked up and handed me a brooch—a red rose with a diamond sitting among the petals.

I pinned the rose on my blouse and stood in the center of the makeshift circle. Trembling but following suit, they all joined me standing within the flaming circle.

Jackson somersaulted onto the ground, a few feet away from the circle. Wearing an ugly grin, and with a terrible gleam in his eyes, he ignored the flaming carpet and started walking toward us, scowling at everyone as we huddled within the protective circle. Jackson started to advance but couldn't breach the circle of flames.

"That won't save you," he sneered. "We'll burn the entire church to the ground, with all of you inside—flamey circle and all! One way or another, you'll die tonight, Alice!" He looked around and picked up a fallen torch and went to grab a candle so he could re-light the charred wood.

As I looked at the blazing flames from the carpet, I reached for the wooden box on the altar and moved toward the flames, stepping out from within the protective circle.

"Alice! What are you doing?" shouted Christian.

I ignored him and tossed the wooden box into the fire and it was immediately engulfed in flames. As it burned, Adrianna's warning came back to me, *"The box cannot be destroyed by fire. Only fanning the flames will unlock its secrets."*

As the box caught fire, a bright light filled the room, a shining glow stunning everyone, including Jackson. The light became so bright we had to shield our eyes. When it finally dimmed, the only remains left of the box was a rose amulet, similar to the one carved on the box-cover, and a dagger made of a very bright, almost white, metal.

"God have mercy," the minister exclaimed. "A holy dagger!"

I ran to pick up the knife and amulet, drawn by the power—a magical power—I could feel emanating from them.

"Alice, don't! You'll burn yourself!" Christian exclaimed.

But when I reached to grab the dagger, it was as cool as marble. "It's okay," I said, turning the dagger over in my palms.

Out of the corner of my eye, I glimpsed Jackson lunging toward me, trusting in the dagger's power, I turned to face him. When mere inches away, I plunged the silver dagger into his dead heart. He let out a deep and disturbing wail then a long sigh and with a peaceful look on his face, he evaporated. I caught a glimpse of his eyes as he went, but instead of hate, I saw they were filled with remarkable gratitude.

"Thank you," Jackson whispered as his spirit rose and flew from the church—finally free.

I looked at the dagger in my hands, shocked that Adriana had been right. I am a Ghost Maven and I've just taken my first step to embracing my true heritage—magical heritage.

"You did it!" Christian said, edging toward the rim of the circle.

Inside, the church still burned, alight from Jackson's torches.

"Oh my God, this fire! We're going to die anyway," someone screamed.

Soon, we were all choking from the thick acrid smoke. It filled our lungs, making it impossible to breathe.

"Get down on the floor," Christian shouted, motioning frantically.

We dropped down onto our knees, trying to inhale what little air existed and crawl toward an exit. We could hear banging on the church door, and I feared O'Reilly and the rest of his men waiting outside—then I recognized the voice.

"Alice? Alice, let me in!" Henry screamed.

"We can't. If we open the door, they'll come in," Christian cried.

I ignored him again and, clutching the ghost slayer in my hands, ran to unbolt the door. Frantically, I fumbled with the latch.

"Don't!" Christian said again more frantically. He started to run toward me, his arms waving, eyes wide.

"I have to," I shouted. The lock was stubborn, but I managed to pry it loose. "Henry!" I screamed when the doors swung open.

His face was bruised, clothes ragged and torn, and he looked like he'd been in a fight or two, but to my eyes—he was the only sight I'd never been so glad to see.

I threw my arms around him and hugged him as though I could absorb him into me. "Are you all right?" I asked, voice quivering.

He nodded. "You have not been injured have you?"

"No, and I killed one of the ghosts," I said proudly.

"We must leave," Henry said, nodding behind him.

I froze when I saw O'Reilly's men circling the church. The lost souls helped Henry and made a valiant effort, but O'Reilly's men were fighters at heart. I feared that if we tried to run, they would easily catch us.

"Wait. There's another way," said Christian, slamming the heavy door shut once Henry made it inside. "Everyone, follow me." Then he began to crawl on his hands and knees through the smoke.

"We're trapped," I said. The smoke suffocated me and I was convinced we would all die—here in this church.

"No we're not!" shouted Christian. He crawled along the aisle to the tabernacle and pointed to a marble slab. "Help me!" he shouted to Henry.

The two of them lifted the slab, exposing a dark corridor that led under the church.

"A secret passage!" I exclaimed.

"Yes. Used by smugglers in the olden days to steal rations."

"Where does it lead?" I asked, curious to find a real secret passageway.

"Under the church and to the cemetery outside," Christian replied. "C'mon, Alice. You go first."

Chapter Twenty-five: The Vault

Henry and Christian lowered me down into the passageway, about a ten-foot drop to the darkness below, so my legs dangled beneath me. I had to jump the remaining few feet, onto the cold, hard floor beneath. Luckily, I didn't twist an ankle. With the passage so dark and musty, I couldn't see much in front of me.

Emily came next. She squealed as they lowered her, until she, too, touched the ground.

"Ugh. What is this place?" I asked, looking around in the darkness at the damp, glistening walls.

"It's an underground vault," Christian shouted from the top. "Come on, Dad. You're next."

One by one, the others were lowered into the vault, though some insisted on being difficult.

"Would you rather stay behind and be burned alive?" Christian asked a complaining Mrs. Prescott.

That silenced the old woman, and she, too, agreed to be lowered into the darkness. Ethan followed Mrs. Prescott, and soon all were safely below, except for Henry and Christian. They jumped the ten feet and landed safely beside us as flames consumed the interior of the church.

"Come on," Christian said, leading the way.

We followed him through the passageway, past several tombs covered with dusty cobwebs. I read the names of some of the deceased, thinking of those who had died while the rest of Pacific Grove had gone on living.

At the end of the passageway, a brick wall reared up in front of us, seemingly a dead end. We searched and searched but could find no likely exit.

"Great," said Henry, exasperated. "What now, Preacher Boy?"

"We go up," said Christian, pointing to the ceiling above.

I looked up at the ceiling—nothing but darkness, Christian started to push on the roof. Once the hidden panel was out of the way, we all witnessed a glimmer of light from edges around the outside.

"An exit!" I exclaimed.

The panel popped open, and Christian urged everyone through. We came out in the graveyard, and the ground underfoot was damp and springy, making it difficult to move. All around us, headstones reared up from the ground.

In the distance, I could hear the cries of O'Reilly's men. The church continued to burn and by now the flames had engulfed the entire roof, likely to collapse at any moment. The rest of the parishioners, including the minister, quickly scattered, running in all directions through the mist.

"What now?" I asked Henry.

"This way," Henry urged, yanking my hand.

I followed, running as fast as I could, breathing hard from trying to keep up with him. Christian, torn between running after his father or following us, decided after a split second to follow Henry, Emily, and me, into the mist.

I heard the shouts of O'Reilly's men as they continued fighting the other lost souls. From their cries, it seemed the sailors were losing.

In the gloom, O'Reilly wailed, "There they are! Don't let them get away!"

My heart leapt into my mouth as we zigzagged through the head-stones. I gripped Henry's hand tightly, afraid to let go.

At the exit of the cemetery, Henry stopped running. "Take Alice with you and head for the lighthouse," he told Christian. "It's the near-est place. The spirit of the lighthouse keeper may protect you from O'Reilly."

"What about you?" I asked.

"I will distract O'Reilly. He is following your scent, tracking you. Give me your jacket," Henry said.

I took off the jacket Christian had given me and handed it to Henry. The night air was cold, and I began to shiver.

He took the jacket in his hands. "I'll join you once I've disposed of O'Reilly."

"What about the other men?" I asked. Some of them had been killed in battle, including the one I had slain with the silver dagger, but others remained.

"Those who are left will retreat. They are cowards, lost without O'Reilly."

"Henry, be careful," I said, sensing the usual dread—fear of never seeing him again.

"I will. Now go!" With that, he vanished, heading back toward the church.

I turned to Christian and Emily, both terribly frightened. At that moment, I realized how much I cared for them. "Come on," I said. "We'd better go. If we follow the coastal path, it will lead to the lighthouse."

The three of us ran through the cemetery gates and headed downhill.

Just stick to the path, and we'll be okay, I said to myself.

We traveled for what seemed like forever, when Christian stopped at the sound of rushing water. "I thought this was the way to the lighthouse," he said, "but how do we cross that?"

I looked to see where he pointed. We were on the banks of a black river that wound its way through the Monterey valley like a thick snake.

"We have to cross it," said Christian. "It's the only way."

I shuddered, looking at the fast-flowing torrent of water. "I can't, Christian. I'm still too terrified of the water. You two go on without me," I said sadly, resigning to my end.

Chapter Twenty-six:

The Lighthouse

The river loomed ahead, menacing in the darkness. I paced up and down along the muddy banks, peering at the shore seeming so far away.

"Come on, Alice. It's only a short swim, and it's our only chance. You heard what Henry said," Emily urged. "We have to get you to that lighthouse."

"I can't," I said. "You know I'm afraid of the water."

"You can," Christian replied firmly. "If you don't, we'll all die."

We could hear O'Reilly shouting in the darkness. Although muffled, he sounded close. I wondered if he figured out Henry tricked him and now was on to my real scent.

"Just go without me," I said. "I'll be all right. I'll hide somewhere. Really, you two should just go."

"Like hell we will," said Christian.

This brought me to reality—I'd never heard him swear before now and it sharpened my senses.

Christian waded out in the water, with Emily in tow, shivering with the cold. They turned back to look at me, pacing on the banks.

"Come on!" Christian urged. "We're not going any farther without you."

I shuddered, took a deep breath, and plunged into the freezing water and before long it came up to my chest. Splashing through, I tried to keep my head up, making a feeble attempt at dog paddling toward Christian and Emily.

When I was within his reach, Christian grabbed my arm and pulled me close to him. "Just hold on to me, and don't let go," he instructed. "I won't let anything happen to you."

He started to swim across, and I tried to help him by kicking my feet, never once letting go of his neck. His strokes were strong, and I could feel his muscles contracting, working hard to pull his own weight and mine. Soon, we were halfway across the river. I tried to look for Emily, and saw she was ahead of us and nearly the other side. Being a nimble swimmer, Emily reached the far bank within a few strokes.

Finally, we lay on the bank, breathing heavily, chests rising and falling as we gasped for air—soaked and exhausted. The three of us were like drowned rats, writhing on the shore.

"We must keep going," Christian said, panting. "We have to get to the lighthouse."

Finally, I managed to sit up. "Okay. I'm good. Let's go."

The fog was even denser on that side of the river because it directly faced the ocean. Underfoot, I felt the spring of green grass, and assumed we were on the golf course. That made it easier to run, and we quickly gained momentum. For a tiny moment, I felt a glimmer of hope.

When I turned around, though, I didn't see my friends. "Christian!" I shouted fearfully. "Emily!"

No answer.

My heart began beating wildly, and I feared the worst. *Did I somehow take a wrong turn in the fog?*

Then I thought I heard a voice sounding like Emily's calling me. I started to move toward the voice, but the closer I got, the farther away it seemed.

"Christian! Emily!" I called again, almost a scream now.

Again, no answer.

Oh God, what do I do now? I felt like sinking into the ground and giving in to defeat.

Sitting in stark terror and awaiting what came next, something caught my eye. A strange green light, ahead about fifty feet, moving slowly in the fog. It had a mysterious glow about it, like an aura. Fascinated, I watched curiously until my mother's words from the séance came forward—*follow the light.*

I trusted and believed in my mother, so I started to run into the unknown toward the strange green light.

Once within ten feet, I could see it was someone carrying a lantern. I tentatively approached, but the figure didn't speak. "Hello?" I asked meekly.

"Alice. . ." said a feminine voice.

"Wh-who are you?" I asked the shadowy figure as I crept forward. I caught a glimpse of her face and saw a girl, around my age with dirty-blonde hair. Her skin looked a pale blue, and I could see the veins in her feet and hands. "Heather?" I asked, incredulous.

The girl stared blankly at me with dull eyes.

"Heather? Is that you?" I asked again.

"Yes," came the reply, flat and lifeless.

"Your mom, she's so worried about you."

"She doesn't need to be," replied Heather. "I'm at peace now."

"What happened to you?" I asked. "The whole town has been looking for you."

"I had an unfortunate accident Homecoming night after fighting with Channing. Ethan offered to drive me home and he took an unexpected detour so we fought. I jumped out of the car and tried to run down the coastal path, back to Pacific Grove, but I slipped on one of those ridiculous heels, and tumbled into the water. Ethan reached out to help me, but he couldn't save me."

Emily had seen an image of the incident only the hands were trying to save Heather, not drown her.

"Are you okay?" I asked, immediately feeling foolish.

Heather gave a small laugh. "Don't I look good for a dead girl?"

"Dead?" I repeated. "Are you saying you drowned?"

Heather nodded. "Sometimes there are accidents, and now I am paying the price for my past deeds in the fourth dimension. I have to atone through service to humans."

"But you had a wonderful life. Everyone loved you, adored you. Even I envied you and thought you were so beautiful."

Heather stared at me; her eyes—once so full of life—looked empty and lifeless. "You envied me? What for? I fooled everyone and my life was nothing like you imagined. Now I am destined to stay in this bay until I atone for my selfishness and abhorrent treatment of others."

"May I ask what abhorrent treatment you speak of?" Recalling Ethan and my conversation.

"Vanity and deceit—a predator's life. The list is longer but since you are not my confessor, I see no need to be specific."

O'Reilly's voice, calling for me through the fog, sounded closer, and I knew he was on to Henry's trick. "You can't outrun me, Alice!" he cried. "I'll find ye. I can smell ye!" O'Reilly's laughter thundered through the fog.

I turned to Heather and pleaded, "Can you help me? I have to find the lighthouse where I'll be safe."

Heather looked at me for a moment, long and steady—then she turned away.

My heart sank.

"Well, are you going to follow me?" She asked over her shoulder.

Relief flooded my being. Half-frozen from fear, I struggled to run but, run I did to keep up with Heather's quick strides. I followed the green light as she led me through the gray mist.

She stopped when the white building loomed ahead. "There," she said, pointing to the lighthouse. "I can't follow you—and I can't help you anymore."

"Thank you, Heather."

"Will you do something for me, Alice?"

"Yes, anything."

"Do not be afraid of anything. But promise you will not suffer my fate?

"I promise."

Heather slowly turned her back and disappeared into the mist.

Sadly, I watched her leave—I would never see Heather again and I felt grateful this would be my last memory.

As I opened the door to the lighthouse, it creaked loudly. I fumbled to find a light switch but when I found them, they did not work. *Ugh! No electricity!* I thought to myself, groping around in the semidarkness looking for the best place to hide.

The Point Pinos Lighthouse was rumored to be haunted, but the thought of more spooks didn't alarm me as much as O'Reilly hunting me down. If Henry was right, the spirit of the lighthouse keeper would protect me.

Again, I remembered Emily's vision of me climbing the tower. I didn't know if there was something I was supposed to do. "Maybe I'm supposed to head up to where the lighthouse's beam will be," I said aloud. "I might find safety up there."

Carefully, I climbed the steps of the lighthouse—nearly two-hundred. As I climbed, I wondered about Christian and Emily, hoping they were safe and O'Reilly hadn't caught up with them. That thought was too terrible to contemplate.

Finally, I reached the top and looked out at the bay. The whole peninsula was shrouded with dense fog. From my vantage point, I scanned the golf course, looking for any sign of Henry, clutching the silver dagger tightly in my hands, hoping I wouldn't have to use it.

A moment later, a dark figure appeared on the grounds below—O'Reilly walked straight toward the lighthouse with a determined stride, powerfully strolling across the golf course. The very sight of him made me cower.

"O'Reilly!" shouted Henry, emerging from the other side of the building as he headed for his former skipper, fists clenched and eyes blazing. "It's *my* soul you want, you fiend!"

"Oh, I'll get thy soul all right," said O'Reilly, "but first I'll take care of the girl. I want thee to suffer for the misery thou hast caused, lad, and thou will watch her die. How's that for vengeance from thine ol' captain, eh?"

"You are as god-awful at being a captain as you were at being a father and husband," Henry taunted. "No wonder your poor wife abandoned you, you cruel, selfish bastard!"

O'Reilly grimaced. "Miserable scum!" he shouted in a rage. "You're just a boy, a cabin boy I found in that horrible little pub, going nowhere. How dare thee judge a captain?"

"Your wife and your child were better off without you," said Henry. "You did them a favor by drowning. In fact, I did them a favor by ridding their lives of you. I'm sure they would thank me."

O'Reilly gave an almighty bellow and charged at Henry who stepped aside at the last moment, prepared for his attack. O'Reilly charged past like an ox, almost disappearing into the swirling mist. When Henry whirled around to face him again, expecting another charge, O'Reilly came at him with everything he had, forcing Henry to the ground.

From the top of the lighthouse, I watched helplessly, trying to think of a way to distract O'Reilly.

O'Reilly threw a punch at Henry, causing him to slip. Henry fell dangerously close to the cliff's edge and O'Reilly was headed to finish him off when a bolt of lightning struck the lighthouse, setting the whole structure aglow with a bright electromagnetic energy. Another flash of light, an explosion, then the second bolt of lightning struck O'Reilly. He cried out in pain, and stumbled back. A surge of current rippled through his body, knocking him backward and he toppled off the cliff into the sea that swallowed him up with a heavy splash. The pull of the tide was too strong, and submerged his body underwater.

Henry limped slowly to the edge of the cliff and peered over. The tide violently crashed in and out, drawing O'Reilly's body into the red mist.

Chapter Twenty-seven:

Morning Tide

Dawn began to break, and the first glimpse of light fought its way over the hills from the east. From the lofty vantage point of the lighthouse, I could see the morning sun, cleansing away the cold, damp fog of the night and bathing the whole town with a brightness and warmth, a new hope.

Huddled at the top, I felt numb, cold, and exhausted. The tide receded, taking with it all the trash brought in from the night's storm. Almost as though it were washing away the horrors of the night before, exorcising my guilt and sins at the same time.

The low-lying clouds dissipated over the sea, retreating back, withdrawing their cold, clammy fingers. From far above, I thought I spied a lone gull, or maybe it was an albatross. It reminded me of the one I'd seen hovering over the island days ago.

I finally found my footing again and clung to the railings as I tried to muster the strength to descend the stairs. Peering down the stairwell, I decided it was safe to climb down, but I still took one step at a time. Soon, I stood at the bottom.

I walked along the beach, watching the tide rush in and out, crunching pebbles underfoot as I strolled. When I looked toward the horizon, I saw that the rock pools were exposed to the sunrise, draped in green and brown seaweed, glinting in the sunlight. Some seabirds picked at the exposed mussels.

I came across the wreckage of a fishing boat that had run aground in the fog. Planks strewn across the shore like scattered bones, and a gaping hole across the stern, but no sign of the crew, living or dead.

I fretted over Henry, Christian, and Emily, hoping they were safe, wherever they happened to be. Squinting through the vanishing mist, I saw the silhouette of someone limping down the path. I recognized him instantly—"Henry!"

He looked younger than ever before. His eyes lively, full of contentment, a disposition absent since I'd known him. In those beautiful eyes, I glimpsed a man released from his demons.

"Henry!" I shouted again. I ran as fast as my legs could carry me and jumped into his arms. I was cold and wet, but in his arms I felt warm and cozy. "Henry! You're safe. You're alive!"

"I'm—alive?" he repeated, chuckling, holding me close, and caressing my damp hair. He was wet and smelled of the sea, but I didn't care as we tried to warm each other with our embrace. "I'm alive? That's a first. How did I manage that?" he joked, releasing an adorable smile.

"You know what I mean. Is O'Reilly—?"

"You needn't worry about him anymore, my love," Henry said, looking into my eyes. "Nothing and no one will ever hurt you again."

Somehow, I believed him. As long as I was with Henry, I felt safe and protected. No matter what life or death had in store for us, at that moment I experienced complete security. The one thing I wasn't sure of—the safety of my family and friends.

As we walked farther down the tideline, we recognized two figures, and we both broke into a sprint.

"Christian! Emily! Thank God you're safe!" I said, running up and hugging them.

Emily had tears in her eyes. "We thought we'd lost you, so we took shelter in a cave down by the beach. We waited until the mist cleared."

"What about O'Reilly?" Christian asked.

"He's gone. We don't need to worry about him anymore." I explained to them what had happened.

"How awful," said Emily, "but thank God you're okay."

We went over all the events of the night before. They noticed the change in Henry, but did not broach the subject.

In the distance, we could see the smoke rising from Pacific Grove, where the remains of the church still burned. Dogs frantically barking, and families searched for loved ones.

The blanket of fog had completely disappeared and the townspeople busily made repairs and overcame the chaos of the dreadful night before—the night the Dead terrorized their streets.

Christian and Emily soon headed home, concerned about their own families. I prayed to God they were safe.

I worried about Dad and Sophie, too, but I lingered behind with Henry. "Come with me," I said.

Henry shook his head. "I'm afraid I can't. I must bid you farewell now, dear Alice," he said sadly.

"But I want to be with you," I said with a shiver. The wind had picked up and blew wisps of sand across the beach.

"Are you cold? I saw a blanket in a fishing boat moored near here. I'll go and fetch it," Henry said.

I looked out to sea as he walked away, desperate for some way for the two of us to be together forever. I knew of only one way I could be with him. I walked to the top of the path and looked down at the crashing sea, where the waves lapped and circled around the rocks.

I closed my eyes and considered my options. Sure that if I drowned, if I gave myself willingly to the bay, I could be with Henry forever. It would mean never seeing my mother again but I consoled myself with the idea she lived in a higher dimension called Heaven. If I drowned myself, I would be alienated from Dad, Sophie and Mom forever. Those are the rules.

I imagined the last few moments of my life—Dad and Sophie, how they would suffer at losing me, especially after losing Mom, too. But when I thought of Henry—how much I loved him and wanted to be with him. Of course I loved my father and sister, and I missed my mother with all my heart, but the love I had for Henry was a different kind of love. He made me happier than I had ever been. I closed my eyes and braced myself for the cold shock of the water.

"Alice! No!"

I turned to see Henry standing at the edge of the rocks. "But it's the only way," I pleaded. "It's the only way we can be together, right?"

Henry shook his head. "No! I will never let you forfeit your life for me."

"But I want to be with you. I love you, Henry Raphael, and I want to spend the rest of my days with you."

"What about your family? Your dad and sister?"

"They'll manage without me," I said, trying to convince myself as well as him.

"Will they?" Henry replied. "How have you managed your mother's loss? Have you not suffered immensely? Do you want to put them through that again?"

Silent for a moment, I stopped to consider the pain I would cause my family if I dived into those lapping waves. Slowly, I edged away from the ledge and climbed over the rocks, until only a few feet from Henry.

"Thank you," he said.

I nodded, but knew I really should thank him.

"You are so brave, Alice, brave and beautiful. I hope one day you will realize just how astounding you really are."

I thought about Adriana's words, and the Ghost Maven, the silver dagger I still had in my pocket and the ancient amulet around my neck. I still hadn't figured it all out, but the one thing I did know was that I loved Henry, and didn't want to lose him. Even if his heart didn't beat for me, mine would always have a beat for him.

"Please don't go," I urged.

"I must, Alice, for it is time," he said. "Those are the rules. I have to go back to my world. The island is waiting for me."

He led me back toward a small fishing boat beached on the shingle shore. Reaching into the boat, he pulled out a blanket and wrapped it around me, then he started dragging the boat into the water.

"What are you doing?" I asked.

"I have to return to the island, I can't stay."

I shook my head and ran toward him. . . "NO!" coming out in a choked sob. Our lips met in a passionate kiss, sweet and long—he tasted like the ocean, salty and powerful.

"Please stay," I whispered.

"I will always love you," Henry replied.

"Me, too. I will never forget you ever, you are my first love," I said.

Henry nodded. He boarded the boat and I watched him as he floated further out into the water—the lure of the tide instantly pulling him out to sea.

But I couldn't let him go and ran into the freezing ocean. . .even the bitter cold couldn't stop me as I chased after that boat, stumbling through the waves in desperation. The boat continued to drift further out and soon I was up to my chest.

Then he was gone.

When the boat became a tiny speck on the ocean, disappearing from view, I took a deep breath and allowed the tears to flow. The anguish in my heart so painful, I found myself choking for breath in between the sobs I cried for Henry, for me, my family and my friends. . . Unsure of my and the town's destiny, I pondered the future and what it held for me as a Ghost Maven. After today, I knew I would never be the same 'Alice'. *After losing Henry, I'm not sure I will ever find that kind of love again.*

Sitting on the beach gazing out over the ocean, I remembered the amulet around my neck. I've had it on since I burnt the box in the church but had no time to examine it closely. I lifted the rose and held it closer, examining the dark, almost black, crystal—the moon's light shining through the kaleidoscope of colors. At first I thought the metal used to shape it was made from silver and tarnished over the years but when I tried to rub a bit of tarnish away, I saw it wasn't silver at all. *Curious*, I thought, *I've never seen a black metal like this.* The part where I tried to rub away tarnish shone as though a new penny.

I wasn't sure of the amulet's power or purpose, but it was the last earthly piece left of my journey with Henry and that made it more valuable to me than any other trinket will ever be. I kissed the rose and stood to get on back to my new life—*or new adventure*, I thought, smiling to myself.

Slowly, I turned and waded back up the beach. I spied a sea otter in the water, trying to pry open a clam with his paws. He pulled the contents out and chewed the meat with his little jaws, whiskers bobbing up and down. The creature looked healthy and happy, and I hoped that was a good sign the plague left with the fog. I thought about Dad and Sophie and got anxious to be with them.

As I walked, I pondered all I'd been through the past few months, what I learned about life and death. I realized everyone had to die sometime: Mom, Dad, Sophie, and me. It was just hard to come to terms with that, because I grew to love Henry in a way I have never loved anyone before now.

*

A week later, we celebrated Thanksgiving at the minister's house. Dad, Sophie, me, Christian and his parents sat around a table loaded with food; everyone shared love, food, friendship, and laughter. I was stuffed with the meal and thrilled to be surrounded by loved ones. I knew that some people, like Mrs. Palmer and Mrs. Prescott, weren't so lucky with Thanksgiving tables flanked by empty chairs and painful reminders of loss. I vowed, right then and there, to tell my family all of what I'd seen, once I felt strong enough to relive the tale, over the pain of losing my beloved Henry.

I woke up early the next day and opened the blinds. The bay sparkled in the distance. I put on my bathing suit and jogging clothes and took a towel from the bathroom. I slipped out of the house before anyone woke and walked down to the beach near Lovers Point.

It wasn't even eight o'clock, but there were a few people down on the beach. A man out for a stroll with his dog, and a dive-master testing his equipment in the shallows. Connor was carrying some wet suits down onto the sand in preparation for a group of high school students.

"You're a brave one going in the water," said Connor. "This is becoming a regular habit of yours."

I smiled. I visited the beach every other morning, but this time, I intended to dive in. "I need the practice," I said, taking off my jogging clothes. My mom bought the swimsuit for me a couple of years earlier, for vacation, and I'd only worn it for sunbathing—never in the water.

I dipped a toe into the water—it was cold, so I wet my limbs in an effort to adjust. Finally, I took the plunge and started to kick. I managed a few breaststrokes in the shallows while keeping an eye on the pier, making sure I didn't swim out too far.

Not entirely over my fear, but I was taking baby steps to get there. I would remember that Henry said I was brave. Also, I learned something very important about life—*when you're swimming, it's important to keep your head above water.*

Epilogue

What I learned later was that when O'Reilly fell backward, he tumbled into the water with a heavy splash becoming submerged in a swell. The strong current swept him out to sea, and from an observer's standpoint, looking up from the cliff, it looked as though O'Reilly perished when the surge of electrical and energetic bolts coursed through his corpse.

When in fact, O'Reilly surfaced a mile out to sea, head bobbing in the water like an inflated soccer ball. Always a strong swimmer, he began fighting to save his soul—remaining afloat despite being battered around by the violent swells.

The dim lights of a small tanker could be seen in the far distance. O'Reilly needed an army, one he could raise to wreak his revenge on Henry and take his wrath out on the residents of Monterey. The men on the tanker, once turned, would be his servants—and he their new captain.

With strong powerful strokes, O'Reilly began to swim toward the ship. Soon he was alongside the stern, grasping a rope that dangled from a lifeboat. Climbing aboard, he stood for a moment on deck, clothes dripping wet, eyes fixed like daggers. With an angry bellow, he marched toward the lights on the bridge.

The fate of the tanker is unknown. . ..

About the Author

Tony Lee Moral was born in Hastings, England in 1971, and later moved to California. He is the author of three books on the film director Alfred Hitchcock. *The Haunting of Alice May* is the first in a series of *Ghost Maven* novels. If you enjoyed this book and would like to read more in the series, please write a review on the Amazon website. You can read more about Tony's books on www.tonyleemoralbooks.com and www.ghostmaven.com